LIVES OF THE MIND SLAVES

SELECTED STORIES

MATT COHEN

The Porcupine's Quill, Inc.

CANADIAN CATALOGUING IN PUBLICATION DATA

Cohen, Matt, 1942-
Lives of the mind slaves: selected stories

ISBN 0-88984-139-X

I. Title

PS8555.O38L5 1994   C813'.54   C94-931606-7
PR9199.3.C64L5 1994

Published by The Porcupine's Quill, Inc., 68 Main Street, Erin, Ontario NOB ITO, with financial assistance from the Canada Council and the Ontario Arts Council. The support of the Government of Ontario through the Ministry of Culture, Tourism and Recreation is also gratefully acknowledged.

Represented in Canada by the Literary Press Group. Trade orders available from General Distribution Services in Canada (Toronto) and the United States (Niagara Falls, N.Y.).

Readied for the press by John Metcalf.
Copy edited by Doris Cowan.

'Golden Whore of the Heartland', 'The Sins of Tomas Benares' and 'Café Le Dog' first appeaerd in Café Le Dog (M & S, 1983). 'Lives of the Mind Slaves', 'Living on Water', 'Mirrors' and 'Racial Memories' were first published in Living on Water (Viking, 1988). Minor changes and corrections have been made for this edition.

Cover photo: COMSTOCK/M. & C. Werner.

CONTENTS

GOLDEN WHORE OF THE HEARTLAND

MALCOLM TOTTING tried to kill himself by swallowing sleeping pills – two dozen of them one afternoon before Benton was to arrive to pick Totting up for dinner. When Benton got to the door, it was open. Totting had left a note on the dining-room table saying that he was lying dead in the bedroom. He was extremely sorry to have burdened Benton with such a task, but could he call the police and an ambulance before his body began to smell. The note went on to say that his affairs were all in order, the will written and recently updated, and that the refrigerator had been defrosted by the cleaning lady. It was signed, 'With all best wishes, Malcolm Totting,' and there was a postscript giving the relevant telephone numbers.

After supervising Totting's trip to the hospital, Benton went downtown to the restaurant where they were to have eaten, and sat in the bar drinking one Scotch after another. When he was too drunk to drive he telephoned his wife to explain why he was going to sleep over at Totting's apartment. Then he returned to the bar where he saw a table of his favourite graduate students. After two more doubles Thalia Stewart asked him if anything was wrong.

'I stayed in town because my car broke down.'

'I'll drive you home if you like,' she said.

'I think I'll have another drink.'

'The bar closed half an hour ago.' Her voice was a loud whisper, as if she was speaking through a megaphone. Benton remembered going out to her car, winking at the other students as he climbed into the front seat. She was already on the expressway, driving towards the farm he had described often enough to his class, when he told her that he was staying in town that night, at Malcolm Totting's.

As he stepped out of the car he stumbled and fell on his face. It was a unique sensation: first there was the long, dizzy moment when he knew his balance was lost; next came the urgent but ever-more-useless effort to regain it; and finally, the best part – the long, slow, swoon that ended only when his face and stomach landed in Malcolm Totting's parking space. Fortunately it had been raining all night. Benton made a harmless landing in the wet mud.

'I'll help you upstairs,' Thalia offered.

'I'm okay.'

But he stumbled again. Thalia had to link her arm through his, she was amazingly strong for such a thin and awkward girl, and push him through the lobby and into the elevator. After opening Totting's door and guiding him to the bathroom where he splashed off the mud, Thalia steered Robert Benton along the hall to Malcolm's bedroom. Standing at the foot of the bed, he noticed that the bedspread still held the imprint of Malcolm's drugged body. Then he passed out. When he woke up he was completely lucid, naked under the covers, his arm wrapped protectively around the equally naked body of Thalia Stewart, to whom he had given a B plus on her most recent essay. Her skin was taut and warm, and as he moved his hand along her ribs Benton could feel the soft, vulnerable drumming of her heart. Her face was turned towards him. She was smiling in her sleep. Benton's first thought was that he hoped Thalia hadn't seen the note on the dining-room table.

Benton got out of bed, feeling quite free to wander naked into Malcolm's dining room. The note was on the table. Scribbled at the bottom was a new postscript, 'He's all right, but he has to spend a week in hospital – TS.'

There was a brief moment in which Benton realized there was still time to rescue his marriage. 'Sometimes you have to decide,' Totting had said to him only a few weeks ago, 'which you are going to save – your marriage or your life.' Benton went back to the bedroom and slid beneath the covers. Thalia's body searched out his own, and as he wrapped his arms around her slender back, he couldn't help wondering if Thalia had been Malcolm's mistress too.

The afternoon Thalia announced that she was pregnant, Benton was still living with his wife. He advised Thalia to have the abortion and then finish her thesis.

'Who needs another thesis on Blake. And I won't have

anything truly original unless I go to England.'

'You should go to England,' Benton said. He meant it; he even dared to hope that her love for him would survive the separation and that they would be joined together in a misty future. 'While you're gone I can straighten out my own situation.'

'I'll go,' Thalia offered. 'But I can't have an abortion.'

'Why not?'

'I don't believe in it,' she said, with such determination that Benton, twenty years older than her, suddenly felt that all of his own convictions had been bargained away in a series of compromises too boring to recount.

A year later, Benton was divorced from his wife, and Thalia was in place with the baby, at the farm outside of Toronto. 'I've never lived on the land,' she said. 'Never really lived *on* it.' As if she had spent her whole life floating above the ground and now wanted to come, literally, down to earth.

'You know,' Benton said, 'you really *believe* what you say.'

'Don't you believe what *you* say?'

'Of course,' Benton protested, wondering which of his declarations of love and lifelong fidelity she was now reviewing, 'I believe what I say but, you know, I feel that my life has been so sordid –'

'You like to believe your life has been sordid. You read about F. Scott Fitzgerald too much.'

'Too much, too soon,' Benton murmured.

'You're really a very conservative man,' Thalia declared. 'I know you've never had a dishonourable thought in your life.'

Thalia became the second woman to live with Benton in the white frame farmhouse that Benton himself had rebuilt. But as Benton had explained to Thalia, what really counted to him was not the house but what surrounded it. Over the years the topography of his farm had become the living and breathing map of his own body: its dank depressions, its brief moments of glory, its little nooks of life that existed in defiance of larger forces – these were all so essential to him that he needed to travel over them almost daily in order to believe he was still alive.

The farm itself was located forty miles from downtown

Toronto. At night the lights of the city sent a glow through the southern portion of the sky, so that Benton always felt, no matter how deeply he wandered into the surrounding woods and hills, that he was only the blink of an eye from the city's perpetually humming downtown.

'I love it here,' Thalia said one night. 'While you're at the university I look out the window and imagine that Jonah and I live here all alone, a hundred years ago.'

Thalia made this welcome announcement while they were getting ready for bed. During Thalia's first weekend at the house, Benton had told her its one hundred and forty years of history, including the story of how the wife of the farmer who'd built the house had died, in this very bedroom, during the birth of her fifth child.

'But the child lived,' Benton had rushed on to say, 'and he was the one who kept the farm. Built the big barn out by the pond and drained off the marsh so it could be used for hay and wheat.'

Thalia, pregnant with Jonah, had nodded with what seemed to be boredom, and Benton had been embarrassed with his own moralizing.

But now that Thalia was firmly installed as mistress of the house, Benton found himself suspiciously close to contentment. Warm and secure, he lay under the down comforter with Thalia's head resting on his shoulder, her voice reassuring in his ear. She was, in fact, just telling him once again how much she enjoyed her days when Benton began to hear, along with the sound of the wind scraping along the metal siding he himself had applied, the convulsive shudder that the oil furnace made when the chimney draft stayed open.

'Christ.'

'What? Is it silly for me to be happy here?'

'It's wonderful. I meant that the draft is stuck again. I'd better go fix it.'

'Cold,' Thalia said.

'I'll go.' But he hesitated. The basement had a dirt floor with the massive furnace – an old woodburner converted to oil in honour of the young and tender flesh of both Jonah and Thalia – set up on a cement pedestal. The single lightbulb that was suspended from the stairs threw shadows of old beams and twisted nails around the stone walls; and sometimes Benton wanted to laugh at himself for the additional shapes his eyes invented.

'Leave it,' Thalia said. 'What's the difference?'

Benton switched on the bedside lamp and saw his own enormous shadow spring up on the bedroom wall. 'It's crazy,' he said, 'I know. But I hate to see that perfectly good oil going up the chimney. Don't you think I should fix it?'

'You should. I mean you should fix it so that you don't have to go down there every time the wind blows.' Benton, pulling on his housecoat, couldn't help noticing the way Thalia was starting to imitate his patterns of speech.

The next day, after teaching his Wednesday class in American fiction, Benton was making a list of all the minor chores he had neglected for months when Robyn Marler stepped into his office and closed the door behind her.

The day he first saw her, the previous September, he thought she was part of the year's crop of graduate students. She wore high-heeled shoes that emphasized her tightly skirted legs, and when she walked she switched, like a nervous filly, the long golden hair that hung halfway down the back of her carefully tailored suit.

'Do you mind if I come in?' Robyn asked.

'Of course not.'

Robyn Marler *was* a newcomer to the Department, but not a graduate student: in her forties she had a slender, almost steely body, and a prim, upright neck leading to a lined and weathered face which was undeniably a record of the dissipation which was her academic specialty. That is, she had written a book about Coleridge and Wordsworth in which she claimed that Coleridge was the greater poet because he was willing to burn his brains out on drugs, while Wordsworth confined himself to the stimulation of the damp countryside and his sister's incestuous ministrations.

This book, which Benton had somehow read even before Marler was invited to be Visiting Professor, had been published by a prestigious American house, and was translated into enough languages to use up two lines of her *curriculum vitae.*

Marler sat in the student visiting chair, crossed her legs and lit a cigarette.

'Terrible weather,' Benton said. 'It doesn't always get this bad.'

'I never go outside,' replied Marler. 'Except for walks. I take a walk every day.'

'So do I,' Benton said. It was easy to imagine Robyn Marler walking. With her brisk stride, smoking non-stop, she would whip herself up and down the street until she returned exhausted to her apartment. He could imagine the apartment, too, because it was sublet from Malcolm Totting who had risen from the ashes of his unsuccessful suicide to be awarded a sabbatical, springing free not only the apartment, but also the salary and the office that the renowned Robyn Marler was now occupying.

'The thing is,' Marler said, 'if you don't mind me getting to it ...'

'Go ahead.'

'I want to stay on after this year, and I was wondering if you could tell me how.'

Benton blushed, a sudden flash of heat rushing through him as if he had just seen Robyn Marler in a ridiculous and obscene position.

'Why,' Benton finally asked, 'why would someone like you want to stay in Canada? Don't you feel cut off from –'

'One of my students,' Marler explained. 'I've fallen in love. He's only in second year and I don't think he's smart enough to change universities ...'

Benton felt his blush grow yet deeper. Then he saw that Robyn Marler was starting to grin.

'Sorry,' she giggled, 'I never learned to tell the truth. You didn't believe me, did you?' She laughed.

Benton found himself laughing, too.

'Actually, I just came by to see if you'd join me for lunch.'

She laughed again, her laugh extending itself into a surprising little-girl giggle, and Benton couldn't help laughing with her.

By the time Benton got home the sun had already set, leaving only a thin red souvenir along the horizon. As soon as he got out of the car, Benton set out on his walk, running from the driveway to the road so that Thalia wouldn't have a chance to shout at him.

Once over the first hill and out of sight of the house, he slowed rapidly. His breath was irregular and choking; the three Scotches he had drunk with Robyn Marler threatened to make their own dash for freedom.

Shouldn't drink, he admonished himself. *I know I shouldn't drink.* Three years previously, on his fortieth birthday, Benton had found out that he had a mild case of diabetes; nothing serious, the doctor had said then, Benton's only symptom being persistent fatigue.

'It's all right,' Benton said. 'F. Scott Fitzgerald had diabetes. His doctor told him not to drink, too.'

'Who's he?'

'I don't know. I guess I could look it up. No one ever asked me that before – who was the doctor of F. Scott Fitzgerald?'

'No,' Benton's doctor said gently, 'I didn't mean who was the doctor.'

'A writer,' Benton said. 'Fitzgerald. They made movies out of his books. I teach a course on him.'

'*The Great Gatsby,*' the doctor suddenly supplied.

'That's it.'

'He was an alcoholic, wasn't he?'

'I'm not,' Benton said, suddenly irritated, his mind filled with a picture of Fitzgerald sitting in an airplane toilet, drunkenly trying to force a syringe into his thigh. 'Will I have to take insulin?'

'Exercise and diet.'

Two miles from the house Benton was sober again, and he turned around to go home. Thalia would be waiting for him, supper made in one of the copper pots he had given her last Christmas. Benton realized he had forgotten to eat lunch. He reached into a pocket for a cigarette, then began walking again, trying to imagine now what would happen if he invited Robyn out for dinner. She didn't have a car, he remembered her saying; she would have to stay overnight. Near the house,

Benton stopped and looked over a rocky hill to a barn that had been gradually falling down, walls buckling a foot at a time, for the entire ten years he had lived on the farm. He realized he had been thinking that Thalia would be jealous of Robyn, because Robyn was an active and independent woman with a career of her own while Thalia, once a pretty and awkward girl with a halo of scholarships and a promising academic future, had under Benton's care evolved into a beautiful and somewhat bored young woman who looked after a baby and tried to remember to work on her thesis in her spare time.

'You know,' Robyn Marler said, 'you really are an extraordinary person to be buried away in a place like this.'

'And where,' Benton asked, 'should my light be shining?' They had developed the habit of a daily visit to report on departmental gossip, commiserate on the stupidity of students and bureaucrats, and smoke one another's cigarettes.

In fact, Benton thought, the compulsive smoking of each other's cigarettes was a pervasive theme, a clear line that extended so markedly through their meetings that it deserved special mention – a term paper, or perhaps a thesis: 'Oral Substitution and Sublimation as Practised by the Department of English.' But, the question was, for what were the cigarettes a substitute? Because although Benton enjoyed the idea that they were putting bits of each other into their mouths, he had no desire to touch or kiss or, even less, taste the actual parts of Robyn Marler. With her lined face, the colour of seasoned oak, and her thin, stringy-looking hands, she gave the impression that beneath her concealing and smartly tailored clothes was the sinewy body of a cat grown past catting. Robyn Marler was, as Benton had explained to Thalia, not only a cat grown past catting, but a single woman past the point of being on the make. There was, Benton said, no word for her at all. With her dyed-blonde hair, her fingers smoked to the colour of kippers by her filterless cigarettes, her tense movements and flashy smile, she had reached a strange no-woman's-land between spinster and dame.

'Your intense light?' Robyn asked, in a tone that was beginning to make Benton feel slightly uncomfortable. Then she shrugged her shoulders. 'That's the problem these days. It's easy to hate where we are; but there's nowhere worth lusting after.'

'It's not so bad here,' Benton said.

'No, it isn't really.' She reached, they were in Benton's office, for one of Benton's cigarettes. He couldn't help noticing that her fingers were cleaner today, as if they had been pumiced. According to her impressive *curriculum vitae* Robyn was forty-six years old, only three years older than himself. But every time he found his eyes riveted on her masculine hands, the unsuggestive lines of her suit, the tiny but intricately detailed pouches under her eyes, he couldn't help feeling guilty about inspecting his new friend this way. Especially guilty, he knew, because he assumed that Robyn was sexually desperate enough to regard him as an attractive male, even if his intense light was placed under a provincial bushel. In fact, from feeling like a pariah at the beginning of the year, Benton had progressed, under Robyn's encouraging gaze and her carefully dropped comments, to being convinced he was almost respectable. Of course he was not going to win a popularity contest, though that defeat – in such surroundings – was no serious wound. But he *was* liked and sought after by graduate students, the prettiest and most intelligent of whom he had somehow captured on a full-time basis; he had tenure and was paid a large salary to work a few hours a week for eight months of the year; he was known for his professional competence; and his University Press book on F. Scott Fitzgerald, although not translated, still earned occasional praise for its elegance of style and its sympathetic understanding of Fitzgerald's passive character.

'And anyway,' Benton said, '*you* came here. That says something for us.' The Department had been pleasantly shocked when its Chairman, returning from a conference in Los Angeles, intimated that the Visiting Chair might be occupied by Robyn Marler, the distinguished Coleridgean who was on a leave of absence from Princeton. Before she arrived, there had been jokes that Robyn Marler and the Chairman must have conceived one of those unlikely convention passions where Circe melts even the stiffest of Puritanical collars.

'I didn't mean to sound ungrateful.'

'Ungrateful,' Benton said. 'It's we who should be grateful. Why would you want to spend a year in Toronto when you might have been in England, Europe ...' He cut himself off, realizing that he had done it, asked the question he had promised himself to avoid because it was obvious to him and everyone else that Robyn Marler must have chosen to spend a year in Canada either because she was financially distressed beyond the need for an ordinary prestigious fellowship – which surely she could have had – or because her stress was an emotional one and she needed, after the well-publicized death of her well-publicized husband, a place where she could both hide and be looked after, a refuge that wasn't lonely, a sort of benevolent mental institution.

'You see,' Robyn said, her voice still flat, 'I had a ... disagreement ... with the Dean while my husband was ill.' Hugh Walpole Marler had been notorious for the wonderfully malevolent cartoons he had drawn for the *New York Times Book Review*. Whenever a book was to be panned, Marler was employed to sketch the author in a state of dementia. When he discovered he had terminal cancer he wrote an article saying that approaching death made him realize that the hatred he had exercised on various writers had so poisoned his heart that he felt absolutely indifferent to everyone, even his own family.

'Anyone can disagree,' Benton said.

'It wasn't a disagreement on policy matters. It was more of a personal confrontation. He didn't actually fire me, I should say. What happened was that I offered my resignation, and he accepted it.'

Robyn lit a new cigarette while her first was still smoking, and her hands moved with such agitation that Benton was sure he was about to hear a story that he didn't want the burden of knowing.

'That was that,' Robyn said. 'I wasn't joking when I said I'd like to stay. But since then I've been offered another job. An old friend in Pennsylvania.' She stood up and quickly brushed her hand through her dyed-blonde hair. The gesture was so unusual and girlish that Benton also sprang to his feet.

'We should go to lunch,' Benton said.

'I'm going home,' Robyn replied. 'I have to prepare for a seminar this afternoon. And anyway, I'm afraid I'd be depressing company today.'

'Don't be silly.' Benton began to panic at the thought of Robyn, depressed, in Totting's apartment. 'I absolutely insist.'

'No, really, *I* absolutely insist.' For a moment Robyn looked at him, her smile beginning to flash as it did when she was about to make one of her off-putting remarks. But her lips only parted sadly, and then she gave a smile of such vulnerable sweetness that Benton was paralysed. Before he could speak, Robyn was out of the office and into the hall, her boots on the marble floor melting quickly into the Department's lunchtime rush to the Faculty Club.

'You see,' Benton explained to Thalia, 'she's amazingly vulnerable. It must have taken a lot of courage for her to move here.'

'You should invite her out,' Thalia said. 'She must be terribly lonely so close to Christmas.'

'Dinner would be nice,' Benton said.

'Why not have her for the weekend?' Thalia asked. 'All you do these days is mark papers. I wouldn't mind the company and you could use an excuse to rest. I'm worried about you.' She got up from her chair and stood solicitously beside him, putting her palm on his forehead as if to test his temperature. Jonah, who was trying out a highchair for the first time, threw his apple sauce on the floor and screamed. Thalia bent over and kissed Benton: once, twice. It was the way, he remembered, that she used to lean over and kiss him the week they stayed at Totting's apartment, making love and visiting Malcolm at the hospital. Thalia had not been, it turned out, Totting's lover; in fact she had never been anyone's lover at all. 'I saved my whole life for you.'

'You shouldn't say those things.'

'They're true.'

That night Benton woke up in a sweat. He put on his dressing gown but the nervous sweat kept flowing like a river down his backbone, dampening the crack between his buttocks, making him shiver as if he were starting the flu.

The furnace was rattling away but that wasn't the problem:

he had been dreaming about the kiss Thalia had given him at the supper table, the full press of her lips against his own. But in his dream the lips had belonged to the sad, wise, mouth of Robyn Marler. Thalia had been a virgin but Robyn, Benton knew, was anything but. In the dream he had felt himself, like a hippopotamus sinking gratefully into soft mud, diving happily into the total corruption of Robyn Marler; with her honey-blonde golden whore hair and her wise-dirty smile she embraced and drew him into the sweet drugged heartland of New York vice and corruption. And in fact those very words, golden whore of the heartland, had been on his tongue as he, dreaming, returned Robyn's kiss and pressed himself eagerly against her – already wondering what the neighbours would say when Thalia and Jonah disappeared, were replaced by this American goddess redolent of the thousands of bodies that had eagerly lusted after her.

Benton went downstairs to the living room and poured himself a glass of brandy. The truth was, he now accused himself, that he had known from the very moment Robyn Marler had walked into his office six weeks ago that he was going to sleep with her, that he was going to have an affair with her that might or might not be sweet but would certainly be guilt-ridden and would certainly wrench him away from Thalia; and he also had known, he now forced himself to admit, that this affair would be as unpleasant for Robyn as it would be for himself, that she and Thalia would both be wounded, possibly even destroyed.

'But why?' Benton said aloud. '*Why bother!*' He had poured himself a second drink and was dialling the number of his only true friend, Malcolm Totting, when he realized the call would be answered not by Malcolm but by Robyn.

'Jesus,' Benton said, hanging up the receiver.

It would have happened, he realized, on this very day if he had offered to take Robyn home. Not only was her apartment Malcolm's, but it was also the scene of his initial tryst with Thalia. And, to tell the truth, there had been a few times in his married years when parties at Malcolm's had ended with himself and one woman or another sleeping it off on Malcolm's capacious Victorian couch.

Maybe, he suddenly thought, it was a psychological thing, a need to defy his own best friend. 'I am not,' Benton had once shouted, filled with derision for his wife, 'a member of the human potential movement! What most shrinks need is a good crap.'

The brandy began to settle in his stomach and Benton began to settle also; gradually, the dream was replaced by the comforting view of the room he had lived in these past ten years, the books he had read and placed in the shelves his hands had awkwardly made. It wasn't true, he said to himself; Robyn didn't want him and he didn't want her. It was natural for adults to be sympathetic to and interested in each other. Such a minor attraction – one that was really a repulsion – didn't have to pull him into a *danse macabre* that would destroy his life.

And as he reassured himself and lit a cigarette, another disturbing idea flitted by: he didn't have to worry, he could change wives, change houses, even change medical regimes and it wouldn't matter – it didn't threaten his life at all, it barely even affected it.

Benton stood up and walked to the window. The dark glass threw back his own reflection, and despite everything he looked tall and thin, as fit as he had been twenty years ago. The whole autumn he had walked as the doctor prescribed, and had confined his drinking to the social minimum. The complaints he once had – fatigue and occasional dizziness – had entirely disappeared. He remembered thinking that he was going to die because it would be unfair to live past the lifespan of the person from whom he had made his money. But now, at forty-three, he was older than F. Scott Fitzgerald had ever been. 'He died not of drink but of work,' Benton had written in his biography, a book that portrayed F. Scott Fitzgerald not as the madcap alcoholic Zelda wanted him to be, but as a man whose sincere desire to stick to his last had been corrupted – but only temporarily – by desire. The desire for fame, for the touch of beautiful women, the release of alcohol, and, most of all, the drunkenness of love.

Now, in his living room, Benton remembered how clearly he had understood that love was corrupting and evil. This understanding, fuelled by his frequent separations from his wife, had pushed him through draft after draft of the Fitzgerald book. 'It must be a work of love,' Totting joked once. 'No,' Benton protested, 'it's only hate.'

Benton poured himself a third brandy. It was amazing the way a man could drift away from himself. He stood up again, so pleased to be remembering his own lessons that he couldn't help pacing the room. Outside he now saw a car driving by, its white headlights scanning the snowbanks. For a moment Benton was afraid that it was lost and in trouble, and was going to turn up his own driveway. But it went on, slowly following the road that led only to the houses of a few farmers who had to get up at five in the morning to do the milking. *It must be a doctor*, Benton thought, *someone must be sick*. He started towards the hall, as if he would go upstairs and get dressed, ready to help. But he was too drunk, he had lost touch with who was sick and who was well, and if Thalia knew these things, as his wife used to in intricate detail, she did not pass the information on to him.

But even the car, like a stranger walking through his own living room, could not shatter Benton's feeling that for once the world was in its place.

The weekend, to begin with, was a disaster. Thalia had insisted upon it, despite Benton's protests, and she had even gone so far as to call Robyn herself – inviting her to come Saturday afternoon, picked up by Thalia in town after her massage, and thus guaranteed to arrive in time for a walk around the farm before dark and the commencement of eating and drinking. For this, Thalia had decided, there would be two other couples: a pair of graduate students called Stephan and Lilly Hartmann, who had been finishing their ph.d. theses for close to a decade and acted as surrogate parents to young initiates like Thalia; and Milton and Elaine Totting – Milton was Malcolm's older brother and taught in the Biology Department, while Elaine had achieved a small reputation as a vegetarian psychic.

This guest list was invented by Thalia, who said that she didn't mind the idea of a dinner party, but she wasn't going to have a group of Benton's enemies over from the English

Department just to impress Robyn Marler who was, after all, as well as being a single woman badly deserving company on a weekend so near to Christmas, also an American who, strictly speaking, should never have been offered a job at a Canadian university when there were probably hundreds of equally qualified Canadians getting a lot lonelier driving cabs or waiting in unemployment lines.

At the last moment, Saturday morning, Milton Totting telephoned to say that he and Elaine had both come down with the seasonal flu and would be unable, sorry, to come, much as he had been looking forward to meeting with the renowned Miss Marler of whom he had heard many wonderful things. Listening to Milton compose his long and pompous sentences, Benton wondered how the two Totting brothers could be related.

'For God's sake, don't tell Milton,' Malcolm had said, his first words when they took off the oxygen mask. 'It's an old Celtic custom that you shouldn't have to hire your own undertaker.'

By Saturday afternoon at three o'clock, Benton had finished cleaning the house, had changed Jonah for the sixth time that day, and was trying to decide, as he had been for three hours, exactly what he should wear. He wanted a costume that was essentially formal, clothes which would announce to Robyn Marler that here was a man to be taken seriously, a man who wore a suit in his own home the way a Spanish peasant wore a shirt and tie when he stepped out to trim the hedges; a man in possession of his life who *could not be dislodged without the gravest consequences*. At five minutes to three, in fact, he was wearing the dark-blue suit that he had not worn since his wedding, and was sitting downstairs with a very light drink, reading the most recent *Times Literary Supplement*, airmail edition, and keeping one eye on Jonah who, in an excess of splendid good behaviour, was sitting happily in the centre of the living room floor, his tiny little fingers laced together, enjoying the feeling of the sun shining on his face.

At that moment, Benton remembered that he had promised to take Robyn for a walk around the farm. In fact he had already planned numerous anecdotes to tell her that would, on the one hand, be amusing and therefore welcoming, so that she would feel he truly wanted her to be sharing his house for a few days, and on the other hand a little on the staid and humourless side, just like Milton Totting. This combination would allow her to see that, drinks in the afternoon aside, he really was a very boring fellow, certainly not worth the trouble of a brilliant and widely translated writer whose book was a surprise bestseller in Japan; it might even demonstrate what an extraordinarily dull and serious person he was, a complete zero in fact, redeemed only by his desperate existential commitment to the faulty but beautiful Thalia Stewart, a commitment that could not be breached for one second without both betraying a helpless young mother and corrupting beyond repair what little was left of his own worthless moral fibre.

Unfortunately, Benton realized, racing up the stairs, all these noble intentions were going to be wasted if he didn't change, not even a totally insufferable asshole would dress up in his wedding suit to take the golden whore of the heartland for a walk in the barnyard.

He had his suit pants off and his jeans half on when he heard the kitchen door open. Jonah shrieked and, pulling on his jeans, Benton rushed stocking-footed to rescue his son.

'Sorry,' Milton Totting said, standing at the doorway to the living room. Benton reached for Jonah, whose happiness had been changed by Milton's arrival into total terror.

'It's all right,' Benton said, stooping to swing Jonah into his arms. 'Strangers make him nervous.'

'We felt better and decided to come up for the afternoon, anyway. I tried to telephone but the line was busy.'

'Party line,' Benton said automatically, 'the woman up the road is on the phone a lot these days. The other night her husband slipped and broke his leg.'

'Elaine is out in the car,' Milton said. 'I just thought I would come in first to make sure you were ready to receive us.'

'Bring her in, for God's sake, I was just –' Here Benton looked down at his shirt, his tie, his unzipped jeans.

Milton nodded and went out again. Benton, this time with Jonah under one arm, rushed upstairs to take off his tie and substitute the heavy cableknit sweater that Thalia had given him the first Christmas after they had met.

When he returned to the living room Milton and Elaine were standing and looking at his books. Elaine had a red nose, which Benton recognized as the nose she developed from crying during her fights with Milton, and Milton had a bruise under his right eye which Benton hadn't noticed before.

'Let's have a drink,' Benton said into the silence.

Milton and Elaine both turned towards him at once.

'I don't know, old man,' Milton began.

But Elaine cut him off and held out her hand.

Soon they were armed with three stiff Scotches, and as the grey December sky filled with snow, Benton calculated his chances of getting the Tottings drunk and battling again before dark, so they would leave before the evening proper commenced.

'Have you heard from Malcolm?' Milton asked.

'A card or two,' Benton said. 'Oh, and there was a letter.' This letter was his first lie of the afternoon. It was, he thought, in honour of Robyn – whom he was now eagerly awaiting, because she would surely soften the problem of these unwanted Tottings.

'I haven't heard at all,' Milton said gloomily.

'He doesn't like to write Milton,' Elaine added. 'He confuses Milton with his father.'

'I thought your father was dead.'

'That's why he uses Milton. He's far too immature to stand on his own, and thank God he doesn't get himself fired by taking out this authority problems on the Dean. Really, he ought to give Milton a portion of his salary for keeping him stable.'

Benton found that his Scotch had disappeared and he went into the kitchen to get himself another. When he got back Elaine was sitting on the floor, beside Jonah.

'He *is* cute,' Elaine said.

'He is,' Benton agreed.

'It's too bad you didn't have children with Penny.'

'Just as well now,' Benton said. 'It would have been hard on the children.'

'Don't you think you would have stayed married?' Elaine

looked around the room. Benton recognized the moment – she and Milton had come out to the farm often enough when he was married to Penny, and after the marriage broke up they had tried to console and patch up. Of course Benton hadn't told them about Thalia, but it wouldn't have mattered if he had. Milton considered graduate students to be expendable fodder intended for the amusement of the faculty – as long as they had paid their tuition.

'No,' said Benton, 'of course not.' But he was distracted because he had seen, through the window, Thalia turning up the drive.

'I would never get divorced,' Elaine said, as Benton headed once more out of the living room and into the kitchen, this time to start heating Jonah's formula.

Milton followed him into the kitchen and stood behind him while Benton put the bottle and the pot of water onto the stove to heat.

'We didn't know whether to come,' said Milton in a low voice.

'It's nice to see you, and Thalia would have been so disappointed.'

'Elaine hasn't been feeling herself lately. She's been thinking of changing doctors.'

'You should take it easy on her,' Benton said, turning around to see, behind Milton's surprised look, Robyn and Thalia stumbling in the door.

At the sight of Robyn, her arms around a brown paper bag of groceries, marching in confidently as if she were already mistress of this house, Benton's stomach pumped a vigorous dose of fear into his system, and he could feel the sweat spring out along his back.

'Take these,' Thalia instructed, handing her own shopping to Benton. 'I hope the red wine didn't get too cold. God, the massage almost killed me today. When he put his fingers into my spine I thought I was going to scream.'

'You said he was a fairy.'

'Now he says he wants to get interested in women.'

'I want to go for a walk before it gets dark,' Robyn announced.

'You take her,' Thalia said. 'I'll go put Jonah down.'

Benton stood paralysed, only his head moving as it nodded back and forth to listen to the commands of the two women. Perhaps, he thought, they might have already discussed him, his own particular will-less state, and settled his fate between them. That thought he found comforting: if only they could decide between them what was best, a solution that made *them* happy, then he was certain he would go along.

'Well, come on,' Robyn said. 'What are you waiting for?'

While Benton put on his boots and coat, he asked Milton and Elaine if they would like to tour the barns. 'I don't know why you'd want to,' he added. 'They don't look any different than the last time.'

'We should go home,' Elaine said. Since telling Benton she would never get divorced she had been standing and chewing her lip in the kitchen doorway.

'Stay,' Benton said. 'I insist.'

'We weren't going to come at all,' Milton repeated, but by this time Benton had finished dressing and was pushing Robyn out the door in front of him, so that all he could do was turn and call back, 'I'm glad you did, help yourself to another Scotch before Thalia gets down.'

Outside, the sky was already starting to turn dark. Across the frozen snow the wind was blowing from the north, starting a quick ache in the earlobe where Benton had once gotten frostbite.

It was already too late to walk around the land. But instead of taking Robyn to the barn where the sheep and cows were, Benton led her to the chicken coop, a small, low-ceilinged building with a tiny row of windows facing south. He opened the door and made Robyn go ahead into the blackness. Then he followed her in, Switching on the light. Instantly there was a bizarre glare of white: Benton had put a floor in the old coop and insulated the walls in styrofoam. His plan had been to finish, before winter, construction of a studio where Thalia, in a place where she couldn't be interrupted by Jonah, would finish her thesis.

'Nice,' Robyn said.

'It's not done yet.'

She turned to him. The room was small, smaller even than Benton's office at the university. He noticed that Robyn was wearing a thick fur coat, in which he would have liked to bury himself, and that her face seemed ten years younger.

'It's very nice just the same,' Robyn said. 'I really think so.' She took a couple of steps, which brought her across the room.

'I meant to finish it sooner. I don't always get things done.' The light came from a bare bulb hanging on two wires taped into the ceiling fixture. There were, along the walls, jagged rectangular holes cut for further outlets. Thalia liked to use an electric typewriter, and while he was doing the wiring Benton had tried to imagine different places where she might want to sit, ways she would position the light. The idea of Thalia out in this chicken coop that he had converted to a study for her thesis gave him pleasure. All the while he worked on it he held fast to the image of himself in the house, surrounded by the smell of the soups he was going to learn to cook, Jonah crawling on the living room carpet, while outside, Thalia – who after everything was said and done had surely not become pregnant with Jonah just to force him out of his marriage – finally picked up the thread of her life, the thread that Benton had broken the night Malcolm Totting tried to kill himself.

'You love Thalia very much,' Robyn said. She was giving him her sad smile again.

'I guess I do,' Benton said. 'No, that sounds silly. I do love her. I *really* love her.'

'I believe you.'

'Well, I guess it *is* true then.' He smiled. The room was cold, but not nearly so cold as outside, and it came into his mind that they could lie down on the insulated plywood floor and go to sleep under Robyn's thick fur coat.

'I loved my husband very much,' Robyn said. 'I was very sad when he died.' She was wearing her sad smile almost permanently now, and she spoke her words very slowly and carefully, as if they were an emotional arithmetic at which Benton was a slow learner.

'I'm very sorry he died,' Benton said.

'I don't think he went to heaven.'

'No.'

'I don't think he went anywhere.'

'No.' Benton realized that his face was wet. It really *was* too bad that Robyn Marler's husband had died. If she loved him. She had reached out for him and he had been taken away. 'I'm sorry,' Benton said.

'It's not your fault.' Robyn smiled, only this time it was not her sad smile, but the flashy one that snapped like electric fingers.

'Well,' Benton said, 'people will be wondering where we are.'

'We're here,' Robyn said. 'You've been telling me how much you love Thalia, how sorry you are that my husband died.'

Benton looked down at his boots. The snow had melted into little black puddles. 'Actually,' he said, 'I think it was you who was telling me.' Saying the words made him feel sick to his stomach, the way he used to feel when he quarrelled with Penny.

'You'll forgive me,' Robyn said. Not a statement, but not entirely a question. A hope. She had stepped forward and put her hand on his canvas parka. 'Will you forgive me?'

If he kissed her, Benton knew, his world would end. The slender thread connecting him to Thalia, keeping him on this absurd farm from which he could see, hear, almost *smell* the city, would snap, and he would be plunged into the river of Robyn Marler, her untrustworthy New York eyes and smile, the thundering vacuum of her too-successful soul.

And yet, Benton had to admit to himself, he was forty-three years old and he knew what it was like when a woman asked him to kiss her. This wasn't it. Robyn Marler, the much translated Coleridgean who was also a defenceless and bereaved widow, was not closing her eyes and turning up her lips, she was not opening her eyes wide and sizzling his nerves, she was not pressing stray parts of herself against him and giving him hints that there was more to come. She was just asking him to forgive her for a somewhat nasty remark.

'Of course,' Benton said, 'there's nothing to forgive. Please.' And then he stayed, without moving, while Robyn led the way out, ducking slightly at the low door.

Outside, the sky had turned from dark to black. Mounted on a hydro pole was a light which illuminated the hard-packed snow paths between the house and the buildings. As he walked behind Robyn Marler, Benton breathed the cold air deep into his lungs, his heart fairly leaping with exultation. He had done it, truly *done* it; for the first time in his life he had looked into the eye of desire and had been able to turn around and walk away.

Benton opened the kitchen door for Robyn, feeling so much the master of the situation that he let his hand fall against her coat. She neither responded nor withdrew, only waited patiently while he fumbled with the latch. And then the door was open and he could hear Thalia's happy laughter from the living room; she was standing by the fireplace, a glass of wine in her hand, waving it towards her friends, the Hartmanns, who must have arrived while he was in the chicken coop with Robyn. And while Benton kicked off his boots and went to make new drinks for himself and Robyn, he could see the Tottings sitting sullenly on a sofa. The three young people had probably made them feel old and out of place, and Benton experienced a happy satisfaction at the thought that he, though older than Milton Totting, felt perfectly at ease with the younger generation.

When he entered the living room, the fireplace was roaring and spitting with the cedar he had split for it that morning. As he came up to her, Thalia passed a joint to him – no doubt courtesy of the Hartmanns – and after taking a demure puff he passed it on to Robyn, who sucked down the smoke with such greedy force that the fire split apart a seed and made it explode with a spark that tore open the paper and surprised Robyn into dropping it.

'Professor Marler!' Stephan exclaimed admiringly. He started another joint at which Robyn again took her turn. After it had made several rounds, Benton carried it over to the Tottings.

'Thank you, Benton, but not tonight,' Milton said, as though it were a telephone conversation. 'We really must go.' Thalia had put on a record, one of her favourite raucous English bands who dyed their hair purple, and Benton could barely hear Milton's voice above the noise. 'We just meant to drop in, you see, but I thought we'd wait until you came back to the house.' This he said disapprovingly, as if he knew it was only a matter of time before he and Elaine, dropping in on a Sunday afternoon, would find Benton and Robyn cosily ensconced while poor Thalia and Jonah were buried out in the back field.

But before Benton could reply, Thalia was leaning over the Tottings, insisting that they absolutely *must* stay, that she would even change the music to suit them, and without waiting for a reply she sprang over to the record player and put on a suite of oboe sonatas.

Benton, whose head was swirling from what he realized must be close to half a bottle of Scotch, as well as a number of healthy lungfuls of what Hartmann had whispered to be 'real Cambodian shit', felt as though he had been suddenly hurled from the centre of the storm which he had just faced down, the decadent lust of the ravaged widow, into a deep and languid tropical swimming pool, an aqueous jungle of low moaning sounds. And yet, amazingly, Milton looked happy; a greasy purr was lighting up his face. Even Elaine was smiling and lighting a new cigarette while sipping primly at the ice water to which Milton must have confined her.

'You will stay,' Benton said. His body broke in half as he leaned over them, plucking from Milton's diffident hand its empty glass; yes, good, the Tottings were staying, it was important that they stay because this was Thalia's event, Thalia's weekend. Somehow it must be a dazzling triumph, a riot of non-stop fun.

'That's right,' Milton replied, 'a riot of non-stop fun.'

'I must have spoken aloud,' Benton said.

'A dazzling triumph of reason,' Milton said.

In his hand Benton held Milton's glass. He clamped his teeth around his tongue so that Milton could not hear him say how desperately, how deeply, how with incredible and total sincerity he wished that his best and only friend Malcolm were here in place of this leather-stuffed fart of a brother.

'You know, Benton,' Milton leaned over, 'I don't think that I've ever understood until this evening exactly why my brother values you so much. You have a thick skull, but beneath it you're such a fine person, a truly *fine* person.'

'Fuck you,' Benton said. His words were like bubbles and he hoped, hopelessly, that they would burst through the surface of the swimming pool.

'Fuck,' Milton said. 'A fine word. Benton, get me another fucking glass of Scotch, will you?'

'Fuck you,' Benton said, but this time he managed to get himself turned and aimed in the direction of the kitchen. Drunk, it was amazing, the Scotch had absolutely gone to his head. It seemed now like years since he had been on the wagon, years since he had been properly drunk, so long ago that he must have been a different person then, a carefree married man who went alone to the occasional party at his best friend's apartment and got drunk and sang old Beatles songs and stayed up half the night until settling into some innocent infidelity on the couch that was there for exactly that purpose. And even in the morning after those drunks, he never felt remorse, guilt, fear of getting caught; he would wake up ready to roar, wake up with the fire blazing in him, and rush into Malcolm's kitchen to stoke himself with coffee for the exhilarating day.

Drink, fire, air: in those days he had been like an eagle; now he was stuck on the farm, rooted as Thalia called it, living on the land – yes, he was on the land all right, he had been squashed to the fucking ground until he could feel the earth grinding up through the yellowing soles of his feet. Earth and water, he was diving down with age, this new drunk was the drunk of the second half of his life. Under the horizon where the sun would never rise, where his heart was filled with earth and water. 'You know what,' he whispered to Thalia; he was in the kitchen now and had walked up to her despite the fact that she was leaning back against the sink, eyes closed, happily letting Stephan Hartmann put his arms around her, 'I feel like a vegetarian tonight.'

Thalia opened her eyes – he had forgotten what a fierce green they could be – and stepped into him, away from Stephan's shadow, her arms now around his own neck the way she used to kiss him. 'Benton, we're having *stew* tonight.' And then, giggling as she pushed him back, all the way across the kitchen from the sink to the refrigerator, pressing herself against him and biting his ear, she whispered, 'Benton, you're so drunk; Benton, you're not mad at me?'

'I love you, stupid.'

'I love you.'

She kissed him and he held her tight, wrapping his arms around the slender back of this beautiful stranger while she bit his ear and made little knives of desire shoot through his fingers.

Then suddenly she whirled away, skimming across the kitchen like a skinny dancing heron, bowing not to Stephan but to Lilly, who was holding out her pudgy arms to her. And as Thalia rushed into Lilly's embrace Benton turned to Stephan, to exchange a shrug, but Stephan was laughing so hard that his eyes were squinted into tiny blind sparks.

'You're all drunk,' Benton said, but quietly, sad to see that they were all still birds while he was reduced to burrowing through the earth; and feeling suddenly teary and self-pitying he poured Milton half a glass of Scotch. If Milton had one gene in common with his sorely missed brother, surely this would set it free. And then, opening the freezer to get the ice cubes he scraped his knuckles, and when he turned to ask Thalia to kiss them better she was already behind him, her stealthy hands sneaking up his sweater to scare him. He shrieked in loud delight.

'Are you all right?'

'Fine, really fine.'

'You're sure?' But just as her repeated question made him unsure, her hands squeezed him again and the knives of desire came back, he was a bird with them after all.

When Benton got back to the living room Elaine had changed the music again, back to the raucous British, and had thrown off her shoes to dance with Stephan, who was smoking another joint. She had unwound her black hair from the bun she always wore. It swung around her shoulders like a witch's mop as she danced, except that she wasn't really dancing, she was just kicking her heels up into the air and waving her arms around like a crazy woman, singing along to the music while

Stephan passed her the joint and laughed in encouragement.

'Some party,' Milton said.

For some reason this made Benton realize that it had been ages since he had seen Robyn. He turned his head around the room so quickly that he staggered. As he fell towards the floor he kept twisting, and as he did he saw Robyn coming down the stairs, smiling and quite at ease as if she had come from her own room – which of course she had, since she was staying for the weekend – and then Benton heard the doctor's voice telling him that it wasn't good for diabetics to get drunk, and he saw an image of a graph, his blood sugar going up and down like a rollercoaster, up and down to one knee with his leg twisted beneath him – there was a moment when he felt himself beginning to black out the way he had that first night with Thalia – but the moment became a loud popping sound, it was the sound of his own clarity bursting through the surface of the swimming pool, and he could feel his eyes jumping open with the pressure, his ears hurting, and in a completely controlled sequence to his fall he began to unwind himself, amazing himself as he gradually got to his feet, grinning at Robyn whose eyes had never left his, whose large and violet eyes were the depths through which he had been swimming, whose eyes now watched him in that same detached and sad way he had first seen in his office, and smiling first at her and then at Milton, Benton rubbed his leg and said, 'Sorry, I must have twisted my ankle, sometimes it goes like that.'

'You didn't spill a drop.' Milton Totting's pompous voice declared this with such approval that Benton realized that his wish had come true: Milton wasn't such a bad fellow after all. Beneath that swollen grease was a person worth having to dinner.

'No,' Robyn said, 'he didn't spill a drop.'

Now she was standing close to him, much closer than she had in the shed, and her eyes, he hadn't been mistaken when he saw her from his fallen position, were truly burning; she, too, was drunk, stoned, the golden whore of the heartland was on the rampage and Benton could see her passion exploding like violet ribbons from her eyes.

'You really are amazing,' Robyn said. She was wearing a silk dress of dark scarlet that was tied modestly at the neck and at the wrists, and she put one of her hands on his arm. For this occasion all the nicotine had been scrubbed away, but Benton was still aware of the used, hide-like skin that had been leathered by empire and corruption, by the same decades he himself had travelled through, by losing to life first, and then to death.

'You think too much,' Robyn said. She had dropped her voice into a private murmur meant for him alone.

'I believe in thinking.'

'I don't,' Robyn said. And she looked to Milton and in the same tone asked: 'Do you?'

'No,' he said, then looked over at his wife. His bruised eye had taken on a dark and pleasantly shiny hue.

'There you go,' Robyn said. 'I told you you were amazing and I was right.'

In the middle of the night, Benton woke up. One minute he had been asleep and the next he was lying on his back, body rigid, eyes staring at the ceiling. He breathed deeply, felt his muscles relax. The fear was in his stomach, a nauseous feeling that wanted to be thrown up. He reached his arm out, turned very carefully to see who he would find lying beside him. But it was only Thalia, her breathing deep and regular. He shifted slightly in the bed to discover if she was naked. She was, good: when she was angry with him she wore a nightgown to bed.

Benton, feeling better, sat up and reached for a cigarette. Once he had quit smoking for six years. When he would wake up, drenched with sweat, the fear was that he had given in and smoked a cigarette.

Through the window he could see bright patterns of stars. That meant, he knew, that it would be very cold outside. As the thought entered his mind, like a switch, the furnace went on. For a few seconds the house shook like a ship in a storm. But instead of instructing himself to go to the hardware store, Benton now calculated that almost half the heating season was over. During the Christmas holidays he would call a repairman to clean the motor and fix the faulty hinge.

His gaze fixed on the shining metal roof of the chicken coop. He could remember, with perfect clarity, going out to

LIVES OF THE MIND SLAVES

show it to Robyn. Sentences had been exchanged: he couldn't remember the words, but the sequence of feelings came back – somehow, as he was doing the exact right thing, the proper thing that he had decided, he had nevertheless slid into her embrace.

Benton spat out a long spiral of smoke. Along with everything else, the fine, stoned feeling he'd had was coming back. He felt good. Alive. He had survived some terrible temptation, a temptation even more difficult than not smoking a cigarette, and now the sky was so proud of him that soon it would break apart – the way it used to fifteen years ago – and show him another day. He got up out of bed and put on his housecoat. At this moment, stretching it across his broad shoulders, he almost wished he had succumbed, had fallen to the charms of the great golden whore, taken America itself in his arms so that he could, in his drunkenness, have mixed his own corruption with her yellowed skin, taken her in his arms and then risen up out of them, like right now, risen before the dawn and driven back to his faithful, waiting Thalia.

He stepped out of the bedroom and walked downstairs. His feet knew the way in the dark and soon he was in the kitchen, brewing up a cup of coffee the way he used to. The coffee was like a hot slap against his tongue. It poured down his throat and fired up his belly. The kitchen was a mess of heaped plates and dirty pots. He took a swallow from an open bottle of wine, spat it into the sink, then carried his coffee into the living room.

Now he remembered the second trip out to the kitchen coop – for a moment he panicked with the memory, afraid that the had lost his hold after all. Then the picture came back: after he and Thalia had seen the Tottings to their car, he had insisted on showing Thalia exactly how he intended to fix the chicken coop as her studio.

They had stumbled inside, but he didn't switch on the light. He just closed the door behind him and threw his arms around her, desperately wanting to beg her forgiveness. But of course there was nothing to be forgiven for; he didn't dare explain that he had almost kissed Robyn Marler. Thalia, drunk, wanted to make love on the floor, had even wrestled him to the cold plywood. But he had been too dizzy, so they just sat silently in the dark, their backs squeaking against the styrofoam, looking out at the sky.

'I don't care,' Thalia whispered fiercely. 'I feel so close to you tonight.'

Then they went back to the house. Robyn had gone up to bed in their absence and the Hartmanns, suddenly lucid and sober, were carrying dirty glasses and ashtrays into the kitchen. 'Don't,' Thalia protested, but they had insisted on at least cleaning the living room; and now, sitting in his favourite chair, beside the bookcases he had made, Benton felt that certain grim sense he had sometimes at Malcolm's house, the last one awake, the mourner sitting in the party's morgue, remembering the triumphs and disasters, trying to add up the score so that it came out in his favour.

It was all right, Benton said to himself. It *was*. Every time his mind went back to the moment he had sat on the floor with Thalia he felt tired and listless. But when he remembered the time with Robyn, a raw nerve pulsed. He *had* managed to resist her. He had turned her down, even if she had been the one to apologize, and she would never forgive him. So he would never have to turn her down again.

Benton stood up. He had never been so drunk in his own house. Suddenly he felt overwhelmingly exhausted. Every step was painful, his muscles felt bruised from the inside. He walked slowly to the kitchen, turned out the light, then started up the stairs.

At the bathroom he pushed open the door to brush his teeth. Even as the door began to move, he realized that the light was on. He hated to waste electricity. As that thought was forming, the smell of steam and perfume swept it away, but he didn't have the presence of mind, despite what Robyn had said about his compulsive thinking, to actually do anything but continue to open the door, thoughtlessly following one strange clue after another like a dog who will run a trail until he bashes his brains into a tree. And then the door was open and he saw Robyn Marler, standing stark naked on the rug beside his bathtub.

'Excuse me,' Robyn said, 'I didn't think to bring my housecoat.'

'It's all right.'

Robyn then stepped, as she had been about to, into the bathtub, and as Benton watched, slid down into the water until she was lying, full length, on her back.

The party had washed away the lines on her face, her body was slender and perfectly formed – she might have been Thalia's smaller twin. Her skin was a smooth and dazzling ivory, with a young, glossy sheen as though it had been made from the whites of rare eggs.

'Well,' Robyn said.

'Well,' Benton repeated. All the fearfulness that had attacked him the past two months was now gathered together and raging in his nerves. Even his own choked breath sounded like Thalia, rushing in to discover this lurid scene.

'Well,' Robyn said. 'I feel like a character in an Italian movie.'

'I was just on my way to brush my teeth,' Benton said.

'That's a good idea,' Robyn said. 'Why don't you brush your teeth?' Her breasts were bobbing on the water like small pear-shaped lifeboats.

Benton took his toothbrush from the rack. It was a bright-blue plastic with white bristles. He covered them carefully with toothpaste, all the while looking away from Robyn, then bent over the sink. In the mirror he saw Robyn staring at him.

'I'm sorry about this afternoon,' Robyn said.

'Don't –'

'Sometimes I get lonely for a man.'

Benton lifted the toothbrush towards his mouth. Robyn shifted in the bath, sending tiny whorls of water from her nipples.

'Many men must find you –'

'Not so many,' Robyn said.

'I do,' Benton said. He turned and, still holding his tooth-brush, walked out of the bathroom, closing the door carefully behind him, and continued down the hall to the bedroom. Thalia was lying awake in bed, the lamp on, reading.

'What's everyone doing?'

'I made some coffee,' Benton said. 'Robyn's taking a bath. I walked in on her by mistake.'

'I hope Jonah doesn't wake up.'

Benton took off his housecoat, put his toothbrush in its pocket, and lay down beside Thalia, pulling the covers over himself. Thalia switched off the lamp and curled beside him. Benton, on his back, was conscious that he was staring at the same spot on the ceiling that he had looked at when he woke up. He also wished that he hadn't woken up. Thalia, putting one leg across his thighs, rested her head on his chest.

'Do you mind?' Thalia asked sleepily.

'No.' In the dark he could hear the furnace starting to shudder again, his own heart skipping with it, struggling to break free.

Winter light splintered from the white snow, from the plate glass windows of the offices banked next to his own, from the white scrubbed stone of the university buildings. Long brilliant shards pierced his office, threw themselves against his own white-painted walls, lay like spears across the photograph of the American writer.

One of these days, Benton thought, one of these days soon, he himself was going to break apart under the force of all this harsh and glaring energy. But for now he was alive, safe and still.

He was sitting in his office, his pre-Christmas appointments with students finally finished, and he was looking at the picture of F. Scott Fitzgerald. It was a signed photograph. Benton had found it in a second-hand bookstore in Paris when he was researching the book. In it, Fitzgerald was still young and full of juice, the wide-set eyes hungrily staring out at the world, eager to swallow and record, to render the vision in prose as clear as a dream, as sparkling as champagne, as hopeful as the hopeful mornings he must have had waking with Zelda, heart popping open with love.

Remembering the prose of Fitzgerald, the shock of reading each perfect line, Benton stood up in surprise. Twenty years ago, when he had been seized by the dream of words, the perfect surface of Fitzgerald's language, he had wanted to write not a biography but a novel of his own. In those days, too, he had been living in Toronto.

When Robyn came into his office Benton was looking out the window to the snow. He turned around, and even before her name came into his mind he saw that her hair had been cut to shoulder length.

'What happened?'

'Am I early?'

'Your hair.'

'Oh, that. Do you like it? I've wanted to cut it for years but Hugh always insisted he would leave me if I did. Today is the second anniversary of his death and I thought, instead of crying all day, that I would go to the hairdresser. How do you like it?'

She stopped suddenly, searched in her purse for a cigarette. She had never before mentioned her husband by name and Benton found himself stepping towards her, as though she would have to be consoled.

'Stephan was the one who talked me into it,' Robyn said.

'Stephan?' Benton repeated. Despite himself he felt a flare of jealousy.

'When I told him about Hugh's loving my long hair Stephan said that I was being like a primitive widow, throwing herself on her husband's funeral pyre.'

'When did he tell you this?' Benton said stupidly, hating himself as he heard the words.

'At lunch,' Robyn said, 'the other day. He wanted me to read the first chapters of his thesis.'

'A brilliant student,' Benton said. 'Quite exceptional.' He sat down. Robyn's face, which used to be half hidden by the tidal waves of her long hair, now looked pretty, younger, more vulnerable. The colouring, too, had been renewed, so that the sharp light from the window was muted and golden in the wisps of hair that curled about her shoulders.

'I admire Jews that way,' Robyn said. 'They always have such a sinister twist of mind.'

Benton felt a blush starting, the way it had the day Robyn had pretended to be having an affair with a student, and he wondered if once again she was saying something to test him. But even as he expected her to laugh and apologize her mouth moved into that sudden flash of a smile, like a fencer flicking his sword to see if the tip had drawn blood.

'What are you doing this afternoon?'

'I was going to do my Christmas shopping today,' Benton said. 'I left my car to get repaired. It's not going to be ready until this evening.'

'Let me come with you. I always feel so stupid buying presents. You can encourage me to be extravagant.' Again she smiled, but this time it was the sad-wise smile she had shown him a week ago in the chicken coop, the smile he had imagined on her face as he turned his back on her in the bathroom. The following morning it had been Thalia, at the breakfast table, who brought up the incident.

'Benton tells me that he interrupted your bath.'

'I always like company in the bathroom,' Robyn had said. 'He could at least have brought me a drink.'

'It's silly how easily men can be embarrassed,' Thalia had continued. 'Nothing is more natural than being naked.'

Now Benton stood up. 'We'll go shopping,' he said. 'Then we can have a drink before it's time for me to pick up my car.'

'I don't want to waste your whole afternoon,' Robyn said hesitantly.

But as she spoke Benton felt as though one of the blades of light had slipped between his ribs. He stopped, suppressing a gasp, reached one hand out to the bookshelf to steady himself. He was in love with Robyn Marler. How could he not have known? Since the day he had met her he had been happy only in her presence, had thought of nothing and no one but her, had centred his daily existence on their apparently chance and casual meetings.

'What's wrong?'

'Nothing,' Benton said. He straightened up. The physical pain was gone but the calm white light of the room was now a swirling rainbow of turbulent colours. *I've had a heart attack,* he thought to himself, *an attack of the heart.*

'Are you feeling sick?'

'Not at all, no. It's just that I've been sitting in my chair all afternoon. I'm getting to be an old man, dizzy every time I make a sudden move.'

'Don't make any sudden moves,' Robyn said. She was standing very close to him, her arm linked through his to support him. Looking down to her face Benton saw the violet eyes of Robyn Marler turning slowly upwards, opening wider as if to grasp exactly what was happening.

'I'm all right,' Benton said. 'Let's get outside, into the air.'

A few minutes later they were walking across the snow-covered common of the campus. The afternoon sun that had been so dazzling only a few minutes before was now masked by thin yellow-white clouds, and though the sky was half clear, snow was falling. The wind gusted it into eddies, whipped it like sand across their faces.

Soon they were at the subway entrance. And by the time they were riding up the escalators of the Eaton Centre, Benton felt that he could breathe again, that the scene in his office was safely behind him, stored away with other scenes with Robyn, other embarrassing incidents from other moments in his life.

Through his body he felt a warm and buzzing hum, as if his blood had turned to sweet honey: the feeling of love released. When Robyn turned to ask his advice about a blouse for her sister, her voice rang through him like a low bell. And when he bought a sweater for Thalia he held it in his hands and squeezed the soft wool between his fingers as though it was Robyn he had in his hands, Robyn's skin he was wanting to warm, Robyn's pleasure he was hoping to excite.

Passing through the crowd they were sometimes squeezed together, sometimes separated by other bodies. The warm press of Robyn's shoulder and breast, her sudden absence, became the rhythm of Benton's breathing. Once she stopped to look in a window and Benton, wandering in his daze, was almost a hundred feet away before he realized that the rhythm was broken and she was out of his sight.

By the time they were finished shopping it was six o'clock. 'It's time for me to go now,' Benton said.

They were in the middle of the shopping mall, surrounded by a crowd so thick that they were now permanently pressed together. Benton, trying to step away, felt suddenly as he had that night on his farm. He was looking desire in the eye, and he was walking away from it.

'Goodbye,' Robyn said.

When Benton got to the garage they told him that they had been trying to phone him at his office. Something to do with the carburetor, a missing part that would take an extra day.

'I need the car,' Benton said. 'You should have told me it might take longer.'

'You can have mine,' the manager said, 'if it's that bad.'

'No. It's not that bad.'

He left the garage and walked down the street to a hotel where he and Malcolm had often gone to drink when they were graduate students. But when he went into the bar, Benton saw that the old wooden tables and chairs had been replaced by stuffed armchairs and sofas: the place looked like a gigantic living room. In it, laughing and talking, were crowds of happy drinkers, and the sounds of Christmas toasts and singing rolled towards him like a thick fog.

In the lobby he found a telephone.

'I can sleep at my office,' Benton said. 'They promised the car would be ready at noon.'

'Don't sleep at your office, your back will be sore for a week.'

Benton, silent, heard noises in the background. 'Who's there?'

'Stephan and Lilly. They came out to bring us a bottle of wine. Too bad you didn't know about the car earlier, you could have driven with them.'

'I could stay at a hotel,' Benton said.

'Stay at Robyn's. You should know your way around the couch well enough. And you could take her out to dinner. She must be lonely.'

'She doesn't seem lonely.'

'I love you, Benton.'

'I love you.'

'Don't make yourself miserable tonight. I'm sorry about the stupid car.'

'I am, too.'

Now Benton heard the explosive sound of Stephan's laugh. He started to reach for a cigarette, stopped himself, wished Malcolm were back from Paris so he could tell him how at forty-three he was a stupid adolescent again.

'I miss you, Benton.'

'I miss you, too.'

'I wish you were here, right now.' Benton, thinking that Stephan Hartmann was hearing this soft and seductive voice, turned uncomfortably in the phone booth. In the hotel lobby he could see a drunken couple. The man was wearing a camel-hair coat, open to reveal a dazzling white shirt, an expensive-looking tie. The woman was leaning against him, smiling as though for an advertisement. Her teeth were white and gleaming, her eyes shone adoringly, but most spectacular of all was the dark fur she wore: sleek and oiled it glowed with life, as though it still belonged to some incredibly powerful and vital beast.

'Don't worry about me,' Thalia said. 'I'm fine here. Have a good time at dinner.'

'Sit down,' Robyn said. 'Or stand if you prefer.'

Benton, the door of Malcolm Totting's apartment already firmly closed behind him, kicked the snow from his galoshes. Then his cold fingers struggled with the buckles – the old-fashioned kind that Thalia had looked at with awe, as though he were wearing a Chippendale – before stepping into the living room.

'I keep forgetting,' Robyn called from the kitchen, 'that this was your friend's apartment. In fact, Malcolm Totting left me a note saying that if there was anything I couldn't work I should get in touch with you. It was actually a very charming note. I wish I'd saved it.'

'Malcolm is famous for his notes.'

Benton stood for a moment in the centre of the living room. His eye had been drawn to the corner where, unexpectedly, Robyn had placed a small, waist-high spruce tree. Around it was spiralled a long silver chain, and at its foot, surrounding the ceramic pot, were heaped dozens of Christmas cards – some open for display, others still in their envelopes.

Now Robyn emerged from the kitchen. 'I made your Scotch with ice, but without water. I can't get used to Toronto's water – it doesn't taste poisonous enough.'

They sat down, facing each other over Totting's coffee table.

'Your health,' Robyn said.

'Merry Christmas.'

Benton leaned back, lit a cigarette.

'You scared me this afternoon in your office, I have to admit. A friend of mine once had a heart attack that way. He was over for dinner, Hugh had gotten him awfully drunk, and when he stood up from the table he just swayed for a moment, clutched his chest, then fell to the floor. At first we thought he was joking. "Just like Lawrence," Hugh chortled. But then it turned out he'd had a serious attack.'

Benton, staring at Robyn and feeling the blade between his own ribs again, slowly lowered his glass.

'He didn't die,' Robyn said. 'Not that night. But a couple of years later ...'

She stopped. Benton saw her eyes turning towards him once more, opening wider as they had during the afternoon, trying to comprehend what was happening to him. Again the colours of the room broke apart. He rubbed his eyes, but it was as if he were wearing those trick prism glasses he'd once had; nothing wanted to stay in its place. Benton picked up his glass again, tilted it back, and drained it. The whisky was sour against his tongue and throat. He stubbed out his cigarette, started a new one. The doctor had warned him against smoking and drinking so heavily again. And he had virtually given up walking, too. The daily five miles had become a quick, weekly turn around the farm.

'It must be wonderful to have a young child.'

'It is,' Benton said. 'Things happen, you never expect them.' After Jonah had been born, Thalia, thin and too narrow in the hips, had bled profusely for a week. Like a white flower bleeding whiter, Benton had thought vowing to protect her from anything bad that might ever happen to her, especially himself.

'You have a nice home, you and Thalia, a nice family.'

'I know.'

'Are you afraid of losing it?'

Benton looked at Robyn, whose violet eyes were now huge and round, staring into his once again.

'*Are* you afraid?'

'Yes.'

'Don't be afraid, Benton. You don't have to be afraid of me.'

'I'm not afraid of you, Robyn, I'm afraid of myself.' As he said these words he felt the room jerk into focus. It was like the night in the chicken coop, the night Robyn had started to teach him this simple emotional arithmetic that seemed to be her specialty. One is one. One and one are two. Two minus one is one again.

'I wanted to be friends with you, Benton. I didn't want to hurt you.'

'You haven't hurt me.'

'I'm in love with you, Benton.'

'No.' Even as he said it, the word surprised him. It choked out of his throat, of its own volition, then seemed to lie between them, an unwanted stone. 'I mean,' Benton said, but he didn't continue. What he had started to say was that what he feared was not her love for him, but his love for her. But to say it would make it true, would make him responsible for the consequences. 'Keep your thoughts to yourself, when it comes to romance. Then, when they pass, you can mourn for them alone.' This had been Malcolm Totting's advice. Two years older than Benton, Malcolm had crossed the line of his fortieth birthday at a dead crawl, flayed by every crisis in the book: broken marriage, faltering health, professional insecurity, sexual hot flashes. By the time his sabbatical arrived he had barely the energy to get to Paris. Privately, Benton suspected that Totting was going to Paris not to renew his French, eat wonderful food, do research, or get drunk at cut-rate prices – but to contemplate the romance of his failed suicide.

'What do you mean?'

Benton tried to imagine Thalia out at the farm. In Stephan's arms. In Lilly's arms. In the arms of Stephan and Lilly together.

'I mean,' Benton said, 'that I am in love with you, too.' He looked across at Robyn and tried to smile. 'I feel like such an idiot. Why are we sitting here saying that we love each other? Can't we eat dinner or something?'

'Let me make you an omelette, Benton. Eggs satisfy the nerves.'

Benton stood up. For the third time in the past few months he felt himself beginning to blush. This time it caught him entire. He could feel his feet heating up, the gaps between his toes filling with sweat, the rush of hot blood turning his legs into pillars of fire, the invasion of his groin, a hot and itching sensation spreading across his belly. And at the same time he saw his hands had turned beet red, his ears were burning, even his lips seemed swollen and unable to move.

'Benton –'

'No –'

And then he had her in his arms, was squeezing her fiercely against him, crushing her into his chest so that he could feel her own heat joining to his.

'It took me a long time to get you here,' Robyn whispered, when they were finally at the door to the bedroom.

I've been here before, Benton couldn't help thinking. But he said nothing. Instead he stared at the bed as though the blades twisting at his ribs could open his eyes, too, make them see beneath the antique quilt with which Robyn had covered the bed to the imprints of the bodies that had already lain there.

Then he turned to Robyn. In the broken light of his love, her face was like an icon's, dangerous and sharp.

'I can't do it,' Benton groaned.

'Can't do what?'

'I can't leave Thalia for you. I'm too old, too tired, too –'

'Benton, Benton. You must think I'm such a bitch.'

'What are we going to do?'

'Live our lives, Benton, as friends, lovers, never hurt each other. Promise?'

He had taken a room for himself at the hotel, explaining carefully to the bored clerk that because his car had broken down he had no luggage but the single Christmas present he had bought for his wife during the snowstorm. When he got to the room his hand trembled as he tried to insert the key. The key dropped to the carpet and, bending over, Benton wondered how he had reached that point of nervous exhaustion where he was afraid to rent a hotel room without making excuses.

The first thing he did was to take a bath. Soaking in the hot water he reminded himself of other irregular episodes that had been followed by this same cure, as if the poisons of alcohol and illicit sex could be removed only by direct skin contact with soap: a pore-by-pore cleansing guaranteed to wash away hangovers of every variety. When the telephone rang he was in the midst of rinsing his hair. But he leapt to answer it, grabbing a towel on his way. A man's voice, thick and stumbling with Christmas spirit, asked for Helen. Benton cut the voice off, saw that despite everything that had happened it was only midnight, and dialled his own home number.

He was about to hang up when Thalia answered on the sixth ring.

'Benton,' he said. 'I mean, it's me.'

'Hello, you.'

'Are they still there?' Benton felt so jealous that he began to shiver.

'Just going to sleep. Where are you?'

'At the hotel.'

'I miss you,' Thalia said.

'I miss you.' Benton pulled the towel more tightly around his waist.

'Did you have dinner with Robyn?'

'Yes.'

'Benton, is anything wrong?'

Thalia's voice was suddenly awake now, alert. Benton was reminded of the times when, still married, he used to wait until his wife was asleep and then creep downstairs to telephone Thalia. That was after she had told him she was pregnant, during the month-long interregnum between her announcement and his actual final separation. Those phone calls had been like secret dreams; long, whispered conversations during which Benton listened with one ear to Thalia's sleepy loving voice while the other wavered like an antenna to catch the first suspicious creak on the stairs. 'You can't fight women,' Malcolm Totting had told him repeatedly. 'Women are professionals at love.' 'Love, yes,' Benton once replied, 'but men know how to betray.' 'Don't overreach yourself on that,' Totting had advised.

'Benton? Are you there?'

'I'm here,' Benton said. 'Sorry, there *is* something wrong.' He paused and for a brief moment he actually believed that he was going to blurt it out like a schoolboy, pass the burden to the ever-accommodating Thalia who, left on her own, might find other ways to amuse herself. 'I feel terrible,' Benton said. 'You know how I hate hotels.'

'Poor Benton. Have you been drinking?'

'The usual.'

'You were going to stop drinking, doctor's orders.'

'I still am,' Benton said. 'After Christmas, I promise. Nothing but mineral water and tomato juice.'

'I wish you were here,' Thalia said. Her voice was fully awake and Benton realized that a wall of sorts had already grown up between them – a glass wall, perhaps, that was not even visible in the full light of love, but a wall, nonetheless, one that they would have to scale each time they wanted to be close, make love, trust.

'I'll come first thing in the morning, as soon as the car is ready.'

'Love you,' Thalia said, suddenly absent. But Benton, his own suspicions alerted, thought he could hear whispers behind her. Perhaps it was Hartmann going to the refrigerator, or even making faces to tease poor Thalia about having to talk to the staid and aging lover who had snatched her from the midst of youth and placed her, alone, in the middle of nowhere while he stumbled around downtown Toronto having his mid-life crisis.

'Benton, are you sure you're all right?'

'I'm tired,' Benton said. 'Let's spend tomorrow in bed, the way we used to.'

As he hung up Benton realized that the bar would still be open, so he dressed again and went downstairs. In the elevator he decided that right after New Year's he would cut out everything but beer and the occasional glass of wine. Reassured by this resolve he ordered coffee and a double brandy: the coffee to snap him out of his depression, the brandy to put him to sleep.

By the time he went to bed he was, in fact, drunk;

unpleasantly so. Three double brandies buzzed angrily through him, an unwanted extra skin between himself and the starched sheets.

Twice he picked up the telephone to dial Robyn's number; the third time he let it ring twice before he hung up. Then he turned on his stomach, bit into the pillow to keep his thoughts from forming, and fell into a deep sleep full of half-seen dreams and warnings.

'The greatest tragedy is a life unlived,' Stephan Hartmann said, and in his mouth the words took on such irony that they seemed to float at a miserable half-mast, barely hovering above the coffee table in Robyn Marler's living room. Benton, caught framed in the kitchen doorway, stopped and almost turned. For two hours Hartmann had been compulsively ranting to Robyn. First about his thesis, then on various subjects of departmental gossip. His hands couldn't stop moving, and under his thatch of black hair his face was red with enthusiasm. He had arrived at the apartment without calling in advance and when Robyn had answered the door he'd barged right through, nodding at Benton as if to acknowledge not only Benton's unexplained presence on a Wednesday afternoon but the whole new changed order of things. *He's been taking drugs*, had been Benton's first thought; but now Hartmann seemed under the influence of only a very boring type of pep pill.

From the refrigerator Benton took a beer for himself, a tin of apple juice for Robyn. Hartmann was already on his fourth cup of coffee.

It was late January, almost exactly a month since the afternoon he had gone Christmas shopping with Robyn; but so much had changed in that month he could hardly recognize himself. In the mornings when he dressed, his back often to Thalia, he was surprised to find his body fitting into the same old clothes. Even Jonah seemed not to have noticed that Benton's insides had been mysteriously rearranged: he still hugged Benton with abandon, clung to him in the middle of the night when he woke up with bad dreams, smiled at him with foolish happiness when he suddenly appeared from around some unexpected corner.

A month ago, Benton remembered as he poured Robyn's apple juice into a glass, he had promised himself to stop drinking at New Year's. But now liquor was the least of his problems, merely one of the many lubricants he used to get himself through the various sticky patches of his day.

When Benton came into the living room Hartmann suddenly turned to him and said, as if he had been waiting all afternoon to deliver this essential line: 'You are a good man. You *were* bad, like the rest of us, but now you are good. That's why it hurts.'

'It doesn't hurt,' Benton said, putting the glass of apple juice on the coffee table in front of Robyn. He stood above Hartmann, his palm protectively cupped around his beer bottle.

'I understand,' Hartmann said. 'You don't have to explain anything to me.'

Benton sat down. Hartmann's eyes were trained on him like the open mouths of weapons. 'It's your life,' Hartmann said. 'I understand completely.'

Sentences crowded to Benton's tongue, but he didn't want to fend Hartmann off with a sharp reply; he wanted instead to lose himself in a sudden explosion of force, to meet the challenge of Hartmann's phoney stare with a slap that would send Hartmann flying across the room, out the door, out of his sight forever.

It was Robyn who finally broke the silence. She picked up Hartmann's hand and patted it consolingly. When she let it go Hartmann made a fist, like a child about to have a tantrum. 'It's time to go now, Stephan.'

Hartmann jerked to his feet, his coffee unfinished, a cigarette still burning in the ashtray. 'Benton,' he said, 'you can't just –' And then Benton knew that Thalia had sent him, after all, that there were no more mysteries: just Thalia at the farmhouse, listening to the furnace shudder, looking out at the snow, crying into the telephone. 'What are you going to do?' Hartmann asked.

Robyn leaned forward to stub out Hartmann's cigarette. A button had come loose, and her dark shirt opened onto her smooth white skin, skin that felt as smooth and deep as it had first looked that night in the bathtub, and because they had gotten dressed so hastily when Hartmann came to the door she was wearing nothing under the shirt. Almost her entire breast was exposed, like a lost animal suddenly surfacing in a place it didn't belong. Benton, his mouth open to reply to Hartmann, found his attention caught by this unexpected intruder: *help me*, it seemed to say.

Hartmann's eyes were swinging back and forth from Benton to Robyn. The silence had prolonged itself so long that Benton found it quite natural to lift the bottle of beer to his mouth, take a swallow, set the bottle down, and then reach into his pocket for his cigarettes.

'What am I going to do?' Benton said, blowing smoke into the little triangle that their faces made. And finally looked at Hartmann, let his own eyes settle into Hartmann's the way a teacher finally seizes hold of his class. 'For God's sake, Hartmann, you are surely the last person in the world who has the right to demand an explanation.'

But even as Hartmann was going out the door, Benton wondered what sense his words could possibly make, even seem to make. Was he implying that Hartmann had slept with Thalia? With Robyn?

'I can't hurt Thalia,' Benton said. He put out his old cigarette, lit a new one. It was essential to have the entire possibility stretching out in front of him. He walked to the window of the apartment hoping to see Stephan fade reassuringly from sight, but of course the street was too far away, only tiny cars crawling along and ant-like figures twisting amongst each other on the sidewalk.

The light in the room was breaking apart again, the way it always did these days. It made Robyn's golden hair shine brighter.

'I can't afford to love,' Benton said.

Robyn stepped towards him. It was up to her, he thought. Things had gone too far. They were out of his hands. He had known it the night in the chicken coop, when he had tried to do his duty, like a man. Now it was up to the women: they could divide him up in whatever way was most convenient, following the lines of theory or love, it was really their decision.

'You look tired,' Robyn said. She lifted her hand. Her palm slid underneath his shirt. Her fingers felt warm and alive against his bare chest. 'Benton,' she said. He had a sudden vision of them underneath a sheet, swimming in a tent of darkness, her body like a cool sea washing over him.

Totting came back early. Benton drove to the airport to pick him up. It was snowing heavily, and they had to plough the runways to keep them clear. By the time Totting's plane was allowed to land it was after midnight, and Benton, sitting on a moulded plastic seat in the Arrivals lounge, felt stunned with fatigue.

Totting emerged from Customs carrying only one suitcase. He was having the rest shipped in a trunk, he said. After only a few months away he seemed a different person: hair that had been greying was now almost entirely silver, he was thinner, and wore more expensive clothes.

'I felt better,' Totting said. 'I decided to come home before I got depressed again.'

The highways were deserted and as they drove towards the farm Benton was excruciatingly aware of the sharp edge his headlights made against the falling snow, the humming of his tires on the snow-packed pavement.

'Has anything happened?'

'Nothing much,' Benton said. For a moment, in a sudden burst of panic, Benton wondered if Thalia or Hartmann had written to Malcolm, begging him to rescue their friend from a fatal error.

'I met a lot of people,' Totting said. 'I think that's what made me better.'

After a week, one afternoon when they were out walking through his farm, Benton told Totting about his affair with Robyn Marler.

'How did it end?' Totting asked.

'I just told her it was over,' Benton said. Only that morning, he didn't bother to add, while he was at the university picking up a batch of essays. Robyn had come into his office, closed the door behind her, then stood nervously at his desk, gazing at the picture of Scott Fitzgerald. She looked unhappy. In fact, every day she was a little unhappier than the day before.

'I'm sorry,' Benton found himself saying.

'It's not your fault.'

'Let's give up now,' Benton said, 'while we can.'

Robyn had turned away from him and walked out of the office. Remembering the sound of her leaving, Benton found that he had allowed his eyes to be filled by the sun. He blinked. In this bright light the white strands of Totting's hair lay like pale prisoners across his scalp. He looked like an old man; even his skin had started to separate into layers, like French pastry.

'Are you staying with Thalia?'

'I'm going to try.'

'Love is the worst,' Totting said.

THE SINS OF TOMAS BENARES

A NARROW, three-storey house near College Street had been the home of the Benares family since they arrived in Toronto in 1936. Beside the front door, bolted to the brick, was a brass name-plate that was kept polished and bright: DR TOMAS BENARES.

Benares had brought the name-plate – and little else – with him when he and his wife fled Spain just before the Civil War. For twenty years it had resided on the brick beside the doorway. And then, after various happinesses and tragedies – the tragedies being unfortunately more numerous – it had been replaced triumphantly by a new name-plate: DR ABRAHAM BENARES. This son, Abraham, was the only child to have survived those twenty years.

Abraham had lost not only his siblings, but also his mother. The day his name-plate was proudly mounted Tomas could at last say to himself that perhaps his string of bad fortune had finally been cut, for despite everything he now had a son who was a doctor like himself, and who was married with two children.

By 1960, the Benares household was wealthy in many ways. True, the family had not moved to the north of the city like many other immigrants who had made money, but during the era of the DR ABRAHAM BENARES name-plate the adjoining house was purchased to give space for an expanded office and to provide an investment for Abraham Benares' swelling income as a famous internist. The back yards of both houses were combined into one elegant lawn that was tended twice a week by a professional gardener, an old Russian Jew whom Tomas Benares had met first in his office, then at the synagogue. He spent most of his time drinking tea and muttering about the injustices that had been brought upon his people, while Tomas himself, by this time retired, toothless, and bent of back, crawled through the flower beds on his knees, wearing the discarded rubber dishwashing gloves of his son's extraordinarily beautiful wife.

Bella was her name. On anyone else, such a name would have been a joke; but Bella's full figure and dark, Mediterranean face glowed with such animal heat that from the first day he met her Tomas felt like an old man in her presence. Of this Bella seemed entirely unaware. After moving into the house she cooked for Tomas, pressed her scorching lips to his on family occasions, even hovered over him during meals, her fruity breath like a hot caress against his neck. After her children were born she began to refer to Tomas as 'grandfather', and sometimes while the infants played on the living-room floor she would stand beside Tomas with the full weight of her fleshy hand sinking into his arm. 'Look at us,' she said to Tomas once, 'three generations.'

A few years after the birth of his daughter, Abraham Benares was walking with her down to College Street, as he did every Saturday, to buy a newspaper and a bag of apples, when a black Ford car left the street and continued its uncontrolled progress along the sidewalk where Abraham was walking. Instinctively, Abraham scooped Margaret into his arms, but the car was upon him before he could move. Abraham Benares, forty-one years old and the holder of the city intercollegiate record for the one-hundred-yard dash, had time only to throw his daughter onto the adjacent lawn while the car mowed him down.

The next year, 1961, the name-plate on the door changed again: DR TOMAS BENARES reappeared. There had been no insurance policy and the old man, now seventy-four years of age but still a licensed physician, recommenced the practice of medicine. He got the complaining gardener to redivide the yard with a new fence, sold the house next door to pay his son's debt, and took over the task of providing for his daughter-in-law and his two grandchildren.

Before reopening his practice, Tomas Benares got new false teeth and two new suits. He spent six months reading his old medical textbooks and walked several miles every morning to sweep the cobwebs out of his brain. He also, while walking, made it a point of honour never to look over his shoulder.

On the eve of his ninety-fourth birthday Tomas Benares was

sixty-two inches tall and weighed one hundred and twelve pounds. These facts he noted carefully in a small diary. Each year, sitting in his third-floor bedroom-study, Tomas Benares entered his height and weight into the pages of this diary. He also summarized any medical problems he had experienced during the year past, and made his prognosis for the year to come. There had once been an essay-like annual entry in which he confessed his outstanding sins and moral omissions from the previous year and outlined how he could correct or at least repent them in the year to follow. These essays had begun when Tomas was a medical student, and had continued well past the year in which his wife died. But when he had retired the first time from practising medicine and had the time to read over the fifty years of entries he had noticed that his sins grew progressively more boring with age. And so, after that, he simply recorded the number of times he had enjoyed sexual intercourse that year.

Now, almost ninety-four, Tomas Benares couldn't help seeing that even this simple statistic had been absent for almost a decade. His diary was getting shorter while his life was getting longer. His last statistic had been when he was eighty-six – one time; the year before – none at all. But in his eighty-fourth year there had been a dozen transgressions. Transgressions! They should have been marked as victories. Tomas brushed back at the wisps of white hair that still adorned his skull. He couldn't remember any detail at all of the supposed events. Perhaps he had been lying. According to the entry, his height during that erotic year had been sixty-four inches, and his weight exactly twice that – one hundred and twenty-eight pounds. In 1956, when he had begun compiling the statistics, there had been only one admission of intercourse, but his height had been sixty-five inches and his weight one hundred and forty.

Suddenly, Tomas had a vision of himself as an old-fashioned movie. In each frame he was a different size, lived a different life. Only accelerating the reel could make the crowd into one person.

He was sitting in an old blue armchair that had been in the living room when Marguerita was still alive. There he used to read aloud in English to her, trying to get his accent right, while in the adjacent kitchen she washed up the dinner dishes and called out his mistakes. Now he imagined pulling himself out of the armchair, walking to the window to see if his grandson Joseph's car was parked on the street below. He hooked his fingers, permanently curved, into the arms of his chair. And then he pulled. But the chair was a vacuum sucking him down with the gravity of age. Beside him was a glass of raspberry wine. He brought it to his lips, wet the tip of his tongue. He was on that daily two-hour voyage between the departure of his day nurse and the arrival of Joseph. Eventually, perhaps soon, before his weight and height had entirely shrunk away and there were no statistics at all to enter into his diary, he would die. He wanted to die with the house empty. That was the last wish of Tomas Benares.

But even while his ninety-fourth birthday approached, Tomas Benares was not worrying about dying. To be sure he had become smaller with each year, and the prospect of worthwhile sin had almost disappeared; but despite the day nurse and the iron gravity of his chair, Tomas Benares was no invalid. Every morning this whole summer – save the week he had the flu – his nurse, whose name was Elizabeth Rankin, had helped him down the stairs and into the yard where, on his knees, he tended his gardens. While the front of the house had been let go by his careless grandson, Joseph, the back was preserved in the splendour it had known for almost fifty years. Bordering the carefully painted picket fence that surrounded the small yard were banks of flowers, the old strawberry patch, and in one corner a small stand of raspberry canes that were covered by netting to keep away the plague of thieving sparrows.

This morning, too, the morning of his birthday, Elizabeth Rankin helped him down the stairs. Elizabeth Rankin had strong arms, but although he could hardly walk down the three flights of stairs by himself – let alone climb back up – he could think of his own father, who had lived to be one hundred and twenty-three, and of his grandfather Benares, who had lived to the same age. There was, in fact, no doubt that this enormous number was fate's stamp on the brow of the Benares men, though even fate could not *always* cope with automobiles.

But, as his own father had told Tomas, the Benares were to consider themselves blessed because fate seemed to pick them out more frequently than other people. For example, Tomas's father, who was born in 1820, had waited through two wives to have children, and when one was finally born, a boy, he had died of an unknown disease that winter brought to the Jewish quarter of Kiev. So frightened had he been by this show of God's spite that Tomas's father had sold the family lumbering business and rushed his wife back to Spain, the cradle of his ancestors, where she bore Tomas in 1884. Tomas's grandfather had, of course, been hale and hearty at the time: one hundred and four years old, he had lived on the top floor of the house just as Tomas now lived on the top floor of his own grandson's house.

That old man, Tomas's grandfather, had been a round, brown apple baked dry by the sun and surrounded by a creamy white fringe of beard. He had been born in 1780 and Tomas, bemoaning the emptiness of his diary on the occasion of his oncoming ninety-fourth, realized suddenly that he was holding two hundred years in his mind. His father had warned him: the Benares men were long-lived relics whose minds sent arrows back into the swamp of the past, so deep into the swamp that the lives they recalled were clamped together in a formless gasping mass, waiting to be shaped by those who remembered. The women were more peripheral: stately and beautiful, they were easily extinguished; perhaps they were bored to death by the small, round-headed, stubborn men who made up the Benares tribe.

'We were always Spaniards,' the old man told Tomas, 'stubborn as donkeys.' *Stubborn as a donkey,* the child Tomas had whispered. Had his mother not already screamed this at him? And he imagined ancient Spain: a vast, sandy expanse where the Jews had been persecuted and in revenge had hidden their religion under prayer shawls and been stubborn as donkeys.

And they hadn't changed, Tomas thought gleefully, they hadn't changed at all; filled with sudden enthusiasm and the image of himself as a white-haired, virile donkey, he pulled himself easily out of his chair and crossed the room to the window where he looked down for Joseph's car. The room was huge: the whole third floor of the house save for an alcove walled off as a bathroom. Yet even in the afternoon the room was dark as a cave, shadowed by its clutter of objects that included everything from his marriage bed to the stand-up scale with the weights and sliding rule that he used to assess himself for his yearly entry.

From the window he saw that his grandson's car had yet to arrive. On the sidewalk instead were children travelling back and forth on tricycles, shouting to each other in a fractured mixture of Portuguese and English. As always, when he saw children on the sidewalk, he had to resist opening the window and warning them to watch out for cars. It had been Margaret, only four years old, who had run back to the house to say that 'Papa is sick', then had insisted on returning down the street with Tomas.

Two hundred years: would Margaret live long enough to sit frozen in a chair and feel her mind groping from one century to the next? Last year, on his birthday, she had given him the bottle of raspberry wine he was now drinking. 'Every raspberry is a blessing,' she had said. She had a flowery tongue, like her brother, and when she played music Tomas could sense her passion whirling like a dark ghost through the room. What would she remember? Her mother who had run away; her grandmother whom she had never known; her father, covered by a sheet by the time she and Tomas had arrived, blood from his crushed skull seeping into the white linen.

They had come a long way, the Benares: from the new Jerusalem in Toledo to two centuries in Kiev, only to be frightened back to Spain before fleeing again, this time to a prosperous city in the New World. But nothing had changed, Tomas thought, even the bitterness over his son's death still knifed through him exactly as it had when he saw Margaret's eyes at the door, when Joseph, at the funeral, broke into a long, keening howl.

Stubborn as a donkey. Tomas straightened his back and walked easily from the window towards his chair. He would soon be ninety-four years old; and if fate was to be trusted, which it wasn't, there were to be thirty more years of anniversaries. During the next year, he thought, he had better put some effort into improving his statistics.

He picked up his diary again, flipped the pages backward, fell into a doze before he could start reading.

On his ninety-fourth birthday Tomas slept in. This meant not waking until after eight o'clock; and then lying in bed and thinking about his dreams. In the extra hours of sleep Tomas dreamed that he was a young man again, that he was married, living in Madrid, and that at noon the bright sun was warm as he walked the streets from his office to the café where he took lunch with his cronies. But in this dream he was not a doctor but a philosopher; for some strange reason it had been given to him to spend his entire life thinking about oak trees, and while strolling the broad, leafy streets it was precisely this subject that held his mind. He had also the duty, of course, of supervising various graduate students, all of whom were writing learned dissertations on the wonders of the oak; and it often, in this dream, pleased him to spend the afternoon with these bright and beautiful young people, drinking wine and saying what needed to be said.

In the bathroom, Tomas shaved himself with the electric razor that had been a gift from Joseph. Even on his own birthday he no longer trusted his hand with the straight razor that still hung, with its leather strop, from a nail in the wall. This, he suddenly thought, was the kind of detail that should also be noted in his annual diary – the texture of his shrinking world. Soon everything would be forbidden to him, and he would be left with only the space his own huddled skeleton could occupy. After shaving, Tomas washed his face, noting the exertion that was necessary just to open and close the cold water tap, and then he went back to the main room where he began slowly to dress.

It was true, he was willing to admit, that these days he often thought about his own death; but such thoughts did not disturb him. In fact, during those hours when he felt weak and sat in his chair breathing slowly, as if each weak breath might be his last, he often felt Death sitting with him. A quiet friend, Death; one who was frightening at first, but now was a familiar companion, an invisible brother waiting for him to come home.

But home, for Tomas Benares, was still the world of the living. When Elizabeth Rankin came to check on him, she found Tomas dressed and brushed. And a few minutes later he was sitting in his own garden, drinking espresso coffee and listening to the birds fuss in the flowering hedges that surrounded his patio. There Tomas, at peace, let the hot sun soak into his face. Death was with him in the garden, in the seductive buzz of insects, the comforting sound of water running in the nearby kitchen. The unaccustomed long sleep only gave Tomas the taste for more. He could feel himself drifting off, noted with interest that he had no desire to resist, felt Death pull his chair closer, his breath disguised as raspberries and mimosa.

At seventy-four years of age, also on his birthday, Tomas Benares had gone out to his front steps, unscrewed his son's name-plate and reaffixed his own. In the previous weeks he had restored the house to the arrangement it had known before his original retirement.

The front hall was the waiting room. On either side were long wooden benches, the varnished oak polished by a generation of patients. This front hall opened into a small parlour that looked onto the street. In that room was a desk, more chairs for waiting, and the doctor's files. At first his wife ran that parlour; after her death, Tomas had hired a nurse.

Behind the parlour was the smallest room of all. It had space for an examination table, a glass cabinet with a few books and several drawers of instruments, and a single uncomfortable chair. On the ceiling was a fluorescent light, and the window was protected by venetian blinds made of heavy plastic.

After Abraham's death his widow, Bella, and the children had stayed on in the Benares household, and so on the morning of the reopening Tomas had gone into the kitchen to find Bella making coffee and feeding breakfast to Joseph and

Margaret. He sat down wordlessly at the kitchen table while Bella brought him coffee and toast, and he was still reading the front section of the morning paper when the doorbell rang. Joseph leapt from the table and ran down the hall. Tomas was examining the advertisement he had placed to announce the recommencement of his practice.

'Finish your coffee,' said Bella. 'Let her wait. She's the one who needs the job.'

But Tomas was already on his feet. Slowly he walked down the hall to the front parlour. He could hear Joseph chatting with the woman, and was conscious of trying to keep his back straight. He was wearing, for his new practice, a suit newly tailored. His old tailor had died, but his son had measured Tomas with the cloth tape, letting his glasses slide down to rest on the tip of his nose exactly like his father had. Now in his new blue suit, a matching tie, and one of the white linen shirts that Marguerita had made for him, Tomas stood in his front parlour.

'Dr Benares, I am Elizabeth Rankin; I answered your advertisement for a nurse.'

'I am pleased to meet you, Mrs Rankin.'

'Miss Rankin.' Elizabeth Rankin was then a young woman entering middle age. She had brown hair parted in the middle and pulled back in a bun behind her neck, eyes of a darker brown in which Tomas saw a mixture of fear and sympathy. She was wearing a skirt and a jacket, but had with her a small suitcase in case it was necessary for her to start work right away.

'Would you like to see my papers, Dr Benares?'

'Yes, if you like. Please sit down.'

Joseph was still in the room and Tomas let him watch as Elizabeth Rankin pulled out a diploma stating that she had graduated from McGill University in the biological sciences, and another diploma showing that she had received her RN from the same university.

'I have letters of reference, Dr Benares.'

'Joseph, please get a cup of coffee for Miss Rankin. Do you –'

'Just black, Joseph.'

They sat in silence until Joseph arrived with the coffee, and then Tomas asked him to leave and close the door behind him.

'I'm sorry,' Elizabeth Rankin said. 'I saw the advertisement and ...'

She trailed off. It was six months since Tomas had seen her, but he recognized her right away; she was the woman who had been driving the car that had killed his son. At the scene of the accident she had shivered in shock until the ambulance arrived. Tomas had even offered her some sleeping pills. Then she had reappeared to hover on the edge of the mourners at Abraham's funeral.

'You're a very brave woman, Miss Rankin.'

'No, I ...' Her eyes clouded over. Tomas, behind the desk, watched her struggle. When he had seen her in the hall, his first reaction had been anger.

'I thought I should do something,' she said. 'I don't need a salary, of course, and I *am* a qualified nurse.'

'I see that,' Tomas said dryly.

'You must hate me,' Elizabeth Rankin said.

Tomas shrugged. Joseph came back into the room and stood beside Elizabeth Rankin. She put her hand on his shoulder and the boy leaned against her.

'You mustn't bother Miss Rankin,' Tomas said, but even as he spoke he could see Elizabeth's hand tightening on the boy's shoulder.

'Call Margaret,' Tomas said to Joseph, and then asked himself why, indeed, he should forgive this woman. No reason came to mind, and while Joseph ran through the house, searching for his sister, Tomas sat in his reception room and looked carefully at the face of Elizabeth Rankin. The skin below her eyes was dark, perhaps she had trouble sleeping; and though her expression was maternal she had a tightly drawn quality that was just below the surface, as though the softness were a costume.

He remembered a friend, who had been beaten by a gang of Franco's men, saying he felt sorry for them. When Tomas's turn came, he had felt no pity for his assailants. And although what Elizabeth Rankin had done was an accident, not a malicious act, she was still the guilty party. Tomas wondered if she knew what he was thinking, wondered how she could not. She was sitting with one leg crossed over the other, her eyes on the door through which the sounds of the children's feet now came. And when Margaret, shy, sidled into the room, Tomas made a formal introduction. He was thinking, as he watched Margaret's face, how strange it was that the victims must always console their oppressors.

Margaret, four years old, curtsied and then held out her hand. There was no horrified scream, no flicker of recognition.

'Miss Rankin will be coming every morning,' Tomas announced. 'She will help me in my office.'

'You are very kind, Dr Benares.'

'We will see,' Tomas said. It was then that he had an extraordinary thought, or at least a thought that was extraordinary for him. It occurred to him that Elizabeth Rankin didn't simply want to atone, or to be consoled. She wanted to be taken advantage of.

Tomas waited until the children had left the room, then closed the door. He stood in front of Elizabeth Rankin until she, too, got to her feet.

'Pig,' Tomas Benares hissed; and he spat at her face. The saliva missed its target and landed, instead, on the skin covering her right collarbone. There it glistened, surrounded by tiny beads, before gliding down the open V of her blouse.

The eyes of Elizabeth Rankin contracted briefly. Then their expression returned to a flat calm. Tomas, enraged, turned on his heel and walked quickly out of the room. When he came back fifteen minutes later, Elizabeth Rankin had changed into her white uniform and was sorting through the files of his son.

Bella said it wasn't right.

'That you should have *her* in the house,' she said. 'It's disgusting.'

'She has a diploma,' Tomas said.

'And how are you going to pay her? You don't have any patients.'

This discussion took place in the second-floor sitting room after the children were asleep. It was the room where Bella and Abraham used to go to have their privacy.

'At first I thought maybe you didn't recognize her,' Bella started again, 'and so I said to myself, what sort of a joke is this? Maybe she didn't get enough the first time, maybe she has to come back for more.'

'It was an accident,' Tomas said.

'So you forgive her?' Bella challenged. She had a strong, bell-like voice which, when she and Abraham were first married, had been a family joke, one even she would laugh at; but since his death the tone had grown rusty and sepulchral.

Tomas shrugged.

'I don't forgive her,' Bella said.

'It was an accident,' Tomas said. 'She has to work it out of her system?'

At thirty, Bella was even more beautiful than when she had been married. The children had made her heavy, but grief had carved away the excess flesh. She had jet-black hair and olive skin that her children had both inherited. Now she began to cry and Tomas, as always during these nightly outburst of tears, went to stand by the window.

'Well?' Bella insisted. 'What do you expect me to do?'

When she had asked this question before, Tomas advised her to go to sleep with the aid of a pill. But now he hesitated. For how many months, for how many years could he tell her to obliterate her evenings in sleeping pills.

'You're the saint,' Bella said. 'You never wanted anyone after Marguerita.'

'I was lucky,' Tomas said. 'I had a family.'

'I have a family.'

'I was older,' Tomas said.

'So,' Bella repeated dully, 'you never did want anyone else.'

Tomas was silent. When Abraham brought her home he had asked Tomas what he thought of her. 'She's very beautiful,' Tomas had said. Abraham had happily agreed. Now she was more beautiful but, Tomas thought, also more stupid.

'It is very hard,' Tomas said, 'for a man my age to fall in love.'

'Your wife died many years ago ...'

Tomas shrugged. 'I always felt old,' he said, 'ever since we came to Canada.' All this time he had been standing at the window, and now he made sure his back was turned so that she wouldn't see his tears. The day Abraham had been killed he had cried with her. Since then, even at the funeral, he had refused to let her see his tears. Why? He didn't know. The sight of her, even the smell of her walking into a room, seemed to freeze his heart.

'If there was –' Bella started. She stopped. Tomas knew that he should help her, that she shouldn't have to fight Abraham's ghost *and* his father, but he couldn't bring himself to reach out. It was like watching an ant trying to struggle its way out of a pot of honey.

'If there was someone else,' Bella said. 'Even a job.'

'What can you do?' Tomas asked, but the question was rhetorical; Bella had married Abraham the year after she had finished high school. She couldn't even type.

'*I* could be your receptionist, instead of that –'

'Nurse,' Tomas interrupted. 'I need a nurse, Bella.'

'I can put a thermometer in someone's mouth,' Bella said. 'Are people going to die while you're next door in the office?'

'A doctor needs a nurse,' Tomas said. 'I didn't invent the rules.'

'There's a rule?'

'It's a custom, Bella.'

He turned from the window.

'And anyway,' Bella said, 'who's going to take care of the children?'

'That's right, the children need a mother.'

'We need Bella in the kitchen making three meals a day so at night she can cry herself to sleep – while the murderer is working off her guilt so at night she can go out and play with the boys, her conscience clean.'

'You don't know what she does at night –'

'You're such a saint,' Bella said suddenly. 'You are such a saint the whole world admires you, do you know that?'

'Bella –'

'The holy Dr Benares. At seventy-four years of age he ends his retirement and begins work again to provide for his widowed daughter and his two orphaned grandchildren. Has the world ever seen such a man? At the *shul* they're talking about adding a sixth book to the Torah.' She looked at Tomas, and Tomas, seeing her go out of control, could only stand and watch. She was like an ant, he was thinking. Now the ant was at the lip of the pot. It might fall back into the honey, in which case it would drown; or it might escape after all.

'You're such a saint,' Bella said in her knife-edge voice, 'you're such a saint that you think poor Bella just wants to go out and get laid.'

She was teetering on the edge now, Tomas thought.

'You should see your face now,' Bella said. '*Adultery*, you're thinking. *Whore.*'

'It's perfectly normal for a healthy –'

'Oh, healthy *shit!*' Bella screamed. 'I just want to go out. Out, out, *out!*'

She was standing in the doorway, her face beet-red, panting with her fury. Tomas, staying perfectly still, could feel his own answering blush searing the backs of his ears, surrounding his neck like a hot rope.

'Even the saint goes for a walk,' Bella's voice had dropped again. 'Even the saint can spend the afternoon over at Herman Levine's apartment, playing cards and drinking beer.'

Tomas could feel his whole body burning and chafing inside his suit. *The saint*, she was calling him. And what had he done to her? Offered her and her family a home when they needed it. 'Did I make Abraham stay here?' Tomas asked. And then realized, to his shame, that he had said the words aloud.

He saw Bella in the doorway open her mouth until it looked like the muzzle of a cannon. Her lips struggled and convulsed. The room filled with unspoken obscenities.

Tomas reached a hand to touch the veins in his neck. They were so engorged with blood he was choking. He tore at his tie, forced his collar open.

'Oh, God,' Bella moaned.

Tomas was coughing, trying to free his throat and chest. Bella was in the corner of his hazed vision, staring at him in the same detached way he had watched her only a few moments before.

The saint, Tomas was thinking, *she calls me the saint*. An old compartment of his mind suddenly opened, and he began to curse at her in Spanish. Then he turned his back and walked upstairs to his third-floor bedroom.

In the small hours of the morning, Tomas Benares was lying in the centre of his marriage bed, looking up at the ceiling of the bedroom and tracing the shadows with his tired eyes. These shadows: cast by the streetlights they were as much a part of his furniture as was the big oak bed, or the matching dressers that presided on either side – still waiting, it seemed, for the miraculous return of Marguerita.

As always he was wearing pyjamas – sewing had been another of Marguerita's talents – and like the rest of his clothes they had been cleaned and ironed by the same Bella who had stood in the doorway of the second-floor living room and bellowed and panted at him like an animal gone mad. The windows were open and while he argued with himself Tomas could feel the July night trying to cool his skin, soothe him. But he didn't want to be soothed, and every half hour or so he raised himself on one elbow and reached for a cigarette, flaring the light in the darkness and feeling for a second the distant twin of the young man who had lived in Madrid forty years ago, the young man who had taken lovers (all of them beautiful in retrospect), whispered romantic promises (all of them ridiculous), and then had the good fortune to fall in love and marry a woman so beautiful and devoted that even his dreams could never have imagined her. And yet it was true, as he had told Bella, that when he came to Canada his life had ended. Even lying with Marguerita in this bed he had often been unable to sleep, had often, with this very gesture, lit up a small space in the night in order to feel close to the young man who had been deserted in Spain.

Return? Yes, it had occurred to him after the war was finished. Of course, Franco was still in power then, but it was his country and there were others who had returned. And yet, what would have been the life of an exile returned? The life of a man keeping his lips perpetually sealed, his thoughts to himself; the life of a man who had sold his heart in order to have the sights and smells that were familiar.

Now, Tomas told himself wryly, he was an old man who

had lost his heart for nothing at all. Somehow, over the years, it had simply disappeared; like a beam of wood being eaten from the inside, it had dropped away without his knowing it.

Tomas Benares, on his seventy-fourth birthday, had just put out a cigarette and lain back with his head on the white linen pillow to resume his study of the shadows, when he heard the footsteps on the stairs up to his attic. Then there was the creak of the door opening and Bella, in her nightgown and carrying a candle, tiptoed into the room.

Tomas closed his eyes.

The footsteps came closer, he felt the bed sag with her weight. he could hear her breathing in the night, it was soft and slow; and then, as he realized he was holding his own breath, he felt Bella's hand come to rest on his forehead.

He opened his eyes. In the light of the candle her face was like stone, etched and lined with grief.

'I'm sorry,' Tomas said.

'I'm the sorry one. And imagine, on your birthday.'

'That's all right. We've been too closed in here, since –' Here he hesitated, because for some reason the actual event was never spoken. 'Since Abraham died.'

Bella now took her hand away, and Tomas was aware of how cool and soft it had been. Sometimes, decades ago, Marguerita had comforted him in this same way when he couldn't sleep. Her hand on his forehead, fingers stroking his cheeks, his eyes, soothing murmurs until finally he drifted away, a log face down in the cool water.

'There are still lives to be lived,' Bella was saying. 'The children.'

'The children,' Tomas repeated. Not since Marguerita had there been a woman in this room at night. For many years he used to lock the door when he went to bed, and even now he would still lock it on the rare times he was sick in case someone – who? should dare to come on a mission of mercy.

'I get tired,' Bella said. Her head drooped and Tomas could see, through her nightdress, the curves of her breasts, the fissure between. A beautiful woman, he had thought before.... He was not as saintly as Bella imagined. On certain of the afternoons Bella thought he was at Herman Levine's, Tomas had been visiting a different apartment, that of a widow who was once his patient. She too knew what it was like to look at the shadows on the ceiling for one year after another, for one decade after another.

Now Tomas reached out for Bella's hand. Her skin was young and supple, not like the skin of the widow, or his own. There came a time in every person's life, Tomas thought, when the inner soul took a look at the body and said: Enough, you've lost what little beauty you had and now you're just an embarrassment – I'll keep carrying you around, but I refuse to take you seriously. Tomas, aside from some stray moments of vanity, had reached that point long ago; but Bella, he knew, was still in love with her body, still wore her own bones and skin and flesh as a proud inheritance and not an aging inconvenience.

'Happy birthday,' Bella said. She lifted Tomas's hand and pressed it to her mouth. At first, what he felt was the wetness of her mouth. And then it was her tears that flowed in tiny, warm streams around his fingers.

She blew out the candle at the same time that Tomas reached for her shoulder; and then he drew her down so she was lying beside him – her on top of the covers and him beneath, her thick, jet hair folded into his neck and face, her perfume and the scent of her mourning skin wrapped around him like a garden. Chastely he cuddled her to him, her warm breath as soothing as Marguerita's had once been. He felt himself drifting into sleep, and he turned towards the perfume, the garden, turned towards Bella to hold her in his arms the way he used to hold Marguerita in that last exhausted moment of waking.

Bella shifted closer, herself breathing so slowly that Tomas thought she must be already asleep. He remembered, with relief, that his alarm was set for six o'clock; at least they would wake before the children. Then he felt his own hand, as if it had a life of its own, slide in a slow caress from Bella's shoulder to her elbow, touching, in an accidental way, her sleeping breast.

Sleep fled at once, and Tomas felt the sweat spring to his skin. Yet Bella only snuggled closer, breast and hips flooding through the blanket like warm oceans. Tomas imagined reaching for and lighting a cigarette, the darkness parting once more. A short while ago he had been mourning his youth and now, he reflected, he was feeling as stupid as he ever had. Even with the widow there had been no hesitation. Mostly on his visits they sat in her living room and drank tea; sometimes, by a mutual consent that was arrived at without discussion, they went to her bedroom and performed sex like a warm and comfortable bath. A bath, he thought to himself, that was how he and Bella should become; chaste, warm, comforts to each other in the absence of Abraham. It wasn't right, he now decided, to have frozen his heart to this woman – his daughter-in-law, after all; surely she had a right to love, to the warmth and affection due to a member of the family. *Bella*, he was ready to proclaim, *you are the mother of my grandchildren, the chosen wife of my son. And if you couldn't help shouting, at least you were willing to comfort me.*

Tomas held Bella closer. Her lips, he became aware, were pressed against the hollow of his throat, moving slowly, kissing the skin and now sucking gently at the hairs that curled up from his chest. Tomas let his hand find the back of her neck. There was a delicate valley that led down from her skull past the thick, black hair. He would never have guessed she was built so finely.

Now Bella's weight lifted away for a moment, though her lips stayed glued to his throat, and then suddenly she was underneath the covers, her leg across his groin, her hand sliding up his chest.

Tomas felt something inside of him break. And then, as he raised himself on top of Bella the night, too, broke open; a gigantic black and dreamless mouth, it swallowed them both. He kissed her, tore at her nightgown to suck at her breast, penetrated her so deeply that she gagged; yet though he touched and kissed her every private place; though they writhed on the bed and he felt the cool sweep of her lips as they searched out his every nerve; though he even opened his eyes to see the pleasure on her face, her black hair spread like dead butterflies over Marguerita's linen pillows, her mouth open with repeated climax, the night still swallowed them, obliterated everything as it happened, took them rushing down its hot and endless gorge until Tomas felt like Jonah in the belly of the whale; felt like Jonah trapped in endless flesh and juice. And all he had to escape with was his own sex: like an old sword he brandished it in the blackness, pierced open tunnels, flailed it against the wet walls of his prison.

'Bella, Bella, Bella.' He whispered her name silently. Every time he shaped his lips around her name, he was afraid the darkness of his inner eye would part, and Abraham's face would appear before him. But it didn't happen. Even as he scratched Bella's back, bit her neck, penetrated her from behind, he taunted himself with the idea that somewhere in this giant night Abraham must be waiting. His name was on Tomas's lips: Abraham his son. How many commandments was he breaking? Tomas wondered, pressing Bella's breasts to his parched cheeks.

Tomas felt his body, like a starved man at a banquet, go out of control. Kissing, screwing, holding, stroking: everything he did Bella wanted, did back, invented variations upon. For one brief second he thought that Marguerita had never been like this, then his mind turned on itself and he was convinced that this *was* Marguerita, back from the dead with God's blessing to make up, in a few hours, a quarter century of lost time.

But as he kissed and cried over his lost Marguerita, the night began to lift and the first light drew a grey mask on the window.

By this time he and Bella were lying on their stomachs, side by side, too exhausted to move.

The grey mask began to glow, and as it did Tomas felt the dread rising in him. Surely God Himself would appear to take His revenge, and with that thought Tomas realize he had forgotten his own name. He felt his tongue searching, fluttering between his teeth, tasting again his own sweat and Bella's fragrant juices. He must be, he thought, in Hell. He had died and God, to drive his wicked soul crazy, had given him this dream of his own daughter-in-law, his dead son's wife.

'Thank you, Tomas.'

No parting kiss, just soft steps across the carpet and one creak as she descended the stairs. Then, the face of his son appeared. It was an infant's face, staring uncomprehendingly at its father.

Tomas sat up. His back was sore, his kidneys felt trampled, one arm ached, his genitals burned. He stood up to go to the bathroom and was so dizzy that for a few moments he had to cling to the bedpost with his eyes closed. Limping and groaning, he crossed the room. When he got back to the bed there was no sign that Bella had been there – but the sheets were soaked as they sometimes were after a restless night.

He collapsed on the covers and slept dreamlessly until the alarm went off. When he opened his eyes his first thought was of Bella, and when he swung out of bed there was a sharp sting in his groin. But as he dressed he was beginning to speculate, even to hope, that the whole episode had been a dream.

A few minutes later, downstairs at breakfast, Tomas found the children sitting alone at the table. Between them was a sealed envelope addressed to 'Dr Tomas Benares, MD'.

'Dear Tomas,' the letter read, 'I have decided that it is time for me to seek my own life in another city. Miss Rankin has already agreed to take care of the children for as long as necessary. I hope you will all understand me and remember that I love you. As always, Bella Benares.'

On his birthday, his garden always seemed to reach that explosive point that marked the height of summer. No matter what the weather, it was this garden that made up for all other deprivations, and the fact that his ninety-fourth birthday was gloriously warm and sunny made it doubly perfect for Tomas to spend the day outside.

Despite the perfect blessing of the sky, as Tomas opened his eyes from that long doze that had carried the sun straight into the afternoon, he felt a chill in his blood, the knowledge that Death, that companion he'd grown used to, almost fond of, was starting to play his tricks. Because sitting in front of him, leaning towards him as if the worlds of waking and sleeping had been forced together, was Bella herself.

'Tomas, Tomas, it's good to see you. It's Bella.'

'I know,' Tomas said. His voice sounded weak and grumpy; he coughed to clear his throat.

'Happy birthday, Tomas.'

He pushed his hand across his eyes to rid himself of this illusion.

'Tomas, you're looking so good.'

Bella: her face was fuller now, but the lines were carved deeper, bracketing her full lips and corrugating her forehead. And yet she was still young, amazing: her movements were lithe and supple; her jet-black hair was streaked, but still fell thick and wavy to her shoulders; her eyes still burned, and when she leaned forward to take his hand between her own the smell of her, dreams and remembrances, came flooding back.

'Tomas, are you glad to see me?'

'You look so young, Bella.' This in a weak voice, but Tomas's throat-clearing cough was lost in the rich burst of Bella's laughter. Tomas, seeing her head thrown back and the flash of her strong teeth, could hardly believe that he, a doddering old man, whose knees were covered by a blanket in the middle of summer, had only a few years ago actually made love to this vibrant woman. Now she was like a race-horse in voracious maturity.

'Bella, the children.'

'I know, Tomas. I telephoned Margaret; she's here. And I telephoned Joseph, too. His secretary said he was at a meeting all afternoon, but that he was coming here for dinner.'

'Bella, you're looking wonderful, truly wonderful.' Tomas had his hand hooked into hers, and, suddenly aware that he was half lying in his chair, was using her weight to try to lever himself up.

Instantly Bella was on her feet, her arm solicitously around his back, pulling him into position. She handled his weight, Tomas thought, like the weight of a baby. He felt surrounded by her, overpowered by her smell, her vitality, her cheery goodwill. *Putan*, Tomas whispered to himself. What a revenge. Twenty years ago he had been her equal; and now, suddenly – what had happened? Death was in the garden; Tomas could feel his presence, the familiar visitor turned trickster. And then Tomas felt some of his strength returning, strength in the form of contempt for Bella, who had waited twenty years

LIVES OF THE MIND SLAVES

to come back to this house; contempt for Death, who waited until a man was an ancient, drooling husk to test his will.

'You're the marvel, Tomas. Elizabeth says you work every day in the garden. How do you do it?'

'I spit in Death's face,' Tomas rasped. Now he was beginning to feel more himself again, and he saw that Bella was offering him a cup of coffee. All night he had slept, and then again in the daytime. What a way to spend a birthday! But coffee would heat the blood, make it run faster. He realized that he was famished.

Bella had taken out a package of cigarettes now, and offered one to Tomas. He shook his head, thinking again how he had declined in these last years. Now Joseph wouldn't let him smoke in bed, even when he couldn't sleep. He was only allowed to smoke when there was someone else in the room, or when he was outside in the garden.

'Tomas. I hope you don't mind I came back. I wanted to see you again while – while we could still talk.'

Tomas nodded. So the ant had escaped the honey pot after all, and ventured into the wide world. Now it was back, wanting to tell its adventures to the ant who had stayed home. Perhaps they hadn't spent that strange night making love after all; perhaps in his bed they had been struggling on the edge of the pot, fighting to see who would fall back and who would be set free.

'So,' Bella said. 'It's been so long.'

Tomas, watching her, refusing to speak, felt control slowly moving towards him again. He sat up straighter, brushed the blanket off his legs.

'Or maybe we should talk tomorrow,' Bella said, 'when you're feeling stronger.'

'I feel strong.' His voice surprised even himself – not the weak squawk it sometimes was now, a chicken's squeak hardly audible over the telephone, but firm and definite, booming out of his chest the way it used to. Bella: she had woken him up once, perhaps she would once more.

He could see her moving back, hurt; but then she laughed again, her rich throaty laugh that Tomas used to hear echoing through the house when his son was still alive. He looked at her left hand; Abraham's modest engagement ring was still in place, but beside it was a larger ring, a glowing bloodstone set in a fat gold band. 'Tomas,' Bella was saying, 'you really are a marvel, I swear you're going to live to see a hundred.'

'One hundred and twenty-three,' Tomas said. 'Almost all of the Benares men live to be one hundred and twenty-three.'

For a moment, the lines deepened again in Bella's face, and Tomas wished he could someday learn to hold his tongue. A bad habit that should have long ago been entered in his diary.

'You will,' Bella finally said. Her voice had the old edge. '*Two* hundred and twenty-three, you'll dance on all our graves.'

'Bella.'

'I shouldn't have come.'

'The children –'

'They'll be glad to see me, Tomas, they always are.'

'Always?'

'Of course. Did you think I'd desert my own children?'

Tomas shook his head.

'Oh, I left, Tomas, I left. But I kept in touch. I sent them letters and they wrote me back. That woman helped me.'

'Elizabeth?'

'I should never have called her a murderer, Tomas. It was an accident.'

'They wrote you letters without telling me?'

Bella stood up. She was a powerful woman now, full-fleshed and in her prime; even Death had slunk away in the force of her presence. 'I married again, Tomas. My husband and I lived in Seattle. When Joseph went to university there, he lived in my house.'

'Joseph lived with you?'

'My husband's dead now, Tomas, but I didn't come for your pity. Or your money. I just wanted you to know that I will be in Toronto again, seeing my own children, having a regular life.'

'A regular life,' Tomas repeated. He felt dazed, dangerously weakened. Death was in the garden again. He was standing behind Bella, peeking out from behind her shoulders and making faces. He struggled to his feet. Only Bella could save him now, and yet he could see the fear on her face as he reached for her.

'Tomas, I –'

'You couldn't kill me!' Tomas roared. His lungs filled his chest like an eagle in flight. His flowering hedges, his roses, his carefully groomed patio snapped into focus. He stepped towards Bella, his balance perfect, his arm rising. He saw her mouth open, her lips begin to flutter. Beautiful but stupid, Tomas thought; some things never change. At his full height he was still tall enough to put his arm around her and lead her to the house.

'It's my birthday.' His voice boomed with the joke. 'Let me offer you a drink to celebrate your happy return.'

His hand slid from her shoulder to her arm; the skin was smooth as warm silk. Her face turned towards his: puzzled, almost happy, and he could feel the heat of her breath as she prepared to speak.

'Of course I forgive you,' Tomas said.

CAFÉ LE DOG

LET US SAY it is April in Paris, which means that the sun is rising early and strong, more than enough to burn the skull out, so if you are still dizzy and pie-eyed from the night before, there are worse places to have your coffee than Café Le Dog. I won't say exactly where it is, just to be difficult, but if you happen to be near Boulevard Raspail, perhaps only a few steps from the Montmartre cemetery, then you might stumble upon this place.

The name of the owner is Gaston Fournay. He comes to sit and talk with me now, though he didn't used to. He's got a face made up of little cushions: round, puffed cheeks, drooping jowls, an underjaw like a bullfrog's. Don't ask me how he shaves. I've never put the question to him, either.

I said pie-eyed in the morning, and since I am no ordinary drunk – or if I am I don't want to know – the implication is that the night was filled with wonderful poetic visions. But before we dive into the bitterness of art, the lot of the poet in this century of shit and machines, let's just forget it.

On the other hand, like all cynics, I was once an idealist. In my teenage years, for example, I played football and read poetry. And when I came to Paris I was still full of literary dreams. The first thing I did was to rush over to my uncle's place, a publishing house specializing in police novels and under-the-counter pornography. He was in his office. I had to stand outside the door while he completed his telephone conversation. Even with my flawed French, it was easy to understand that he was having an argument with his mistress. Then I was let into his office. He was the exact opposite of my mother: fat instead of thin; darkly hairy instead of pale and refined. He was wearing a hat, and his office smelled of French cigarettes.

'You're the boy,' he said. 'What do you want?'

Last night was pretty bad. It started here in the afternoon pleasantly enough. I had a couple of beers with Gaston's sister, Marie, and then we decided to go for a walk along the Seine and maybe celebrate Friday night at a cheap seafood restaurant where they know us.

Don't get the wrong idea. Marie and I are old friends but not romantic. That is to say we see in each other derelicts who can never be revived, but we are willing to give each other a little human comfort, if you know what I mean, but not too often. Anyway, you get the picture: vagabonds of indeterminate sex toppling towards a common destiny, but still sufficiently dignified to resist a mass grave. Or maybe it would be enough to admit that I can look her in the eyes, but only when we are in a public place. Have you ever noticed that you can tell true love because the smell of the truly beloved never offends? The fact is, I admit it, I could go on like this forever. But I've learned not to.

Why am I still in Paris, you probably want to know? To see me, you would know right away that I am a foreigner. What betrays are the British tweed jackets that I always wear. At first I wore them because, living in one cheap hotel after another, I had a tremendous fear of losing my passport. Fifty times an hour I would pat my pocket to be sure it was still there. Then I moved to the room where I still live, a room not so far from Café Le Dog, and I hid my passport under a floor-board. That made me feel like a real Frenchman, but I kept wearing the tweed jacket anyway, because I had gotten used to its protection. Besides, I am a tourist at heart, in the worst way. Not for seeing sights – I'm such a snob that I've never even *been* to the Louvre – or experiencing strange places: the truth is that I am one of those people who always feel more comfortable in someone else's house, someone else's life, someone else's dreams and beliefs.... Why go on? You get the idea – I'm addicted to explaining things until my explanations fall inside themselves and begin to mumble and stagger about drunkenly, searching for a graceful exit.

I came to Paris in desperation and my uncle gave me a job in his publishing house. But after a few years he died and his company went bankrupt. Meanwhile, my bad poetry had appeared: three embarrassing little volumes that I buy up from bookstores and destroy whenever I have some spare cash.

'A poet,' people used to say, admiringly, when I was

introduced at parties. I learned that a woman who accepts you as a poet also accepts your basest desires. At first I was flattered. I thought it was my genius they admired. Then I realized that they didn't care who I was, what they really admired was the spectacle of themselves risking venereal disease for the chance to spend a night disguised as a Muse.

'Maybe you will write a poem about me,' they would often say the next morning. Sometimes I did, even while they were eating breakfast. But they never wanted to read it – and when they did they were always disappointed. I don't blame them. Basically, I am like other poets in one way at least: I hate everyone. The portraits, therefore, were never too flattering.

Don't mistake me. I don't think that I am some truth-seeker while the rest of humanity walks around in blinders. What bullshit that is. If I am a poet – which I am not – it is only because I am socially maladjusted in a poetic direction. I am also socially maladjusted in other directions, but as a neurosis, poetry offers a career.

To this aspect of my existence Marie is indifferent. Thank God. With her I feel like a real person. A total asshole, but without pretensions. To put it even more bluntly, if possible, Marie and I have an understanding: we understand that we are both losers in the game of life, that we never even knew what the game of life was, that somehow we ended up middle-aged and ugly and completely unnecessary, but that's life so we might as well enjoy it.

Maybe I am being unfair here to Marie. Just as she is indifferent to my poetry, perhaps there are things about her which I have missed. But I do think that Marie is basically a good person. Let me go further. When the rest of us are sweating in Hell, Marie will probably be in Heaven. Firstly, because she is a woman – despite everything you hear about them most are probably goody-goodies on their way to a higher reward – and secondly, because she has already suffered enough, why torture her further?

To return to something I hinted at: Marie is smelly. That she wears too many clothes and they trap her sweat is probably the reason – but more important is Marie's fundamental desire to repel. Unlike Gaston she has a very nice face, though it has been wrecked for sunlight by her daily two bottles of wine, and even her figure is not bad. Of course she was once quite beautiful: she has shown me pictures of herself when she was employed by various gentlemen as a part-time wife. In those years she probably spent hours a day in the bath, powdering, scraping, and perfuming herself. I wish I could have met her in that era, when I still carried my verses in the pocket which used to hold my passport. But then Marie lost her looks. 'I just sagged one day,' she explains it. She still receives a pension, others would call it blackmail, and at night we often walk by the luxurious house of her last lover and current benefactor. Once we even saw him: driving a German car he wheeled into his steel-doored garage. Marie ran for fear he would think she was snooping but I lingered. Out of the garage came a well-dressed businessman, you know the type – British suit, square, jutting jaw, close-cropped hair, piercing eyes. He looked about sixty. His wife was covered in furs but sulking.

Unlike myself, Marie is a real Parisian. Her family has been here for generations, a long, uninterrupted string of cheap courtesans, nuns, and small shopkeepers. If I were Arletty I would make a movie of her life story; if I were still a poet I would write verses to her courage. But what does poetry have to say about steel-reinforced businessmen? Even in French such a line would be hard to swallow.

Meanwhile it is morning at Café Le Dog. The dog in question is a real one; his name is Claude and he is lying underneath my table with his white head resting on my feet. Claude is named after my alter ego and worst enemy. But, take love where you can get it, as the old song goes. This morning I feel deeply empty, almost poetically so, or perhaps what I am feeling is not emptiness but sadness. I am drinking brandy with my coffee, to thicken the blood, Gaston says.

In front of me is a letter from my mother. It came two weeks ago. *Dear Camille*, it begins. Of course Camille is not my name. If it were, I would be even more depressed than I am. Nonetheless, Camille is what my father called me on his dying day. I was seven years old; the death took place in my father's bed; everything was arranged in the best of taste

despite the fact that it was a rush job. He was sitting propped
up by two pillows, and my mother had dressed him in his silk
pyjamas. She was not yet thirty; he was much older but his illness was sudden and unexpected. A heart attack. It happened
while I was at school, and by the time I got home his fate was
already settled. 'Camille,' he said to me, his voice had a fine
French-horn timbre polished by decades of Cuban rum and
cigars, 'take care of your mother.' Those were his last words,
and to this day no one knows why he called me Camille
instead of Jacob, which is my real name, or even James, which
is my middle name and was my father's first name.

*I am planning to visit you later this spring, when the
flowers have established themselves and the pollen season is over. Your apartment sounds magnificent. How
marvellous it must be to wake every morning to a view
of the Seine. I have often imagined you writing your poetry while gazing at its famous waters. Do you really
have twin black maids? My life here is so boring in com-
parison. But I have spent the whole winter taking
French lessons from Mme Dufresne so now I have only
my wardrobe left to worry about.*

Don't jump to the conclusion that I have lied to my own
mother, although I have, but not the specifics mentioned
above. Firstly, the letters I send to my mother are composed
not by me but by Marie, whose knowledge of English was
gained by reading the entire *oeuvre* of Henry James, twice, in
the American edition. She sends letters to my mother that are
never less than twenty pages long, and sometimes she forgets
to show them to me. Secondly, my mother lives in a nursing
home for the mentally disturbed in Montreal. She shares a
room with the above-mentioned Mme Dufresne, and over the
years they have not only taught one another English and
French, but have taken correspondence courses in Hungarian,
Polish, and medieval Latin.

*Next month this entire block is being torn down for a
new apartment building, and the doctor has said I am*

cured. I have made a reservation to leave on my sixty-fifth birthday, and after that I may never see my country again. To think that for years I have been in the land of the unstable and now I am to become an expatriate in another way. But if life is not one journey after another, Camille, what is it? Now that I am getting ready to set out on my travels, everything that came before seems insignificant. Already I feel as if I have become, in my modest way, part of the scintillating group you have described so generously in your letters. Does Jean-Paul Sartre really ask after me at your Friday night soirées? I have read all of his works that the library here at the home has, and there are dozens of questions I am dying to ask him.

Everyone seems busy: that is the attraction of Paris. Even while I sit and read my mother's letter there are bursts of activity on all sides, as if it were firecracker day in the hearts of Parisians. At this exact moment, for example, Gaston is leaning his elbows on the marble counter he is so proud of, arguing with the butcher about the quality of his *pâté*, the latest political *scandale*, and the fidelity of his dog. Although it is not yet nine in the morning, and the sun is still yellow and clean like a baby egg in the pale blue sky, the discussion at the counter has taken on great urgency. Coffee and various distilled products are being gulped down, cigarettes are being emphatically ground to shreds with twisting, bayonet-like movements. The butcher, in fact, was reputed to be a sadist during the war, a resistance fighter who was himself tortured on many occasions. Even now, at seventy years old, he makes a terrifying sight. Gaston, much younger, buzzes about him like a puffy mosquito labouring to find an exposed vein in the hide of an elephant.

Around the butcher's van, illegally parked in the middle of the street, other vehicles are screeching, cursing, coming within millimetres of total demolition. And surrounding the butcher himself are the various hangers-on, connoisseurs of nothing, over-tired hookers and streetcleaners who make up the early-morning clientele of Café Le Dog. A bit to one side is

Marie, demurely dunking croissants into her bowl of hot milk. Only I am sitting down at a table. I and a few students who don't count, bending over their books. After last night, what am I doing here so early in the morning? Am I so addicted to the dawn, the peculiar kitchen-like smell of early morning Paris, that I have decided to forgo sleep? Has Marie, as a result of our little disaster, left me with the task of writing to my own mother? Am I returning to the scene of the crime to make sure that I am still welcome here, my only home? François Mauriac once said of André Gide that his immorality was merely unforgivable; his truly damning sin was to boast of it in public. That sentiment, no doubt, explains why Mauriac retired from the writing of novels and turned his teacherly attentions to composing the memoirs of his sanctimonious life. In his attack on Gide, he even went so far as to include a chapter saying that Gide's wife was a saint for having put up with him; a saint and a virgin.

Marie, alas, is neither. But she did once say to my that she allowed men access to her body only because it was a crime to deny the one small pleasure she was in a position to give. An old song.

'What about your pleasure?' I asked her.

'That is my own affair.'

Marie, at the bar, offers her cheeks to be kissed by a new arrival. Just my luck, it is Claude St. Foy, one of those scabrous journalists who make this place their hideout from honest work. Even the dog, his namesake, is put off by him. He shifts his head from its hour-long vigil across my instep and growls softly. Claude, the dog, is the great-great-grandson, approximately speaking, of the canine after whom Café Le Dog was named. The invading Americans christened it thus, as if they had never seen a dog in a restaurant before, and the GIs even made a sign, since replaced and electrified, to hang above the counter. On the sign is a picture of the initial inspiration, a large and fierce Dalmatian with black, piercing eyes and teeth that would frighten a rhinoceros. Claude, alas, is a small, living monument to the dangers of breeding in the street. A diminutive beast that could almost fit in the crook of your arm, he is covered by brown, curly hair except for his face, his feet, and the tip of his tail, all of which are white. His good looks and loyal personality are undermined by the fact that over the years he has become an alcoholic. By noon he begins leaping onto the counter and stealing the customers' drinks, the stronger the better; and at a certain peak point – when he is lubricated but not drunk – he scampers from glass to glass, his pink tongue scooping out the liquid at lightning speed. Even drunk, he never upsets a glass before midnight. After that he gets maudlin, staggering about on all fours, cruising, a sad, doggy look attesting to the tragedies he would be only too delighted to relate.

Today, because summer is coming, Marie wears less clothing than usual. A scoop-necked sailor's jersey, a skirt, high heels that show off her perfect legs. A childhood attack of the pox has left her cheeks looking like a bed of gravel, and the effects of wine have already been mentioned, but otherwise she seems unusually young and beautiful today. Twenty years younger, for example, than she looked only a few hours ago, when she was weeping and spitting insults as if the night would never end.

Marie was born the year after the war. She claims her existence began the day the Americans entered Paris. Like me, she was brought up by her mother. But her father did not die, he merely ran away with a troupe of gypsies. 'The war unsettled him,' Marie explained. 'It made him restless. Also he hated my mother because she – it was a matter of temperament. She was from Paris, he from the south. Anyway, a man with Basque blood is almost a gypsy already. If it weren't for the war he would have left long ago, to tell the truth. My real father is the American army. If they hadn't come to Paris in such a splendid way, my father would never have gotten drunk enough to admit desire for my mother again.'

You don't need me to tell you how mysterious are the ways of the heart. Marie's mother, at sixty, is still extraordinarily beautiful. Her fine nose and slate-grey eyes belong also to Marie. But the rest of her features, noble and patrician, are hers alone. Also her creamy, almost transparent complexion, which only a lifetime of abstinence can give. She looks, in brief, like the Mother Superior of an upper-class convent, the kind you can't stop wondering about. In fact I once lived near such a convent in Montreal, and during the summer we climbed trees every day to see if we could catch the nuns sunbathing. Disgusting, but youth is meant to be ridiculous. The convent look is, of course, something Marie has avoided altogether. Yet even in her career as a part-time wife she has always held something back. And I don't mean the pleasure that Marie delights in hiding, because between women and pleasure is a bond invisible to most men. Then what? Perhaps only that little indigestible pebble of fundamental human essence that makes even the most rabid passion choke to death. Or perhaps her heavy exposure to Henry James has caused a set of unpredictable short circuits in her nervous system, some weird syntactic lobotomy that would take a team of psycho-linguists years to unknot.

Despite everything, including her clothes and her smell, Marie is still an attractive woman. She has not only her mother's eyes and nose, but rounded apple cheeks and a smile flawed only slightly by a darkened tooth that should have been replaced by one of her affluent boyfriends. On the other hand, for a woman not yet forty, Marie has let herself slide into some very strange habits. She often talks to herself as she walks, and to see her coming down the street, chattering away with her head wagging back and forth, you would think something more than Henry James had gotten to her. Also she cries too easily; the slightest mean remark sends her into an orgy of tears. Since retiring from sexual commerce with paying customers, she has lost her social tastes altogether: her only friends are her brother, the customers at the café, and myself.

I am, she claims, the only non-paying client she has ever entertained. But where I stand in Marie's cosmos is unknown to me. In fact, there is that balance between us only too typical of men and women: she understands me perfectly; I find her absolutely opaque.

I was on my third brandy when my mother walked into the Café Le Dog. Forewarned is not forearmed, as they say: I didn't even recognize her. What I saw was a thin old woman, erect, wearing a black coat with a colourful tourist's shawl about her shoulders. She had white hair, lined cheeks, a smear of lipstick on her mouth. Even this I only noticed because before she was through the door Marie had leapt forward to embrace her. Then they sat down at a table and began to weep with happiness while I was still staring at the last line of my mother's letter: *Don't worry about meeting me at the airport. I will come to see you as soon as I have found a suitable hotel.*

They might have sat talking and crying all morning without my recognizing her, but her voice trolled through my mind like a baited hook.

'There you are,' my mother said as I joined them, 'your wife has been telling me all about you.' Then my mother turned away from me and extracted a compact from her purse. She popped it open and looked intently at herself in the mirror. 'Do you think I've changed?'

'Only for the better,' Marie said quickly.

'Thank you, you're a kind girl, everything I could have hoped for.' They were speaking French. It was amazing; my mother's accent was so perfect. The twenty years I had spent in France she had used to even better effect in the mental home, improving herself. Now my mother reached into her purse again, this time pulling out the last of my poetry books. 'I've always wanted your autograph.'

In this memoir, more than modesty forbids me giving samples of my poetry. Believe me when I say it is all terrible. So hopeless, in fact, that under the name of Claude St. Foy, I have turned to criticism and make my living writing book reviews for French newspapers. So bitter and vitriolic are my comments that St. Foy's reviews have often been syndicated. Like most journalists, St. Foy is a complete illiterate, so our collaboration is lucky for both of us: between us we make the perfect critic. In fact, our strange star has risen so high that sometimes we even review French books for the *Herald Tribune*, who marvel at St. Foy's fluent command of written English.

But don't take my bitterness as a sign of failure. In fact, the execrable volume my mother had preserved, *Songs of the Seine*, was quite a success. Written in English, it was translated into French before being published by my uncle. I, of course, though under a pseudonym, was the translator. But my picture is on the back, and I am identified as a Canadian.

Writing and translating the book were only the first steps. Next I used St. Foy's name to give the book a scathing attack in *Le Monde*, correctly calling it a pitiable example of neo-structuralist Canadian drivel. Naturally, this brought the book to the attention of the Canadian government, and an English version duly appeared from a small Toronto press. According to the newspapers, it almost won an award, and I was offered a lecture tour of the Canadian West. I declined, the only act of my life that has been tainted with integrity.

This is not to say I failed to benefit from my Canadian notoriety. Taking lecture offer and newspaper clippings in hand, I dressed in my best clothes and Gaston's best *foulard*, and presented myself at the Canadian Cultural Centre. I wished, I said, a small lifetime pension as a distinguished Canadian poet in exile. For bureaucratic reasons they were unable to grant it. But they did offer me a job cleaning the washrooms on Sundays and national holidays. I accepted. It was, in fact, the savings from this employment that I used to send to my mother to make her life easier in the mental home. Of course I never believed she would be released.

'Does Jean-Paul Sartre really come here every day?'

'He died,' Marie said.

But my mother's voice had carried and now Claude St. Foy was hovering over us, rubbing his hands like an undertaker.

'You should have told me.'

'I didn't want to –'

'I understand,' my mother said. She gave me a radiant smile and I felt like a child again; the way I felt the night after my father's funeral when we came back to our apartment and my mother smiled at me and said, 'Now, Camille, we must be good to each other. We are all we have.'

The first thing we did was to close the door to the bedroom where my father had died. That night and thereafter my mother slept on the couch. She replaced her entire wardrobe, and continued to call me Camille in memory of my father. Even the sheets he had died on remained unchanged until the day, ten years later, that my mother was sent to the mental home. I was left alone. A welfare worker was assigned to me. She opened the door and strode into the bedroom. The window had been left open – my father had died during a heat wave – and now the room was full of cats and birds. Of course we had often heard noises, especially at night, but had been too frightened to investigate. As the welfare worker stood in the doorway to my father's room, I ran out of the apartment and down the stairs to freedom. In a bank account I had three hundred dollars that had been left to me in my father's will. I bought a ticket for Paris and departed by boat the same day. I had my uncle's address, since he wrote to my mother every week, and a well-worn but unautographed copy of Rimbaud's collected poems.

At first drink inflames the brain, but eventually the effect is to scramble it, so that every drinker ends up splashing feebly down the same river of forgetfulness and self-pity. Or perhaps, let's be frank, this is only wishful thinking, and the truth is that I am one of those people who can't hold their liquor.

By the time I had signed my mother's poems and St. Foy had seated himself at our table, I was exhausted and muddied. Every word had to be dredged up and I couldn't hear what the others were saying. Of course, I didn't want my mother to know what a bad way I was in, so I began telling jokes. Soon St. Foy had taken over and was reciting lurid stories I'd heard a thousand times before. My mother was entranced and Marie was smiling, even at me. Another of our disastrous arguments had obviously melted away, into that undercurrent of oblivion that moved us along from day to day – But no! Here is that talk of darkness again. How sentimental we poets, even failed ones, become at the mere thought of death. Even the demise of animals and vegetables becomes the humus of literature. But life is different. For example, the young GIs, drunk no doubt, who hung Café Le Dog from the ceiling, could not have felt that they were being smothered by the wet blanket of life. And, except in these memoirs or when I am complaining to Marie, neither do I. After all, I am still a Canadian citizen. This, in fact, is my last and only hope, the rock my mind clings to in its most desperate moments. Every week, when I have finished my cleaning tasks at the Cultural Centre, I spend a few hours reading the Help Wanted columns of Canadian newspapers. One day, I still believe, I will see advertised a government job that is suitable for me. And then, God willing, let bygones be bygones. I will take Marie home with me to my native land and, if our vital organs are still functioning, give myself over to honest work and raising children under sanitary conditions.

'Aren't we ever going to go home?' By midnight at Café Le Dog even my mother was beginning to wilt. Marie, it turned out, had known she was coming all along, and had even used the transatlantic telephone to confirm the hour of her arrival.

'I didn't know how to talk to a hotel,' my mother said. 'You must have an apartment, a room, even a kennel somewhere to sleep in. Take me to it.'

'Allow me,' St. Foy interrupted. 'My wife and I would be delighted to be your hosts. We have a spare bedroom, entirely furnished in authentic furniture.'

'Forget it,' my mother said. 'I never sleep in a house with a strange man, no matter what the excuse.'

'But I am practically your own son.' He had stuck to her the whole day, such an idiot that he was incapable of realizing that to fall in love with my mother would involve him in a terminal form of incest.

'I'm willing to love you,' my mother declared, 'and to answer faithfully whatever letters you might send.' She stood up.

Only once before had I seen my mother drunk. That was the New Year's Eve before my father died. On that occasion they were both dressed like stars from an old movie: my mother in a long, backless satin dress, my father in a tuxedo. It was long past midnight when they came in. The neighbour who had been watching me had gone home, but I was lying awake, keeping away the ghosts by listening to country music on the short-wave radio. Even from my bed their laughter sounded like the clinking of glasses. I put on my housecoat – I was an only child and they liked to dress me up like a little adult – and came out to investigate. My father had kicked off his shoes and was slouched in an easy chair, smoking a last cigar. He was a businessman whose fortunes had moved in gigantic cycles – during my life always downwards – but to me he always had the fancy clothes and bay-rum aura of a wealthy tycoon. My mother was standing in front of him, her face pink and girlish. She had lifted her dress up to her thighs and was standing on one foot, the other extended like a ballerina's, toe pointed towards the door. When she saw me her eyes opened wide, like a doll's eyes, then very slowly her lips parted. 'I've been meaning to tell you,' she said; and then she toppled over and landed on the floor in an unbreakable sleep. My first book of bad poetry included an unsuccessful sonnet describing this very event; prose, too, fails to convey the heart-stopping pleasure my seven-year-old self felt at being singled out for such an important announcement, even if unmade. Of course, after my father's demise I was chosen all too often, but that is another story.

'Take me somewhere,' my mother whispered to me in English. 'Quickly.'

Having passed the whole day at the same table, drinking brandy in the morning, then switching cautiously to beer for the afternoon before plunging into the celebratory evening bottles of wine, I was in more than my usual fog when we stepped outside. Soon we were walking down Boulevard Raspail – Marie, my mother, myself – the cold April air sweeping us along the sidewalks. We turned into the tiny street where Marie lived, unlocked the door and twisted our way up the stairs to her top floor apartment. Marie switched on the light. She was, you might say, a closet intellectual; or at least her place resembled a closet in which was stored every shred of printed paper that had been generated since Gutenberg's ill-fated inspiration.

'Tell me this is Paris,' my mother said.

'This is Paris,' said Marie.

'It was a wonderful first day,' my mother said. 'But I *was* looking forward to meeting Jean-Paul Sartre. Are you sure he's dead?'

'Absolutely,' said Marie. 'I went to his funeral.'

'Then you *were* good friends.'

'*Copains*. Really. We were like that.' She crossed her fingers, the way she always does when she wants to signal God that she is telling a lie for reasons He would surely understand.

'And he really admired Camille's work?'

'He was devoted.'

My mother lay down on Marie's bed. It was covered with layers of the clothes she usually wore, old newspapers and magazines, two ashtrays, and a set of pillows one of her paying lovers had brought her from Japan. But to all this my mother was oblivious. She pulled the mess over herself, not even taking off her shoes, and lay on her back with her head cushioned on a first edition of *The Golden Bowl*.

'I said to Mme Dufresne that I would come to Paris and see my son Camille. I swore to her that I would speak to him, his friends, his associates, even Jean-Paul Sartre, in their own language whatever it was. I told her I would do all this before my life was over, no matter what.'

'Don't die,' Marie pleaded.

My mother's lips quavered. 'Don't worry,' she said. 'I didn't come all the way to Paris just to die. I only ask that you watch me sleep. If you do I will last until morning and then you will see that your efforts have not been wasted. My life is only beginning.'

'Goodnight, mother,' I said.

'Goodnight, Camille. Your father would be proud of you, despite everything.'

While my mother slept, Marie and I talked in whispers about our pasts, our hatred of Claude St. Foy, the chance that her brother Gaston might fatally wound himself shaving. Eventually, we lay down on the floor and made love. When it was over I suddenly remembered that my mother had asked us to watch over her at all times. But she was still breathing. In the morning the three of us went to Café Le Dog and took our coffee outside. No one in Paris could have been happier.

LIVES OF THE MIND SLAVES

WHEN SANDSTORMS, freezing cold, or sudden bursts of rain caused Nellie to cough or hesitate, Norman would caress the steering-wheel and murmur encouragingly, 'Come on, Nellie. You can make it, Nellie.' Or in desperate circumstances, 'Nelliebelle honey, I love you.' Nellie was a 1962 Ford V8. In her youth she had been maroon, a dark lustrous red endowed with flowing curves and a motor that could snap your neck back when you pressed her pedal to the floor. Those had been Nellie's salad days, the days and nights of her first youth, the years of careful washes and hand-shining, valve-jobs and cylinder refittings, the days when her engine always hummed with clear creamy oil and when her evenings were spent at drive-in movies, her springs gently rocking.

Nellie's first owner had cried real tears when he sold her to Norman. The deal took place in downtown Vancouver, outside a liquor store. That was where Norman saw her first. Drawn by her glowing curvaceous body he stepped closer to look at the FOR SALE sign taped inside a window. He was still wondering whether to copy down the telephone number when a man appeared beside him, kicking the tires, stroking the fins, talking in a low steady mumble which ended, 'You wouldn't believe the loving I had in this car. But now the wife wants a station-wagon for the kids.' The lover was wispy-haired pot-bellied man with a sad smile.

Norman was tanned and streaky blond from a summer planting trees on Vancouver Island. The year before he had been crowned by a PH.D. – an accomplishment rewarded by a job teaching remedial English to immigrants in Halifax. This was followed by his months on the island. There Norman met his first Nellie: a young woman who wore white running-shoes and wanted to make love to him every night all night. Then arrived a letter from the McGill-Queen's University Press offering Norman a contract to turn his thesis on 'The Roots of Symbolism in American Narrative' into a book. Norman was lying on a beach as he opened the envelope. Reading the letter he felt the sun burn brighter. So it was goodbye to Nellie the human and hello to his new drivable Nellie. Destination: three thousand miles across the continent to McGill, where he had earned his degree, for six months of post-doctoral research. He didn't finish the book, but another piece of luck came along – the offer of an actual appointment, one-year extendible, at the University of Calgary. A proud event, his first full year teaching, but due to a sudden plunge in the departmental budget the appointment was not renewed. Fortunately the sympathetic department chairman helped him find a life-saving two-year term as a sessional lecturer at the University of Winnipeg – at a much lower salary than he had been receiving in Calgary. After Winnipeg it was back once more to McGill for another two-year appointment, this time on the understanding that he would, finally, finish his book and – if he did – take his place in the pantheon of the tenured.

Between cities, jobs, universities, was the desert. The desert was emptiness. The desert was life with no future. Also, like any desert, it was dry and thirsty. Although during the day the sun burned hot, the night was cold and scary. Likewise fine weather was followed by storms of obfuscation. Life would have been not life at all had the dry and stormy desert not been punctuated by oases in the form of congenial pubs where fellow mind slaves could always be found. And after the slaking of thirst – so many thousands of mugs of draft had been consumed that Norman had the permanent taste of foam at the corners of his mouth – followed manna. Manna was love. Manna was emotional relief. Manna was the security of flesh compared with the insecurity of jobs with no future, students with no talent, tenured professors with no compassion. Manna was the pressing of body to body, the rites of sex, the point of which was not so much ecstasy – though ecstasy he would not have refused – but the complicity of imperfect nakedness and sex, the sequel of long talks in the darkness about whether life in the desert could ever give way to something better.

At McGill the first time, he had met Elisabeth. Dark, slim, with a brittle pretty face and a sharp laugh, she was a Blake specialist who taught part time and most evenings spent an hour in the pub sipping beer before going home to make dinner for her lawyer husband. Norman was twenty-six then, Elisabeth almost thirty.

The second year in Winnipeg, she showed up again. By this time Norman was himself pushing thirty; and that year he developed the uncomfortable habit of looking closely at himself as he shaved. Lines had started to grow out of the corners of his eyes, his mouth had begun to take a particular downward turn, his hair which had been dramatic during the tree-planting summer was now brown, except at the temples where dustings of grey had mysteriously settled. Worse, the nights at the oases followed by manna/mamma had begun to sour. The love of many gave way to the love of one. When a fourth-year student dazzled and pursued him, he fell in love. After that it was no longer mind over matter, but vice versa. Love and jealousy, storms of passion and lightning moments of pure happiness. Then she had gotten pregnant. The pregnancy was announced in the summer after graduation. The girl, whose name was Ruth, told Norman about it one day at breakfast. As she leaned over her coffee, blue eyes opened wide and trusting – or so Norman believed at the moment – Norman had a picture of himself with a beautiful blue-eyed daughter in the circle of his arms. 'Let's get married,' he said.

That afternoon Ruth broke the news to her parents, who were big givers to the alumni fund. Scenes ensued. The parents, who had envisioned a brilliant academic future for their precocious daughter, complained to their good friend the university president. Ruth decided on an abortion. Norman was informed that although – technically – he had broken no laws and therefore could not be sued, his appointment would be terminated at the end of the following year. By September Ruth, womb scraped virgin clean, was off to graduate school at Harvard while Norman was left to contemplate his disgrace and his future.

When Elisabeth walked into the pub Norman didn't recognize her right away. Her face was fuller, and demarcation lines of bitterness divided eyes and cheeks. As it turned out, she no longer had a husband, but there was a child. It was two years old and like a queen talked about herself in the third person: 'Mona wants a cookie. Mona wants ice cream.'

'Mona wants to talk. Mona wants to sit down. Mona wants television.' Norman took up with Mona. Every Saturday afternoon he called for her; once or twice a week he collected her at the day-care centre, then brought her home and fed her dinner. He told Elisabeth about what had happened to him with Ruth; she told Norman about her marriage. Recounting past disasters, struggling through a difficult evening with Mona, looking at Elisabeth across the kitchen, Norman felt as though he and Elisabeth had constructed for themselves a sort of shelter for battered survivors, an emotional refuge in which they were the patients slowly healing, and Mona, unbeknownst to herself, the physician. One night Norman – to help himself get through a particularly excruciating set of essays – brought over a bottle of Scotch and his six favourite Miles Davis records. Near midnight he became aware that he was upstairs, in the bathroom, splashing water onto his face. He raised his eyes to the mirror; his cheeks looked yellow and numb, which was also how they felt. When he stepped into the hall something in his blood went to sleep. 'Something in my blood has gone to sleep,' he said. Elisabeth was downstairs, listening to Miles Davis. She had her own essays to worry about and, Norman realized, they made her far too busy to be concerned about dormant aspects of his blood. He turned. He looked into Elisabeth's bedroom. She had a large bed and it was empty. Soon he was lying on his back. Time passed. Then he was lying on his belly, on top of Elisabeth. The light from the hall made her eyes glow, and the face that had been growing so familiar now seemed to belong to a stranger.

At the beginning of November Ruth phoned. Just her voice was enough to set him seething, whether with love or despair he had no idea. 'I'm dying without you,' she said. Norman, sitting alone in his half-furnished apartment, looked at his cold wooden floor littered with unread books, indigestible essays, the remains of half-eaten meals. 'I'm dying without you,' she had said. Norman wondering what it was he was doing without her. 'Well?' she asked. Any protective layer he might have formed was now shattered. 'Will you come to see me?'

'Yes,' Norman said, his voice choking. And then Ruth said some things about how she had missed him and what she was eager to do to him when he arrived.

'This will be my most embarrassing moment,' Norman announced to Elisabeth, thinking even as he spoke how odd it was that people like Elisabeth and him, chattels to a system which despised them, were in fact so enslaved that a clever little phrase could grease the stickiest situation. But Elisabeth agreed to take his classes so that Norman could have a long weekend in the Promised Land.

The bus left Winnipeg at dawn. By the time the stony grey light of morning had filled the sky, they were on the highway. Thirty-six hours later he arrived in Boston – palms sweating, clothes soaked in cigarette smoke, stomach knotted from tension and white-bread sandwiches. Ruth, all smiles, received the weary traveller in her scented arms, brought him back to her apartment for a night of passionate love. Just as his stomach began to unwind, the recriminations began. Before Norman could unpack the clothes he had so carefully folded, he was on his way back to the bus station.

The last year at McGill, everything went wrong. First, Norman turned thirty-two. Until then he had been able to believe that the sojourn in the desert was a necessary part of the larger story. And, too, he had discovered no lack of fellow wanderers. Fellow, yes; there was strange fellowship in this life after fellowships, fellowship in the expertise in subjects about which no one else would ever care, fellowship most of all in the curious roles they all played – knights errant of the mind, intellectual mercenaries with knowledge for sale at cut-rate prices.

But the week after his thirty-second birthday Norman discovered he had contracted a 'social disease'. The doctor assured him that it was harmless, relatively speaking, and that a bottle of pills plus a month of abstinence would make him a new man. But they couldn't. Norman had been going seriously with a girl for the first time since Ruth. When confronted with the medical evidence, she admitted she was about to decamp and move in with someone else. 'The thing is,' Norman wrote to Elisabeth, 'this would have been funny a few years ago. The wronged lover comes home to discover that his girlfriend wants to play house with the musician who has just given her VD. But now I'm too old. I don't want my life to be a comedy any more. I want to settle down, be loved, have children, enjoy the fruits of my labours. Is this not the natural destiny of man?'

'No,' Elisabeth wrote back, 'it is not the natural destiny of man – not of man, mankind, men, or you. If nature has anything in mind for you, Norman Wadkins, it is that, like all matter in the universe, you shall be subject to the second law of thermodynamics, to wit: decline, decrepitude, death.'

'Thanks a lot,' returned Norman.

'You missed my whole meaning,' Elisabeth protested. She wrote her letters to Norman on departmental stationery. Nor were her letters posted from Winnipeg, as they had been in previous years. Now they emanated from Vancouver and were complete with weather descriptions. 'Brilliant light. Mountains rising out of mist. Another heart-rending sunset.' Even when it rained, Elisabeth persisted in lauding the softness of the falling water. 'City of mountains, city of dreams,' she called it in one letter. Not just for the scenery, Norman supposed, but also because Elisabeth had arrived at middle age in style: she was in Vancouver as an associate professor as well as being assistant dean of women.

'What I mean is that although destiny has nothing special in mind for you, you could do something for yourself. Awake O Blind and Passive One! Join the club of positive thinkers! Have you ever considered being Saved? How wonderful it would be to know that God Was On Your Side. Failing that, you could at least finish that book. Others would kill for a contract with a good university press – you're sitting on yours like a neurotic student afraid to hand in that really big paper. What are you waiting for, Physician? – heal thyself.'

When spring came he was offered a one-year terminal extension of his sessional appointment. In other words, they would hire him as slave labour for a final year, if he would promise to go away when it was over. Norman telephoned Elisabeth.

'Is that what you want?'

'Of course not.'

'What are you going to do?'

'Tell them to hire me properly or stuff it.'

'Good.'

The next three days Norman spent writing a letter outlining his experience and pointing out that he was doing, for half the price, the work of tenured professors whose qualifications did not exceed his own. Proclaiming his own virtues, Norman found, was a strange experience. At the pub he complained that it made him feel like a prostitute. In fact, writing about himself he discovered that, parallel to his dubious life of intermittent affairs and jobs grasped in desperation, he had enjoyed a scintillating career grooming illiterates across the giant breadth of the country. By the time he had signed his letter and put it in the mail he was convinced that the university would reward his years of diligence with dignity and affluence.

He was wrong. The day he received his letter of refusal from the university he sold his furniture, his stereo, and most of his books; and he traded the proceeds, along with a clunker grandmother Nellie that only started in dry weather, for a Nellie young enough to know the meaning of kilometres. This newish Nellie, Nellie LaBelle he named her because he bought her from a woman in the French department, was a Japanese sedan with a leather-wrapped steering wheel, a built-in cassette player, and – Norman discovered when he was already on the highway – a glove compartment full of yearning country-and-western tapes.

From the day he arrived in Vancouver, the sky was always blue. And from Elisabeth's house he could see the mountains, their snow-peaked tops jutting into the sky like jagged postcards.

The idea was that he would live in the basement apartment as a paying tenant. Even so, Norman felt guilty, and insisted that he help Elisabeth by taking Mona to daycare in the morning and picking her up in the afternoon. Then – the idea continued – while the house was empty he would work on the book. But in fact he preferred sitting in Nellie LaBelle and driving around the city. Sometimes he stopped to explore the parks, eat hamburgers if he was hungry or bored, walk along the beaches or through downtown streets. He took on the shopping so he would have an excuse to drive around the city reading notice boards.

Young girl, 18, seeks babysitting. References.

Three men need woman to share two bedroom apartment. Kitsilano.

Moving and other odd jobs. Phone Ray.

Middle-aged couple, will do anything legal.

Norman imagined himself placing his own advertisement:

Male, non-starter, seeks inspiration. Write Norman.

Easterner, reluctant immigrant, wants to be swept away by passionate young woman with private income. Phone Norman.

Notice-board reader, available 24 hours a day, wishes to be kidnapped by illiterate nymphomaniac for serious caring relationship. Find Norman.

The Farradays, Mark and Heloise, were middle-aged and legal. They did not, however, need to place advertisements. Mark was a one-time physicist who at the age of forty had discarded job, wife, and vocation to become a playboy real-estate developer. Ten years later he controlled millions of dollars of half-used space in Vancouver's new downtown office towers, owned an expensive yacht moored in the company of other such yachts, and was remarried to a professor of women's studies with whom he had produced a perfect pair of twins. These five-year-old twins and Mona met at the university day-care centre and insisted on visiting each other. The parents trailed along. 'I've explained that you're a friend and not a lover,'

Elisabeth told Norman. 'But you don't have to see them if you don't want to.'

Curious, Norman went. The Farradays had a cedar mansion on the water; while the children sequestered themselves inside to watch television, the adults sat on the lawn drinking martinis and exclaiming over the perfect weather and the terrific view of the mountains.

'It drives me crazy, too,' Heloise said to Norman. 'People here talk about the weather as though it were the most important thing in the world. Wait until you've been here a whole year. Summer is always long, winter late, spring early.'

By the time dinner came, Norman was on his fifth martini. 'I'm a beer drinker,' he confided to Heloise in the kitchen. He was also thinking of confiding to her that he found her very attractive, extremely attractive, that in fact he could imagine them melting together. He realized, however, that were he to take his confidences so far, he would have also to add that it was not him speaking, but the martinis.

'Elisabeth tells me you're working on a book.'

'Such is the current excuse for my existence.' Norman said. Then added: 'That was supposed to be clever.'

'I know,' Heloise said, and then raised her eyebrows as if perhaps she realized all sorts of things deep and misty. In theory Norman's excuse for his existence in the kitchen was that he was helping her prepare the salmon steaks. In fact he was standing by the window, waiting for something to happen.

Then Heloise suddenly smiled at Norman, and Norman found himself looking into the eyes of a woman who did not care he had drunk four more martinis than he should have, a woman disarmed, a woman who could love him for himself alone, a woman offering a whirlpool of possibilities.

'Am I drunk? Am I imagining things?'

'Yes and no,' said Heloise.

Norman carried the platter of salmon into the backyard. Mark was standing over the barbecue. He had precise square-fingered hands – hands that were, like the rest of him, perfectly preserved, perfectly in tempo.

Norman placed the steaks on the red-hot grill. 'The flesh sizzled,' Norman said.

'What?' Mark asked.

'It's the sizzle,' Norman said. 'Did you ever wonder what it would be like to walk on coals?'

'I did it,' Mark replied. 'The man around the corner gives lessons. An amazing person, really.'

One day after a morning of nothing and lunch at a health-food bar where he felt comfortable reading the paper while he ate, Norman went walking through a park near the beach. In the centre of the park some teenagers were playing basketball. Norman stopped to watch. 'You want to play?' one of them called out.

Norman looked down at his feet. He was wearing sneakers. He stubbed out his cigarette. 'Sure.'

The first time he was passed the ball he dropped it. For a while after that, he just trotted up and down the court, trying to save his breath and remember who was on his team. Then the ball came to him again and suddenly he was running with it, free, his hand bouncing the ball up and down against the packed dirt as though twenty years had just fallen away. 'Go, go!' someone shouted, and Norman found himself turning to avoid a check, twisting in towards the basket. Then he was high up in the air and the ball was sailing free – sailing past the backboard and into the grass. An explosion of laughter, a slap on the back. 'Nice try, hey, we thought you might be too stoned to move!' And then he was running up and down the court again. As he ran, he was suddenly aware of the encumbrances of time; the layers of flesh that formed a girdle around his belly and hips – one which he wished could now be shrugged off like an unnecessary heavy sweater. Muscles in his legs, his back, his shoulders had softened and forgotten what to do. Dead zones had created themselves in the nerves that connected mind to body. When he leapt for rebounds, he found himself tied down by gravity, his hands batting awkwardly in the air. Nonetheless the ball began to follow him around. But instead of trying to shoot he passed it to his teammates, slowing at centre court while they carried on to the other end. By the time half an hour had passed his lungs felt like wet shopping bags and the soles of his feet were burning.

He crouched, gasping, at the edge of the court while the others, shirtless and muscled, played on. Norman looked at his watch. It was time to pick up Mona. He left without saying anything and drove to the day-care centre. When he arrived he was drumming on Nellie LaBelle's leather-wrapped wheel and singing loudly.

Two days later Norman showed up at the park again. This time he was wearing anti-blister bandages on his heels and an extra pair of socks. For a while he stood at the edge of the game – then the same boy who had welcomed him the first time waved him onto the court. The boy was tall and thin with an unlikely cloud of red hair that sprayed out as he leapt, flattened when he ran. Now Norman noticed how easily he moved, how he controlled the traffic around both baskets, how his team-mates passed to him when they were in trouble, looked to him for the ball when they were in the clear. Norman found himself getting the ball more frequently and twice, when he drove for the basket, he actually managed to hit the rim.

'It's coming back,' the red-haired boy said encouragingly. As though he, eighteen, fluid as mercury, knew what it was to be blocky and awkward, what fifteen years of drinking beer and smoking two packs a day could do to your body.

'Stick' was what the others called him. In every high school in his town there'd been, Norman remembered, a boy called Stick, a tall athlete whose brains resided in the fluid motion of his body. For boys like Norman, non-athletes but willing players, there had been no nicknames; boys like Norman had been only the background against which the more gifted ones could display their talents.

Every day for two weeks Norman went to play basketball in the afternoon. It was something to do, an excuse to leave the house, something for him to dream about in the City of Dreams. That is, when he wasn't dreaming about Heloise. Not so much the charms of Heloise, but the prospect of Heloise. Once, as he'd expected her to, she had even telephoned. It was during the morning, and when he answered she asked for Elisabeth – as though she didn't know that Elisabeth would be at work.

'And you,' she said, 'how are you finding Vancouver?'

'It's still perfect,' Norman replied, surprised at the cool formality in her voice.

'That's good,' Heloise said. And with those words her voice was back to the way it had been that afternoon in the kitchen – breathy, open, waiting for Norman to take the plunge.

Why not? Norman thought, why not now? 'Let's go to lunch sometime,' he could say. Or, 'Have you any sights to recommend?' Or even, 'Will the sky stay blue forever?'

But instead he made his lame goodbye and went down to the basement to make sure he had two pairs of dry socks for basketball that afternoon. Bending over his laundry he felt a twinge in his stomach, a twinge he thought was a pulled muscle at first, but then, when he straightened up, he recognized as a familiar pre-boiling, a bubbling tension that used to start a couple of months before the end of one job and continue until the beginning of the next. 'Phone her now,' Norman said aloud. In the kitchen again, making himself lunch, Norman realized that the tingling in his stomach had actually started weeks ago, the afternoon he had first met Heloise Farraday.

He was slicing cucumber on a cutting-board he had bought at the health-food store. The board was red cedar, its flaming grain brought to a dramatic peak by several coats of oil. He took the moist slices and arranged them in piles. Each pile was a chapter in a junior creative-writing assignment. First chapter: the illicit meeting – accompanied by increased tension and feelings of pleasure; second, the illicit sex – tension to be replaced by pure pleasure; third, the disastrous dénouement – pleasure replaced by tension that increases until Norman loads up Nellie and drives to another city. Grade: C minus. Comments: An idea too often repeated. Norman looked down at the cutting-board. The entire cucumber had been sliced away and now his stomach burned so much that he couldn't eat.

On the last day of the second week Norman noticed there was another stranger watching the game. He was wearing only khaki shorts and running shoes. He had glossy black hair that fell straight to his shoulders, and his skin was darkly tanned. 'Paki,' one of the players said right away.

Norman, running past the stranger, was uncomfortably aware of his stare. 'If *you* can play,' the stranger seemed to be saying, 'then why not I?'

An hour passed. The stranger stood waiting to be invited.

'He wants to play,' Norman finally said to Stick.

'Sure,' Stick said. He beckoned the man forward with a tiny motion of his hand. Soon the new player was running up and down the court. But unlike Norman, he was in excellent condition. Every time there was a loose ball he was there, pouncing on it, dribbling it in a mad frenzy until he got to the basket where he hurled himself upwards and scored.

'Whirling dervish,' someone said.

But no one passed the ball to him, nor did he pass the ball back. Soon it began to seem as if the stranger were a team of his own. Then, during a scramble for a loose ball, Norman was knocked to the ground. When he got up he saw the stranger racing down the court, his frenzied dribble carrying him straight to the basket. Norman brushed off his shoulder. His T-shirt was ripped and the flesh of his shoulder was scraped.

After supper Norman proudly displayed his wound. 'The gladiator returneth unto his home and showeth his blood to the women who weep.'

'You're crazy. I thought you were supposed to be working on your book.' But that night, as Norman was falling asleep, Elisabeth opened the door to his room and joined him in bed.

Later, smoking a cigarette, Norman looked at the ceiling and said, 'I have an announcement to make.'

'The gladiator speaks. All fall silent therefore.'

'You have to promise not to take it personally.'

'Let the sword cut where it may.'

'I feel good.'

'You feel good?'

'I feel good. I hereby declare myself a member of the human race.'

'You need a visa.'

'You told me Vancouver was the City of Dreams and I laughed. I admit it. I thought you were just another Eastern convert to West-Coast boosterism. I thought I knew it all.'

'You did.'

'No, I didn't. I didn't know anything. Now I am here. Now I am lying on my back and looking at your ceiling. Now my muscles are sore and my flesh has been torn by honest exercise. I have just had sexual intercourse for the first time in months and my body is covered in miscellaneous fluids. I feel good.'

'You feel good.'

'And I have had a vision. Yea, after fifteen years or more or less of wandering in the desert. Yea, after morc than a decade of having sand kicked into my face, camel dung dropped on my curriculum vitae, cactus needles stuck into the most delicate of my theorems, I have had a vision.'

'Tell me your vision, master.'

'I have looked into the mirror of the oasis, woman, and I have seen what I am not to be. I am not to be a mind slave, an intellectual, a member of the employed class. I am to miraculously become six-foot-three, superbly co-ordinated, and the best basketball player at the playground. And when this comes to pass I am to be known as Stick.'

'Stick?'

'What surpasseth understanding shall be the bearer of Peace.'

'But in this wasteland there is neither peace nor understanding. Only you and I, my lord.'

'If I were your lord, I would marry you and make you happy ever after.'

'But you are not.'

'I know.'

Saturday the blue sky turned milky with heat and Norman suggested he take Mona swimming. Once he was in the car, habit led him to the park. From his window Norman could see the players moving up and down the court.

Norman looked down at his feet. He was wearing brown lace-up moccasins that Elisabeth had bought him when holes appeared in his running shoes. The moccasins were made from caribou skin and had a strange musky odour. Flexing his toes, listening to the irregular staccato of the basketball against cement, glancing suddenly over at Mona who was sitting quietly with her hands folded and her eyes half-closed, Norman had a sudden desire to try to explain the hopeless logic of his life to her – the Nellie she was sitting in, the Nellies past and future.

On earlier wanderings he had found a special place, a sheltered cove with public access that he preferred to the larger and more crowded beach. Carrying a bag with Mona's things he helped her over the bleached logs until they reached the edge of the water.

Mona took her bucket and shovel from the bag and began digging furiously at the sand. Norman, meanwhile, lit a cigarette and looked out at the gently rolling sea. In the blue light the waves heaved up and down like a serenely obese belly. He undid his shirt, let the sun soak into his skin. After a while he closed his eyes and began dozing to the sound of water slipping in and out of the sand.

The night before, after Elisabeth had padded back to her own room, he had wondered if this summer in Vancouver was in fact the long-awaited exit from the desert – the resignation to his fate that would finally lead to release from bondage. He wanted to settle down; Elisabeth was available and even had a ready-made child. He wanted security; Elisabeth knew about a job in the English Department that had conveniently become vacant – a job that needed to be filled so quickly that there was no time for one of those competitions that drew hundreds of over-qualified wanderers like himself. Easy? What could be easier? Of course he would owe her. On the other hand she would be getting a husband, a father for her child. She had said she wasn't for him – but surely she could be persuaded otherwise, if only he would try to persuade her.

Persuasion, yes – although it wasn't persuasion she was wanting: what she wanted, he knew, was dedication, a proposition emanating not from desperation but from his own free will, from the part of him she had written letters to, the part of him that needed self-help. 'Physician, heal thyself,' she had commanded; now was the moment for the garments of doubt to be cast off, revealing the real Norman Wadkins – lover, father, and husband.

Then as night followed day the inner man would propose to the long-waiting, long-suffering Elisabeth James that they combine in a Pact Against All. Only in Pacts and Alliances could permanent escape from the desert be assured.

Norman imagined himself being masterly. He imagined himself telephoning one of the babysitters who advertised themselves at the Health Food Bar. 'I read your notice,' he would say. 'Would you be free at seven this evening?' He imagined himself with Elisabeth at a restaurant with tablecloths. Over wine, in the light of candles moulded by Buddhist vegetarians, to the crackling of burning logs and the hiss of breaking waves, he would make his pitch. 'Elisabeth, for heaven's sakes, I've loved you this whole time. Let's drop the pretences, darling, my heart is yours.'

Just as he had fixed this perfect scene in his mind, the actors began to change: instead of Elisabeth, Norman saw in front of him Heloise, Ruth, the girl who had advertised her services in the health-food store. The music played louder. Norman felt his heart beat faster. These were women for whom he did not have to cast off the garments of doubt. These were women who tore them from his back. These were women who could bring him brief moments of joy followed by months or years of unhappiness. 'Norman,' Norman said to himself, 'these are the women you have learned to avoid.'

'I want an ice cream,' Mona said. Over the years she had switched into the first person. Norman stood up. As he was dusting off his jeans he heard a noise behind him. The stranger from the basketball court was sliding down the path. He looked briefly at Norman, no recognition in his dark eyes, then walked quickly down the beach and around the corner. Norman followed slowly. Beyond the small sheltered cove was a more inaccessible stretch where huge trees arched out from the last edge of land and hung over the water. In the shelter of those trees were a few huts and lean-tos where people had set up camp for the summer. Feeling like a spy, Norman watched as the stranger went to the first one and ducked inside. A few seconds later he re-emerged, an apple in his hand. Norman backed away before he was seen.

At the top of the path he met the other players. They were

laughing, talking, smoking cigarettes. Stick clapped Norman on the back, the way he always did, then offered Mona a drag from his cigarette. She backed away, frightened. 'Sorry,' Stick said, 'I didn't mean to scare her.' Then he put his hand on Norman's shoulder. His hand was huge, the long fingers that held the ball so lightly now seemed almost inhuman. 'See you Monday,' Stick said. He had small even teeth, a smile that was like a blush.

When Norman and Mona got home, the Farradays were sitting in the living-room, a bottle of white wine had been opened, and the adults were laughing while the Farraday twins played with Mona's toys.

By the time the second bottle was empty, Norman had decided that if the bomb fell right that minute he might grab Heloise and take her downstairs to the safety of his basement bed. Then suddenly the Farradays and their twins had gone off taking Mona with them to spend the weekend at their cabin on the coast.

'I'll make some dinner,' Norman said.

'Let's go out.'

'My treat,' said Norman. And then, unable to stop himself: 'In fact, let's get dressed up and go to a restaurant with tablecloths.'

Another couple of hours, another bottle of wine, and Norman found himself back in his dream of the afternoon. Only this time Elisabeth was with him and he was looking into her eyes, trying to feel love in the pit of his stomach. Or wherever. 'The dream has come true,' Norman considered trying. Instead he said, 'You know, I finished the book revisions last week.'

'You did? When?'

'Wednesday and Thursday nights. I stayed up late.'

'That didn't take long.'

'I guess basketball cleared my head.'

'Are you going to apply for the job?'

'Un-hunh.'

'Is that yes?'

Norman took a sip of water. 'If I get a job, I'll have a salary.'

'That would be one of the benefits.'

'With a salary I could pay more rent.'

'If it's not nepotism, it's bound to be corruption.'

'Whatever happened to ordinary people, struggling to earn an honest dollar?'

'Us,' Elisabeth said.

The waiter was standing above them. 'More to drink?' Norman asked. 'Coffee? Liqueurs?'

Elisabeth laughed. She had a smile, Norman suddenly noticed, like his friend Stick. Small and quiet, well-organized, the smile of generals who watch life fall into patterns around them. But no blush. 'Do you want me to ask you to marry me?' Norman tried to imagine himself saying. But he couldn't say it. He couldn't even imagine it.

When they were in the car again, Norman put on 'Your Cheatin' Heart' and with the music to encourage him drove towards the playground. He parked by the edge of the grass, turned off the motor. Through the open windows drifted the smells of late summer: water, grass, the city's exhaled heat. Nights like this he had parked other Nellies in random spots in other cities; cutting bonds, inspecting tires, running his hands over the steering-wheel, and preparing once more to drive out blindly into nothingness. No, not nothingness, he corrected himself, but onto that long single highway on which the country's cities dangled, uncomfortably separated, uncomfortable at the prospect of each other.

Now he was gripping the wheel, stroking it. Elisabeth's hands covered his. He turned to her. *Now*, he thought, *now is the time to kiss her.* Then his thoughts sloughed away like old ice and he was bent over her, gratefully tasting on her lips the same wine that had passed through his own.

When they got out of the car they were still holding hands. It was a new experience, thought Norman, a sort of trial marriage. He led Elisabeth towards the little cove he had visited with Mona that afternoon. 'I know a place where we could neck.'

At first the moon lit their way, but when they got to the path the light was blocked by trees and they found themselves stumbling over stones and twisted roots. 'The light at the end of the tunnel,' Elisabeth said, just after a fallen log had brought them to their knees – but left them a view of an opening only a few steps away. Norman tried to imagine what Stick might reply if handed such a sentence. Perhaps he would simply redirect it, like an errant pass, to a more likely target.

The tide had gone out, the small beach of the afternoon was now a glistening expanse of wet sand. Still holding Elisabeth's hand Norman stepped towards the water. In front of the shelter he had seen that afternoon a huge fire was burning. The muffled sounds they had heard on the path now resolved themselves into excited talking and singing to the strumming of a guitar.

'Let's go over there,' Elisabeth said. She tugged at Norman's hand and Norman reluctantly followed.

As they drew closer, Norman saw that all the basketball players from the afternoon were clustered around the fire, each accompanied by a case of beer. The stranger was the one playing the guitar; he had his eyes closed and he swayed back and forth as he sang.

'Look who's here.'

'Just dropped by.'

Soon a cold beer was pressed into his hand and Norman was talking to Stick and his girlfriend, a tiny voluptuous creature whose hair was an exact match for Stick's.

'Your boyfriend is a wonderful basketball player,' Norman said.

'He was on the all-star team.'

'Are you going to play at university?'

Stick shrugged his shoulders.

'He's working for my dad. He owns the semi-pro team. Then we're getting married in a few months.'

'You are? That's wonderful.' Norman leaned forward, smiling. He lifted his bottle to toast the event, and raising it to his mouth was aware suddenly of the absolute gravity of the bottle – its weight, its fullness, its cold perfection in containing the holy fermented liquid of communion. 'Is this my second beer? Norman asked.

'I wasn't counting,' said the girl. She gave him a certain kind of look, a look filled with speculation and suspicion, which Norman had not seen for decades but now recognized from his high school years as the look residents give to tourists who are passing through. On their way to university and better jobs, Norman had then thought, but that was before he had gotten lost in the desert.

Norman stepped back from the girl. Beyond the crackling red light of the fire, beyond the slow moon-silvered waves sliding into the wet sand, he could see boats parked in the middle of the channel. Some of them were festooned and blazing, others had only a few identifying red and blue lights strategically placed. To be on a boat, Norman thought, to be riding the water surrounded by nothingness. Across the bay was a glittering stretch of apartment towers. And then, rising into the distance, the jagged silhouettes of the mountains.

His bottle was empty. He took another from a case that seemed to have appeared beside him. The years in the desert had turned him into a beer drinker but his body was unused to mixing beer and wine. As he swallowed he felt his stomach protesting. Another swallow, a more vigorous reaction. Stepping away from the firelight, Norman walked towards the bushes, looking for a place to be sick discreetly. He sat down on a rock, blearily drunk, and watched the channel boats rocking with the tide.

'With a salary I could pay more rent,' he remembered saying. But Elisabeth had refused to rise to the bait: Norman staying, Norman leaving, Norman proposing, Norman failing to propose – she had cleverly contrived to leave it up to him. She had somehow become the sun that had simply to wait and shine while he, the planet, spun helplessly in her orbit.

Norman knew he was drunk. 'I am drunk,' he said to himself. Not because he had had too much to drink – although he had – but because he was trying to hide from the truth. From the truths. Truths that shone as bright as Elisabeth's sun. Other truths invisible and hidden black truths buried like hidden seams of coal. He was drunk, he was hiding and meanwhile meanings were waiting to be deciphered. Careful thought, textual analysis, semiotic deconstruction. These techniques – others too – were available and waiting for him. As he had once explained to an indifferent class, the English professor is a surgeon who operates on the body of the text. Words made the surface – supporting it was a whole anatomy of structures, subtexts, themes, literary devices. And passion? Where did passion fit in? Passion was an idea, a concept, a single arrow in the larger quiver. Or, on the other hand, perhaps it was a word that covered over other words – foolishness, youth, self-destruction. Unless, on the third hand, the hand that wasn't, passion was all that mattered.

Norman let himself slide from the rock onto the more comfortable sand. The strumming of the guitar and the singing had grown louder. He closed his eyes and had a dim vision of the entire human race as over-excited water-bugs, each locked in its own shell, each in a frenzy over nothing. Then he thought of Mona. She was not a waterbug. She clung to his hand every Saturday and sometimes during the week. She laughed when he tickled her and cried when he wouldn't give her two ice creams in one afternoon.

There were the sounds of splashing, of gleeful shrieking as people dashed into the water. Norman stood up. He kicked off his shoes, stripped himself naked. Carefully he folded his clothes on a log then, still holding his bottle of beer, he advanced towards the sea. As he passed the fire he saw Stick's girlfriend look curiously at his naked body. Self-consciously he sucked in his stomach. He peered around for Elisabeth. Then he moved more quickly, first running along the wet sand, then straight into the water.

After a few steps the sand gave way beneath his feet and he was in over his head. Norman released his beer bottle and began to swim towards the boats.

It was years since he had gone swimming. But basketball had given him back his wind, and he felt powerful and strong as he sliced towards the centre of the channel. Then suddenly he was out of breath and gasping. He turned towards the shore. In front of the fire figures were waving – whether at him or at each other he couldn't tell. And then above the pounding of his heart he thought he could hear voices calling him. 'I'm here,' he shouted back. He was surprised at the loudness of his voice. He shouted again. He was treading water. The waves that had been so gentle when he entered the sea now seemed to be pushing harder, slapping against his neck and the side of his head. He decided to rest a moment, floating on his back. When he turned up to look at the sky, the water flowed over his eyes, into his mouth and nostrils. He began swimming again, towards the shore, but a current had gripped him and it seemed no matter how vigorously he swam, the fire was growing dimmer. Once more he rolled onto his back. Ripe clusters of stars hung above. 'This is the way I want to die,' he thought. He could hear music. His body would sink to the bottom of the channel, but his soul was flying into the white sky. He closed his eyes, surrendered himself to this final embrace.

When he woke up he knew right away he was in a hospital, knew right away that the face looking down at his belonged to Elisabeth, knew right away that the tears were coming from Mona. 'I'll do a book on post-death experiences in modern literature' was the next thought. He pictured himself sitting at his tenured desk, smoking filter-tip cigarettes and drinking a small glass of beer.

'Don't worry, I'm all right,' he said. He was holding tightly to Mona's hand, he was crying and couldn't stop. Tears slid down his cheeks and the wetness brought it all back; they had hauled him out of the water and up onto one of the yachts. Wrapped him in a thick towel and given him something to drink. For a few minutes he had stood on the deck in the towel, looking at the shore and chatting as if the whole thing had been a humorous escapade. Perhaps the yacht belonged to Mark and Heloise, perhaps his shivering would stop when the warm flesh of Heloise was finally wrapped around him.

But Heloise did not appear. Nor Mark. It was strangers who surrounded him. Strangers who were looking at him curiously as he realized that nothing on earth could enable him to dive back into the sea and swim home. And he wasn't laughing, he was shivering uncontrollably. He had a first drink, then a second. Someone took him inside and he slid into hot bath. The water burned at his skin but inside his muscles and guts were still frozen, still shaking uncontrollably, and even a third drink and a fourth didn't make any difference.

'I'm a doctor,' someone kept saying. Norman looked up to

see a man bending over him, a young rich-looking man of his own age with a friendly face and thick moustaches. 'I'm going to give you a shot,' he said from under the moustaches. And then the needle had entered his arm, a painful biting sensation that finally softened, sweetened, sent its sweetness and sleep humming through his blood until finally he was only aware that he was lying in the bath, enclosed by warm watery lips, floating in water, on water, the sky ripe and waiting above him.

When he woke up again Mona and Elisabeth were gone. He had a throbbing headache. He was wearing his own flannel pyjamas and a thick terrycloth bathrobe that belonged to Elisabeth. He thought about the book on post-death experiences. He would have to say how good it was, after dying, to be warmed and wrapped by the clothes of others. It made one feel part of the tribe again. It made one feel as though forgiveness was being offered.

In the pocket of his bathrobe Elisabeth had placed a note: 'We love you, Mona and Elisabeth.' The folded corners of the paper dug sharply at his palms, then he realized that even the air was clawing at his skin. Another after-death observation: 'Upon their return to the world of the living, certain individuals are rendered hypersensitive. This manifests itself in reactions ranging from pure sensual pleasure to exaggerated feelings of terror.'

When Mona and Elisabeth returned the next morning, Norman had prepared his proposal of marriage. 'A Provisional Document Detailing Terms of Total Surrender' was the title, but before he could deliver it, he fell asleep.

His sleep was a transparent one. He saw himself lying on his back, hands stretched out to either side. Holding them were Mona and Elisabeth. They flanked him. They pressed their warm bodies against him so that he would be sustained. But Norman Wadkins was not dreaming. He was seeing, foreseeing.

He was foreseeing the future and in that brilliant future were man, wife, and daughter.

In his mind the future was already the past. He had become a full professor, he had purchased new furniture for Elisabeth's living room, he had converted the basement apartment into a combination study and sauna. In addition, he spent two evenings a week playing basketball for a semi-pro team. Not a front-line player, too old for that, rather a high-strung specialist, a pure shooter, a brief explosion of energy that might at any moment be seen skimming down the court, a blur among the slower, more awkward players. And then, when arms reached out for him, he was suddenly airborne, a soaring desert hawk: untouched, untouchable.

MIRRORS

HE COULDN'T help the little symptoms – heart thumping, palms sweating, images sliding out from beneath each other like cards tumbling from a deck. Paranoia, Carolyn called it, with a certain gentle smile that was supposed to soften the word. And so, when he saw the house lights were on, his first feeling was relief.

Then – because it was spring, he would say to himself later, and there was no foliage – his headlights picked out Michael's truck parked at the bottom of the driveway. That would be for her suitcases – his heart accelerated again – and even as he turned from the road into the driveway, cutting motor and lights, he couldn't help anticipating the sight of those suitcases, lined up in a hostile row. Drifting down between the maples he waited until the last moment, only a few feet from the truck, to put on the brakes. Even so, coasting slowly, his wheels slipped on the ice and his car jolted into the truck hard enough to slam his head forward into the steering-wheel.

Outside, Jonathan found himself sucking at the cool air as if air alone could save him. Then, as his head cleared, he became aware of the river's sound: a roar that grew louder, more intense, more layered with backwashes, swirls, chunks of grinding ice as he walked towards it. Until finally, when he lay face down on the bank of the wide river, the trembling earth and rushing water were almost enough to break him open and carry him away.... Almost.

As he was walking back to the house, every breeze seemed heavy with the smells of stirring mud, budding trees, the melting rot of frozen vegetation that had been covered by snow for six months. Easy to imagine the waiting armies of summer, billions of spores sheltered in the earth, lying between grains of soil and preparing to explode.

For a moment Jonathan stayed in the driveway, lighting a cigarette. He was standing beside the stone firepit they used for boiling maple sap down to syrup, but tonight there was no sign that only a week ago the three of them had been by the fire – the best of friends – passing wine and cigarettes from hand to hand.

Jonathan began walking towards the house. Either they had heard him or they had not. The kitchen lights were on; as he stepped in he could see no signs of packing, only the remains of supper on the table. Also a half bottle of wine. Interesting, he found himself noting, it had been years since a bottle of wine had gone unemptied on his table. From the living room there were no sounds of conversation or music. Jonathan wondered what it would be like to go in and see his wife and his best friend going at it on the carpet. Or maybe they preferred the couch. A choice: before it was too late he could turn around, walk out, get back into his car and drive to a hotel in Kingston. He tried to imagine himself at the wheel of his car again. His belly was churning. He went to the cupboard and took out a bottle of Scotch. Found a clean glass, poured himself two fingers and drank it down. Holding the glass he noticed that something unexpected had happened to the tips of his fingers: they were vibrating, on their own, like frog's legs detached from the body. Then he heard footsteps from the living room. They had been in there, after all. A voice talking in normal tones. No moans of sex, no intimate undercurrents, no trace in Carolyn's voice of anything he didn't hear every day. In a few seconds she would be in the kitchen. Glad to see him, no doubt, at least on the surface. Anxious to reassure him that despite everything he had threatened, she was still the faithful and enduring wife. No doubt she would joke at his expense about the stupid trick he had tried to play, coming home two days early from the conference, unannounced, spying like a primitive ape.

The steps had temporarily paused. She would be, Jonathan knew, beside the thermostat. Whenever she stopped at the thermostat it meant she was cold, that she wanted to turn up the heat. And then Carolyn was in the kitchen. They were standing there – Jonathan thought, unable to do anything but think – looking at each other. He was holding the bottle of scotch. She was naked. What she might have been thinking was unknown to Jonathan; her face was so frozen that he started to laugh.

'Please,' Carolyn said. Her arms had been folded across her chest but now, as her face unfroze and she began to cry, she opened them wide.

Then he was back in the car, driving towards Kingston. Driving fast. His window was open; the cold air was to keep him from going crazy; and he was shouting into the wind – 'Bitch! bitch! bitch!' He had left the bitch with her arms spread wide. Tits not what they used to be, to tell the truth, or maybe the harsh kitchen light had failed to flatter. Going up a hill towards town he saw a transport come over the crest. He switched lanes. The transport's high beams flicked at him, then its horn began to blare. Jonathan swerved back into his own lane, pushing the accelerator to the floor. At the top of the hill he paused to make sure the truck was continuing. Then he lit a cigarette, took a drink from the bottle of Scotch which had somehow travelled with him from his kitchen, turned his car around and started driving home. It was all so simple, so inevitable, but as he coasted down the driveway – this time lights on, motor running, blood clamouring for blood, he was shouting again. 'Bitch! bitch! bitch!'

II

The road was uphill from the house, a massive stone relic set on a grassy plateau overlooking the water. Connecting road and house was a narrow dirt driveway bracketed by rows of giant maples.

When spring came the sunlight blazed down from the sky and was magnified by the snow. Under its force the old maples leaked sap from broken limbs and lightning wounds. Jonathan identified with these trees, describing to me the way his own heart was mending and bleeding under the hot sun of his new love. 'Can you believe it?' he would ask, giving me a sweet vulnerable smile I had never seen before, 'the old man is stabbed to the very innards, *bleeding* for his love.' By the time he had abandoned such metaphors the leaves had already popped out of their buds: lime-green baby leaves so dazzlingly new that when the sun hit them, they turned the sky around them the colour of breaking glass.

'Carolyn bought me this hat,' Jonathan said one day. We were standing in the rain under the trees. The leaves had turned brighter yet in the rain and were exploding life into the luminous grey light of the spring afternoon. Sheltering Jonathan from all this action was his new hat, a feather in its band. I thought: how like Jonathan to decorate his new hat with the feather of a dead bird.

Summer twilight. Birds swoop, weaving paths in the cool currents that run with the river. We are on the lawn, our chairs facing the crumpled glassy surface of the moving water. Jonathan is wearing another of Carolyn's gifts, this time a Mexican shirt with a hand-embroidered scoop neck. Around his thick tanned throat is a chain featuring a hammered silver bird, an Incan relic that he discovered on his latest dive into the past.

'Has anyone told you lately that you are a very attractive man?'

Jonathan laughs. I am looking down to the riverbank at a rabbit moving fearfully across the grass.

'You,' Carolyn says, 'I mean you.' Now she is kneeling in front of me, her hands on my knees, her eyes looking into mine. She has broad cheekbones, a narrow sculpted nose created by a Toronto surgeon after she took a swan dive, face first, racing downhill on a bicycle. Today she is wearing her own matching Mexican blouse. I am looking at her and because I have just seen the album of their journey I am reminded of Carolyn in the pictures, Carolyn in fact very beautiful, smiling her big smile, somehow in the foreground of every shot – as if to say that while the others were tourists and suckers she was just going along for the screen test. 'What wrong? You don't have a problem, do you?' She laughs again and this time I laugh with her because this is the line Carolyn fed to a weekend guest I brought to their place – a guest who retreated from the winter regimen of cross-country skiing and snowshoeing to get unforgivably drunk before dinner.

But Carolyn isn't finished yet. She's still kneeling in front of me, still carrying on with her soprano laugh. Carolyn and I look at each other. We have the usual feelings, I have always thought. I am Jonathan's best friend, so she tolerates me. She makes Jonathan happy, so I tolerate her. Of course there's a frosty edge, because Jonathan has told us each things about the other that are less than flattering.

Carolyn says, 'Well, you know, I'm serious. It's time you got over your wife and got involved with someone else.' Pause for dramatic effect. 'For longer than a weekend, I mean.'

'Don't tease Michael. You know he's the original Saturday-night man.'

'That's me.' I stand up and start walking towards the river. What am I supposed to say?

Unable to sleep I listen through the open window for a breeze. Instead: still air, a porcupine crunching noisily through the brush, moths beating against the screen as they fight their way towards the dial of the illuminated clock.

Two fifty-six.

Across the hall Carolyn and Jonathan are in their bed. Jonathan, like me, so drunk that at midnight we were scarcely able to make our usual trek along the river path.

'Better not drive,' Jonathan had said.

'The truck knows its way.'

'And miles to go before I sleep. Get a horse.'

Sliding into the cool linen. Waiting for sleep. Transported into a weird drunken doze, my mind a crippled butterfly struggling in the dark. Then waking up, half sober, soaked in sweat. Pushing down the sheet. Hearing the porcupine, the moths. No human breathing. The night gripping tighter.

Two fifty-seven.

I put on my jeans and go downstairs in search of cooler air.

Soon I am in the living room, settled into one of the comfortable padded chairs in which I have spent dozens of winter evenings emptying the bottle with Jonathan. Until Carolyn came. 'But we must forge on,' Jonathan would insist, more than keeping pace with me. 'Do you know why we have to drink? Drink is to the middle-aged what sleep is to babies. Oblivion, sweet and otherwise. A quick trip to Barbados. Getting sick and hung over is all part of the voyage. Proves you've been somewhere.'

LIVES OF THE MIND SLAVES

Sitting in the dark, bare skin scratching against the uphol-
stery, toes vacationing on a coffee table, I ask myself where I
have been tonight. Barbados? Not exactly. Escaping something? But what? Maybe I have only been drinking away an
otherwise beautiful summer's night. Maybe I have only been
sailing a much-crossed sea, wasting moonlight, Jonathan – as
always – at the helm, me – as always – riding steerage.

With my toes I try to find a package of cigarettes. Then, perfectly timed, a match scraping, a flare in the darkness, a tear-
shaped circle of light. Carolyn.

'Sorry. I didn't mean to frighten you.'

'I couldn't sleep. Must have had too much to drink.'

Carolyn laughs. 'No one keeps up with Uncle Jonathan.'
She stands up, crosses the room, the glowing tip of her cigarette a monster firefly floating through the darkness. 'I took
yours. You want one?'

'Thanks.'

Her hand brushes mine. 'God, it's dark.' She puts the cigarette in my lips, then holds her own to light it. 'You going?'

She settles down at my feet, leans into my leg. It occurs to
me that we have seldom touched: a ritual handshake the first
time we met, a compulsory kiss New Year's Eve.

She is wearing a white shift. I am wondering if I will reach
down to touch it. Then I draw away, settle into the routine of
smoking, breathing, navigating the clouds of tension that are
beginning to gather around us.

She turns. She puts her hand on my belly. Slides down to
the top button of my jeans.

'No.'

'Please?'

Later, sticky with each other, we walk on the lawn holding
hands. Then we lie down again, this time in the grass far from
the house. I write my name on her neck with my tongue, other
tricks I haven't had a chance to try for a long time. After a
while I become aware that I am making a strange noise in my
throat, the contented baby-like humming my daughter used to
make when she was nursing. Carolyn, too, is making noises,
little moaning melodies that match my own.

We are lying on our backs. This time we have gotten our

clothes off. A late-night sliver of the moon has risen to slice through the darkness.

Jonathan was an expert in old pottery, the kind that comes in shards. A professor of archaeology to be exact. Not only had he travelled to Mexico, but to sites all around the world. Relics, souvenirs, framed pictures of curiosities were scattered through his house. Also in the house, not entirely invisible, were his poems. Poetry was not his profession, which was teaching and research; not his hobby, which was renovating and repairing the home he had owned for more than twenty years; not his love, which was Carolyn and her predecessors. It was merely something he did, among other things, the mark of a civilized man, an adornment like his Mexican shirt, a relative neither close nor distant, who was tolerated, despised, and admired. Also, among his many accomplishments, it was the one about which he was vain. Never would Jonathan sink to boasting about his latest honour, to meditating drunkenly on the possibility of another step up the academic ladder, to leaving open on a table – as if by chance – this or that scholarly article. But with his poetry – well – for example: if the bottle had grown empty and a second was at hand; when sleepy drunkenness indicated that the narrow end of the journey was rapidly approaching – then Jonathan might seize a scrap of paper hitherto unnoticed, or even pick up the copy of his book that always seemed to be nearby – and suddenly he was reading to you in a voice amazingly polished, a voice smoothly manoeuvring from one word to the next, a voice rising and falling with the accents of Literature: in brief, the voice not of Jonathan the man whom I knew, but of Jonathan the precocious-seminary-boy-turned-successful-scholar – the voice of the shadow Jonathan, the man-of-the-mind Jonathan who should have surrounded himself with a library and spent his nights reading by candlelight.

When did Jonathan compose his poetry? Travelling from one conference to another, in hotels, invariably while looking at his own face in the mirror.

He offered this unexpected revelation in the tavern where before Carolyn's arrival we had often passed winter Saturday afternoons. I wondered what he saw when he looked at himself. What I saw was a face tanned dozens of times in the tropics, an amazingly gentle face with rounded features, high cheekbones to which sun and alcohol had given a permanent flush of well-being, a broad lined forehead overhung by a thatch of salt-and-pepper hair, a smile stranded between sly and shy.

'I don't suppose you knew I was so vain about my looks,' Jonathan added after his confession about the mirror. *Lonely*, I would have said, but didn't because Jonathan with his sad honest eyes and his sighs as he settled his weight into a chair had become – thanks to Carolyn – one of those people with whom you make certain to communicate every pretence of complete – even careless – honesty, while in fact taking every precaution to avoid the truth.

So I said, 'In your case, vanity is hopeless,' or something like that – the sort of remark men expect from each other.

Jonathan said, 'It's strange being here in the summer. I've never been here in the summer before.'

Between us, on the table, was a pitcher of beer. The tavern was air-conditioned but the pitcher was sweating small streams of water onto the plastic-topped table. Jonathan filled our glasses.

'I suppose you're my best friend,' Jonathan said. 'That makes it hard. One should probably discuss these things with strangers.'

For a moment I tried to pretend to myself that he was still talking about his poems. I lit a cigarette, using it as an excuse to turn my eyes away from him.

'Carolyn told me everything. At least I think it was everything. I suppose you never know.'

'What did she tell you?'

'About your screwing,' Jonathan said. 'What did you think?'

I nodded.

'I'm serious. What did you think she might have told me?'

'I don't know. I was just hoping she hadn't told you that.'

'Is there anything else?'

I shrugged. 'No.' *What else is there?* I had thought of adding, just as a diversion. Also because there was something else: the talk of love, the continually made and then discarded plans to run away, the little tiffs and reconciliations, spates of jealousy, three secret dinners in town, the one all-night tryst we'd managed to arrange when Jonathan was away, my own recent declaration that I couldn't keep sleeping with her, her response that she was relieved and that the whole thing had been just 'physical, cabin fever.'

'The three of us could do it together,' Jonathan said. 'I'm not the jealous type. What do you say?'

'It was my fault. It's all over now. Carolyn loves you very much, Jonathan; you know you mean everything to her.'

Jonathan sipped at his beer. 'You two should go away for a while, think things over.'

I was about to say something back but then I saw that Jonathan's hands were beginning to shake. Strong hands. Hands I now wished would bunch up into fists and send me into at least temporary oblivion.

'We could go out to the parking lot,' I offered.

And then suddenly we were out in the drizzling rain, standing between my pickup truck and Jonathan's Chevrolet with its sheepskin-covered seats. We were wavering back and forth, our feet digging into position, me waiting for Jonathan to make a move.

Jonathan put his hand on my shoulder. 'She asked me to marry her. She said she needed me.'

'She does.'

'I think she does,' Jonathan said. 'That's the crazy thing.' Then he made a mock fist and hit me on the chest, one of those little love-taps men give to each other except that at the last second Jonathan closed his fist and swung his whole bulk into the punch, sending me down into the mud. I was still sitting there when Jonathan walked away, climbed into his car, drove off.

'Good luck, you asshole,' I shouted as Jonathan mothered his car over the curb onto the street. And slapping the mud from my jeans, feeling happy but also sorry for myself at the same time, I couldn't help remembering all the times that Jonathan and I had driven home from this same tavern, zooming along on foaming rivers of beer, Jonathan singing out bawdy songs in his full baritone voice while every few seconds his eyes flicked to the rearview mirror, watching for ghosts.

III

Carolyn sometimes thought about writing a little treatise on her life and loves, *Memoirs of a Timid Woman* or something like that. Something to be found in a desk drawer. Something that could begin: *Like most faculty wives* ... Then she would go on to explain how she had gone to the party – but not officially – with her thesis adviser who was married. That had been something different – a chance romance – not really a romance but a perfect flirtation because she had wanted sex and safety in the same package. *Sex and safety in the same package.* For that, further explanations would be required. A quick trip through childhood, the twentieth century, the Third World War of the Sexes – *you've seen the movies.*

In this movie the girl was a reluctant mistress who had heard too many voices about liberated Amazons crashing through the night. But it was the man who cracked first, threatened to fall in love, tell all to his wife and force Carolyn to run away with him. On the way to the party he had told her that 'everything' was arranged. He was going to spend a sabbatical year in England studying 'the early Wittgenstein'. Carolyn, imagining herself wearing damp woollen long-johns while her adviser chased her through an unheated apartment, was unable to speak. Instead, looking for a permanent exit, she asked Jonathan if he could drop her at her house.

A few days later Jonathan telephoned and invited her to join him at a restaurant for dinner. All very chaste. And very quickly it was established that they were both single and eligible. 'You're *really* not married?' she asked. 'Not living with anyone? Not bound to a secret alliance?'

'Just my pottery,' Jonathan said, 'And my house. In fact, you should come out and see my shards, as they say.'

Then she would tell about the drive to his house, a warm comfortable journey bathed in easy conversation and cigarette smoke. Once there, Jonathan made a fire, showed her his collection, told witty anecdotes about his journeys into the past.

In return she offered the slim tale of her thesis supervisor and how she had behaved so stupidly she was afraid she would fail her course and lose her scholarship.

'A scholarship student in philosophy!' Jonathan had exclaimed. 'Don't worry, they would never take a scholarship away from someone like you.'

'Don't tease me.'

'I'm not,' Jonathan said. 'I'm on the committee.'

After that there was another drink and then Jonathan said it was time he drove her home, before he became a menace.

'I wouldn't mind staying,' Carolyn said. This would look bad in the book, even when she explained that she wanted to stay not because he was on the committee but because he didn't seem to need anything from her.

'I never sleep with students.'

'Oh no, I didn't mean *that*. I just meant you could give me the couch, nice and cosy here by the fire, and in the morning you could drop me off at my place on your way to the university.'

'Spoken like a true lady.'

The visits became regular: once or twice a week, dinner and drinking and conversation. And by midnight she was always alone in her sleeping bag. Buzzing slightly from the liquor, sleepy but not exhausted, she would think about how perfect these evenings were, how sensual rather than sexy, how pleasant it was to fall asleep like an overheated cat in front of the fire.

A couple of months into this routine, the story would continue, Michael appeared on the scene with one of his 'weekend visitors'. At midnight, before anyone yawned, Carolyn said, 'I'll go upstairs now.' Which she did, to Jonathan's room. When he came to bed two hours later, she was still awake, sitting cross-legged on his quilt and reading.

He was in a state she had come to recognize: drunk but still navigating. She closed the door behind him, then switched off the light. Without comment Jonathan undressed and slid into bed. Carolyn followed.

'You can go back to the living room if you want,' Jonathan said. 'Michael takes his girlfriends to the attic. I think he must have a stash of candles and incense up there.' He was lying immobile in his place, not touching her. Carolyn reached out and put her fingers on his ribs. Rough skin, unexpected muscle, a thin layer of sweat.

She began to stroke him very slowly, very carefully, running her hand up and down his side, then across the locked muscles of his wide chest.

'I'm not very good at this,' Jonathan finally said. He was still lying rigid, his hands laced behind his head.

'Do me a favour? Don't worry about the details. Can I lie on top of you? I'm freezing.'

'Let me be the missionary, I'll lie on top of you.'

With these words, *I'll lie on top of you*, Carolyn had always thought the first chapter could end. Or perhaps they were so conclusive in every respect that the second chapter should be a blank, a little opportunity for shared speculation.

Spring and the maples are leaking again, this time into buckets. At the end of the driveway a stone-lined pit. Inside the fire crackles, boiling away the maple sap.

During the day Carolyn tends the fire. She wears a lumberjack shirt Jonathan gave her their first spring. Since then it has been washed and rewashed until the soft cotton surrounds her like a security blanket. Secure, too, is how she feels crouched by the spitting flames, breathing sweet woodsmoke and watching the woodpeckers forage through the old maples.

After work, Michael and Jonathan take over. Splitting wood by the light of the flames. Drawing stumps of cedar closer to the fire, clapping hands for warmth and passing a bottle back and forth. When the moon rises it turns the fields into white glowing sheets. The two men walk down to the river, listen to the boom of the ice cracking under the surging presure of the spring currents.

It's close to midnight before they go into the house. Michael and Jonathan strip off their coats, their thick sweaters. Outside, the fire is down to a bed of glowing embers. Beside it, a small pile of wood, split and stacked, waiting to be fed into tomorrow's flames. They eat. They drink red wine. Michael reaches into his briefcase to show the latest picture of his daughter. After all these years the divorce has finally gone through. Michael's ex-wife has moved to Vancouver taking the girl with her – courtesy of the court.

'So,' Carolyn says, 'you're a free man now.'

'That's it,' Michael replies.

She watches him as he bends over the soup. His face is narrow, his mouth thin. She is not exactly certain what it was about him that made her want him so much.

As always, Carolyn is the first to go upstairs. At the landing she pauses. The men's voices, engaged in perfunctory conversation during dinner, have now relaxed into lower, slower tones. Jonathan laughs – a mumble of agreeable bass notes. Michael's laugh starts later, ends earlier – higher-pitched, sharper, chipping away at the edge of things.

In her bedroom she undresses, puts on the terrycloth robe Jonathan gave her against the winter cold. There was a period when they went to a marriage counsellor, driving all the way to Toronto so no one could possibly find out, going not because Jonathan was unhappy but because what she wanted against the cold wasn't something you could buy in a store but Jonathan himself, his big bear's body keeping out the demons.

On her bedside table there are books, including Jonathan's poetry. Their first winter Jonathan had written new poems, poems about her body, poems he called love poems. In those honeymoon weeks she would lie against him, listening with her ear at his chest as he declaimed verses in praise of her various parts. Sometimes she would giggle as he compared her breasts to Etruscan vases, or her belly to the vast rolling stretches of the Sahara Desert. 'But I'm serious,' Jonathan would insist, and then he would slide his hand into her robe and she would giggle some more and accuse him of using verse to incite indecent acts.

Carolyn moves across the room. The fire is still burning, a red heart bleeding slowly into the darkness. She is standing in front of the window. She sees her reflection: a slender face, white teeth when she smiles, long hair curling down to her shoulders. 'My sad Madonna loves to kiss' had been the first line of one of Jonathan's poems; and now he was talking about a whole new book, one that would be dedicated to their life together, to her. Carolyn looks at herself in the mirror and then, thinking about Jonathan's poetry, remembers what Michael told her. She imagines Jonathan sitting in front of a mirror in a Chicago hotel room.

Through the window comes the sound of wind, of men's voices, of a truck door slamming. Carolyn sees the lights go on, hears the familiar uncertain cough of the motor before it catches, watches the twin red tail-lights of Michael's truck as it slowly climbs the driveway towards the road.

She sits cross-legged on the quilt, opens a magazine, begins brushing out her hair. It is Saturday night. Even as she pulls the covers over her she can hear Jonathan's deliberate half-soused step as he climbs towards her. She closes her eyes. He is breathing deeply; there is a pause while he first remembers the new bathroom he has installed, *en suite*, then decides it would be more discreet to use the old one.

Water runs. Carolyn hears the rambunctious sounds of Jonathan splashing his face to sober up. Through the slightly open window she can smell the last traces of the fire.

Jonathan is in the room. Heavily, he climbs into bed, spreads himself carefully beside her, breathes. Some nights, lying like this, listening to him drift slowly into sleep, Carolyn has allowed her mind to wander down certain illegal trails. One that used to be popular: that in another universe she led a twin existence, one where she spent every night with Michael, not Jonathan; betrayed Michael, not Jonathan; made love with Jonathan, not Michael. Another: that she had left Jonathan and was lying in her own bed, alone in a city with no name, and that the only breathing she had to listen to was her own. A third and now the most frequent but most dreaded: that one of these days or nights Jonathan, having drunk, smoked, and eaten too much for the three decades of his adult life, was going to have a heart attack. Then she would telephone the ambulance, go with him to the hospital. There he would lie again, on his back, barrel chest and belly covered by a white sheet, oxygen mask over his wide generous mouth, eyes staring hurt and frightened at the ceiling. 'There's no hope,' the doctor would mouth to her, out of Jonathan's sight.

Soon Michael would come to join the vigil and they would stand one on each side of Jonathan's bed, waiting for him to expire.

'I wouldn't want to be left alone with Michael,' Carolyn thinks.

'What?' Jonathan shouts. He jerks up in bed. Carolyn, terrified, cringes away from him.

'What's going on? I just want to know what's going on here,' Jonathan's voice cries out angrily.

Jonathan's eyes are closed but he has raised his head and is staring through closed eyelids at the ceiling.

'Tell me!' His fist crashes down on the bed. Then he is shaking his head and shoulders, slapping his cheeks gently with his palms. 'I'm sorry, did I frighten you? I was having one of those dreams again. Can you get me a cigarette?'

'Do you want me to light it for you?'

'Thanks.'

She puts the cigarette between his lips and then, as though it were a caress, slides her hand along his chest to feel his heart. It is beating away, strong and regular as always.

'Night terrors,' Jonathan says calmly. 'Maybe I should stop drinking.'

'You always drink.'

'Catches up with you, I guess. At least, it's catching up with me.' He switches on the light. 'You know what I was dreaming? That you were having an affair with Michael again. That you'd been having it on with him the whole time. God, I was ready to kill the little bastard.'

'And me? Were you going to kill me too?'

'Oh no, I couldn't kill you, even in a dream. I was just going to pack your suitcases and leave them in the snow.' Jonathan laughs and Carolyn laughs with him. 'As a matter of fact,' Jonathan continues, 'I'm not feeling very well. Would you mind going down to the kitchen and getting me a Scotch-and-water? There's a bottle in the cupboard above the freezer.'

'I was dreaming too – that you were sick. Don't be sick, please.' She drops to her knees beside the bed. 'Do you want me to call the doctor, Jonathan?'

While in the kitchen Carolyn convinces herself that there

is something wrong with him, that it was unlucky for her to dream he was sick while he was having his own nightmares, that the colour of his skin wasn't right, that when she gets back to the room he will be dead. But when she returns Jonathan is sitting quietly in bed, wearing his favourite shaggy pullover and smoking another cigarette.

'Feeling better?'

'All better.' He takes the drink, sips at it. 'Now I have something to tell you, Carolyn. Go to the window. Look outside. I don't want you to look at me.'

'Please –'

'Do as I say.'

She turns and walks to the window. The fire has gone out. Nothing outside but the pale snow, the faintly seen shadows of leafless maples, the oblong light cast out from their own room.

'I don't want you any more,' Jonathan says. 'I'm sick of this thing with you and Michael. The secret phone calls, the visits to his apartment when I'm away. The thing is, Carolyn, I used not to mind but now I do. So that's it. It's over. I don't want you any more. Don't worry about your suitcases in the snow. You can stay here for a while, so long as you don't bother me.'

'So long as I don't bother you?'

'That's right. Now you can turn around.'

'Thank you.'

'Perhaps you'd be more comfortable in the living room.'

Carolyn folds her arms over her chest, forces herself to inch across the space between them. Halfway she stops. 'No, thanks, Jonathan, I'll stay here. This is my bedroom, too.' She starts walking again, until finally she is sitting beside him.

Jonathan is holding his glass of Scotch. An hour ago he was drunk, stumbling up the stairs. A few minutes ago he had appeared to be dying. Now, looking at him, Carolyn sees a man totally in possession of himself. The way, in fact, he had seemed when she met him: huge, detached, ever more sober the more he drank; a man who needed nothing but the stone house he'd surrounded himself with, and the few friends and acolytes who moved in his orbit.

'I have a conference next week,' Jonathan says. 'While I'm

gone you can find yourself an apartment and pack your things. If you're worried about money I can leave you a cheque.' His voice is still steady, his hand still wrapped calmly around his glass. But Carolyn, listening for it, can sense the change in tone.

'You said you were drinking too much. Maybe you are. Maybe it's time you did something about it. Think about yourself, Jonathan. Think about what you're doing to us.' Then she lifts her hand and forces herself to lay her fingers against his chest. Begins stroking him very slowly, very carefully, the way you stroke a puppy or a kitten so that they know you aren't ever going to desert them.

LIVING ON WATER

THEY ARE IN A RESTAURANT, Maurice and Judith. The restaurant is called 'Luciano' and is good enough to have been
mentioned, with a knife and a fork, in the red Michelin guide
to Italy.

'Would you like a local wine?' the waiter enquires.

'Please,' Judith says, as though only an idiot would order
anything else. Judith is a poet who has published books and
given readings to university students. Her speciality is love
poems, sharp jabbing unrhymed sequences about men who do
nasty things to women. Over the two years of their relationship Maurice has learned to know her poetry the way one
learns the street names of a new city. For a while she even
wrote poems about him and the sharp jabbing things he did to
her. Maurice was embarrassed, then he learned to like the idea
of himself as a dangerous sex criminal on the loose. After her
book of poems about Maurice, Judith wrote another book, still
love poems, but this time the men were more diffuse. At first
Maurice thought he must have grown, in her imagination, to
the universal man; next he thought she was using this vague-
ness as a screen to write about her previous lovers; finally he
realized she was starting to write about the lovers she would
have after he was gone. Judith denied this. She was also a pho-
tographer and one of their most violent fights occurred when
Maurice found a sequence of photographs showing him naked
and asleep. In these photographs he did not look like a Chairman of the History Department at an important Toronto Sec-
ondary School. He looked like an old wino. He was unshaven,
his mouth was slack and almost drooling, his modest pot belly
sagged to one side and lay beneath his ribs like an unnecessary
pillow. There was an exhibition of these photographs and
Maurice was glad his parents were not alive to hear about it.
One of the pictures was even published in the paper; it was
cropped so that his genitals were hidden, but his thin white-
fringed face lolled at a strange angle as though he had been
decapitated by old age and senility.

The bottle arrives. The waiter sniffs the cork and pours himself a glass which he tests. Maurice remembers an article saying wine from this particular region of Italy has its colour reinforced by dried bull's blood and skim milk powder. During the first course he notices that at every one of the surrounding tables is a couple composed of an elderly man and a young woman. All of the elderly men speak Italian very well, like himself, but their accents betray them as foreigners. All the younger women have the air of being faithful and adoring. During their main course a man comes in alone, and sits at the only empty table in the restaurant. Aggressively he places his own red Michelin on the linen cloth. And despite the fact that he immediately orders two pasta dishes, both specialities of the region, he takes only mineral water, without bubbles.

Following the wine Maurice and Judith drink two glasses of Nocino, a heavy black liqueur made by placing green walnuts in containers of alcohol which are left to ferment in the sun for forty days. Coming out of the restaurant, not exactly drunk, but veiled, he stumbles through the narrow streets with Judith on his arm, almost forgotten. Twice they stop to admire churches already inspected by day, and both times Maurice is aware of his Nocino-thickened blood labouring through his veins. Instead of looking at the churches Maurice listens to his lungs wheezing like a waterlogged accordion, and imagines the stately procession of other elderly gentlemen, with their canes in one hand, their temporary wives in the other, slowly marching back to their respective hotel rooms, where like beautifully embalmed corpses they are laid out on their respective beds, their respective cheeks powdered, their respective lips kissed, their respective eyes closed.

The sound of a fighter plane, a hard tearing noise that ripped apart the sky, woke him up. He had been dreaming of a small spring-fed lake where he had once owned a cottage. In the dream he had driven to the cottage in an unfamiliar car, then stepped down from the car and walked to the beach. The beach was white sand and rock: clearly marked on the rock was the line where the water used to be. Now it had receded several feet, turning the lake into a pond.

'It's still good for swimming,' a voice said. Maurice turned to see an old friend from his cottaging years. Then the new owner, the man who had bought the cottage from Maurice, appeared. He had grey hair, a pocked weather-beaten face that had been friendly, almost unctuous when the sale was being arranged but now was bitter and sour, clearly displeased that Maurice had reappeared. But he nodded to Maurice and then, finally, extended his hand. He was wearing a checked shirt and the kind of gabardine pants favoured by the nearby general store that also sold frozen vegetables and live bait.

'You're back,' he said.

Maurice couldn't remember his name. 'Just visiting.'

'The lake went down.'

'Swimming is still good.'

Other neighbours drifted up to join them. Gradually Maurice felt himself loosening up, the old ties of friendship and love forming again as though he were a stray sheep being re-absorbed into the flock.

It was a bright afternoon, the sun so strong in the blue sky that it shone right through the shallow water to illuminate the entire bottom of the lake. This was white and sandy, as perfectly clean as the most sanitary aquarium, absolutely devoid of plants and fish.

'Beautiful day,' one of the neighbours said. He offered Maurice a cigarette and Maurice accepted, thinking that this was rural life, smoking the product of the land instead of inhaling the soot of cities and the exhausts of a hundred thousand cars. They were all standing together, their arms around one another's shoulders, and Maurice was even thinking of explaining to them that such a brilliant day would be excellent for the fermenting of Nocino – if only they lived in Italy – when the fighter planes began streaking overhead, barely visible black insects exploding across the sky.

He lay in the perfect darkness of the hotel room, fragments of the dream slowly floating to the surface. He was absolutely sober. Beside him Judith was sleeping. Maurice climbed carefully out of bed and walked to the bathroom for a drink. He felt elated. Then he lay down again and stared contentedly up into the blackness. The dream had brought a thin layer of sweat to his skin. As it dried he felt agreeably cool, the kind of coolness that follows a summer swim, the temperature of sanity and clear-mindedness. That such a strong reaction could follow a dream was no surprise to Maurice. Two or three times in his life he had experienced dreams equally vivid, equally forceful. Those dreams he had always remembered in great detail, the way some of his friends used to talk about their experiences with drugs or psychiatrists or, in one case, but this was an exception, a friend claimed his own life had reached its watershed the night he spent with a prostitute in Buffalo – 'She really knew what to do,' the friend had said.

As he settled into this mood of total serenity, Maurice let his mind centre on the dream again, the cottage and the friends. It was coming to him, very slowly, that the cottage he had dreamed was not the one he'd owned with Eleanor but an entirely separate one – one unknown to him in his ordinary life, and that even the friends to whose touch he'd so gladly warmed were complete strangers to his waking hours.

At fifty-three Maurice Rossiter was a thin-faced man with full lips, too-sharp blue eyes, square even teeth, a fringe of white beard. His moustache, also white, curved around his upper lip in an abbreviated handlebar. When he smiled the combined effect was that of one of those wiry white-blue monkeys whose faces are always telling us something we can't understand.

His parents came from a village south of London, and preceding his parents had been, of course, grandparents, and before them, an ever-widening stream of forebears going back, on his father's side, to certain green and misty marshes in Wales. During his moments of ancestor worship Maurice Rossiter pictured them painted blue and dancing out their rituals in front of a roaring fire. At various critical moments in his life Maurice had wished he too could have a bellyful of fermented honey, skin crackling with dye, genitals hanging free, and be lost in the thunder of feet stamping on soft trampled grass.

His mother, Lillian Rossiter, had been born Lillian Silver – an English Catholic by upbringing, but according to family legend the Silvers had been Jewish artisans on the north coast of

Spain before fleeing the Inquisition. So while his Welsh ancestors did their merry dance, Maurice supposed, his Hebrew
genes were being carried by his other ancestors in the desert,
sadly wandering about and awaiting instructions from their
God. Such seasons, too, Maurice had known. And sometimes
it seemed to him that his life was little more than a pendulum
doomed to swing forever between these two extremes.

His parents' view of themselves was less exciting. Lillian,
for example, considered herself a woman of culture. In England she had read socialists' novels and the works of George
Bernard Shaw. Then she and George – Rossiter, not Shaw –
emigrated to Canada. It was the year of the Great Crash and, as
George liked to remind his son after a few drinks, Maurice was
conceived during the steerage-class journey to Montreal.

'Oh, George,' Lillian would cough out, 'What are you telling the poor child.' She was a director of amateur theatricals
and Maurice interpreted her protest as an aesthetic one: she
didn't want the children imagining their parents committing
'the sacred act' in a cabin crowded with other passengers.

'Those were the days' was always George's reply. 'Tempus
fugit.' The thought of the parents huffing and puffing in the
dark, even a populated dark, always raised a laugh from the
children, but Maurice had his eye on a different part of the picture. He was watching the steady rivers of sperm struggling to
find an egg to mate with. He would imagine the sperm, cute
and tiny little tadpoles, racing to accomplish the embryonic
embrace. Some might be cheaters, trying to succeed by block-
ing the others; some would rely on sprinting to victory,
thrashing away at the head of the pack; finally there would be
the marathon sperms, the wise distance-runners pacing themselves for the long haul. Meanwhile, serenely watching the
Celtic dance of the sperm, the egg – a Hebrew Cleopatra barge
of life – would be floating down the fallopian Nile.

During the depression the Rossiters lived in Edmonton, which
had more sun than money. When Maurice finally went to university, a scholarship boy, he reversed his parents' direction
and went East: first to the University of Toronto where he stu-
died history, and then all the way back to England where he

did his graduate work and visited the places his parents had talked about.

On his return to Canada he began teaching high school, a serious young man with a slightly Bohemian beard and an acquired English accent to match. He might have been one of those high school bachelors who grow successively thicker crops of dandruff each year, but he was rescued from this fate by Eleanor Hanson, a striking young woman who conceived an inconceivable passion for the bearded young man with a library full of first editions of the British poets.

At this time in his life, his late twenties and early thirties, Maurice supposed himself to be happy. His parents were still alive – there was a brief but obligatory migration west each summer – and his wife showered him with the kinds of attentions he had never expected.

A decade passed in this fashion. There were no children. And then Eleanor Hanson Rossiter turned to someone else, someone close, a computer engineer who was their neighbour at the cottage they rented every August during the ten years of their marriage.

In a certain indirect way, Maurice had seen it coming. That is, while the exquisite August evenings whittled down towards September, Maurice had noticed Eleanor growing ever more friendly with the computer engineer while the engineer's wife grew ever more sullen.

Over the next few months Maurice's hair turned from black to white. His parents said it looked distinguished but Maurice felt that fate was sending him a message, a message he didn't want to hear, not yet. Instead he concentrated on his hatred of Eleanor. Eleanor's large rubbery breasts squeezed flat by her bathing suit. Those and other of her parts in the hands of her engineer. Eleanor mocking him, using him, discarding him. So he consoled or perhaps revenged himself with what seemed to be an amazing supply of young and willing women. Amazing considering that he had nothing to offer – or at least nothing that he wanted to offer. Then the year Maurice turned forty-five, his parents were killed in an automobile accident.

The news came by telephone, from his sister. When he hung up he found he was crying uncontrollably, and the woman he was with – a colleague from the guidance department who was not even a 'girlfriend' but just a fellow member of the Teachers' Union over at his place to help with a report – began crying with him. It was a total collapse, an instant unstoppable nervous breakdown, and for the next few weeks the only adult he could bear to speak to was this spinsterish colleague he had not even slept with. Finally he realized he had become completely dependent on her. And so he said to this woman – to himself he was already calling her 'the innocent victim' – that he would like to go a month without seeing her, in order to think about their future.

After a couple of weeks Maurice found himself missing her desperately. Sometimes she would telephone him, and though he never telephoned her, he always welcomed her calls and spent long hours exchanging gossips and personal news, all the while tempted to cancel the whole absurd experiment. Until the telephones were once more on their cradles and he was alone in his apartment, the same one he had shared with Eleanor, though missing most of the furniture and the art, looking out on the lights of the city and trying to measure the exact extent of his loneliness and pain.

On one of those nights the telephone rang, but it was Eleanor. After a few introductory remarks about the divorce Eleanor invited him to come to her apartment for a drink. Unthinking, Maurice accepted.

When he pressed the buzzer and identified himself into the intercom he was so nervous he was barely able to squeeze his name out of his constricted throat. And when Eleanor opened the door – more lipstick than he remembered, larger nose, too, but also smaller breasts, he felt so dizzy with sexual excitement that he found himself hanging onto the door-frame to steady himself while she gave him that wise insincere Chiclet smile she had used so frequently during the last years of their marriage.

'You're looking great,' she said, 'but I was expecting you to be more tanned.'

This was a reference to the trip Maurice had made to the Bahamas during Christmas break with a girlfriend.

'It rained,' Maurice said. 'We had to stay inside.'

Eleanor blinked, like a boxer who has been unexpectedly nailed with a sharp jab. Then the smile came back.

'Too bad you never liked to screw,' she said.

Then she laughed, a real laugh, and Maurice laughed with her: this was another of Eleanor's tricks, one she had perfected since the night she had confessed about the engineer. The idea was that they were two old pros, worldly, their bodies and minds had been through the mill, but all in all they were still friends, because when you've seen someone over toast and coffee for ten years ...

'You want a drink? Or are you still living on water?'

'Coffee,' Maurice said. 'If it isn't too late.'

Soon he was sitting in his old armchair, feet up on the hassock where he had rested them a decade ago – when marriage was still new, when the computer engineer was a shadow in the future instead of the past, when he was too innocent to know that a few drinks and a few loose screws could separate his feet from his furniture for years at a time.

'Your health,' Eleanor said. As he turned his eyes up to her face he noticed that he had been sitting with his shoulders hunched forward, his chin down, and that at the same moment he had been lifting up his cup he had been lowering his head, so that he was drinking his coffee the way that his father used to eat his soup – lowering his head towards spoon and bowl with his neck curved like a dog too often beaten.

'How's the new girlfriend? Or do you have one these days?'

'Nothing serious,' Maurice said.

'You were always the bachelor type. I don't know what attracts me to you guys. There must be something wrong with me.'

Then she lit a cigarette, offering one to Maurice.

'I guess you're wondering why I telephoned you.'

'I was wondering,' Maurice said, though he hadn't been. Instead he'd been noticing that the sexual excitement he had felt entering the apartment had by now almost completely translated itself into an unwelcome buzzing through the marrow of his bones, a slightly nauseating sensation that made him want to leave. 'I thought you must want to talk about the divorce.'

'That's it,' Eleanor said. Then she stood up and crossed the room until she was in front of Maurice. For a moment she hesitated, as if unsure what to do. Then she knelt in front of him, the way she used to years ago, before they were married and she used to joke that the chairs weren't close enough. She put her hands on his knees and then, her face contorting, she leaned forward so that her face was between his thighs. Maurice watched his hand as, unable to stop itself, it tentatively reached out, groped in the air, then settled on the back of Eleanor's head. He could feel her breath heating its way through his flannel pants, onto the private skin of his thighs. Beneath his hand her skull felt strangely large and round, solid as a cannonball. Then his hand moved from her head to her neck, which was surprisingly fragile, and as she snuggled her head in closer, his fingers reached down to caress her spine, and then finally, sliding along the soft surrounding flesh, down her spine to the warm plateau at its base, the place where he used to hold her when they used to make love.

The year he turned fifty-one Maurice decided that in two years' time he would take a leave of absence from teaching. To make the waiting pass more quickly, he registered for a night course in Italian. Dressed in his blue serge suit, carrying a briefcase full of exam papers, he turned up for the first evening full of dread that he would be too old to do anything but make a fool of himself.

But after a few months he had zipped through the beginner's classes and could almost understand Italian movies on television. One night he went to a party given by one of the members of the class, a woman about his age – a widow who planned to spend her husband's estate 'travelling through Europe like Henry James.' She was taking classes, she revealed, not only in Italian, but also in French and Spanish. 'Romance is my speciality,' she confided to Maurice after the second glass of wine in her impressive penthouse apartment. 'When are you going to Europe? It's a pity we can't travel together but what would people say?'

On his way out the door Maurice's legs tangled with a cat streaking down the hall. 'Stop it,' a voice called out. Maurice, who'd had cats as a boy, reached down and picked the creature up. It came willingly into his arms and was purring contentedly on his shoulder when the owner of the voice, a young woman carrying a wicker basket, appeared.

'Just hang on for a moment. Would you mind carrying it? I'm afraid it won't go back in the basket.' So he took it to the elevator and then down the elevator to the parking lot where the young woman, her name was Judith, had her car. He had to get in the car with her, so the cat wouldn't escape, and then she offered to drive him home if only he would carry the cat once more – please – from the car into her apartment. She explained that she had promised to keep the animal for a friend who was going – of all places – to Italy for a vacation, but that the cat, when she came to collect it, wouldn't let her pick it up.

'It's the most ridiculous thing. I mean, she only likes men, it turns out. I don't know why he didn't get his brother to take it instead.'

After Maurice brought the cat into her apartment, the ground floor of one of those downtown houses near the university, she offered him 'a cup of coffee, or something,' which turned out to be a glass of Scotch. And then she said: 'Well you've seduced the cat, what about me?' Maurice, awkward, began to blush, but before the blood could find its way to his cheeks she was kissing him, then she took his hand and pulled it under her sweater.

The parting was at least dramatic. To admit less would have been uncharitable. It happened one night in a hotel in Florence, a small *pensione* whose name Judith had gotten from a friend and carried with her in her book of addresses for, she claimed, at least five years. 'Who would have ever guessed,' she asked, as they came to the building's undeniably charming façade, 'that I would be staying here one day? I mean, you can imagine the state I was in when I wrote down the address.' Maurice, who knew he was supposed to be imagining a scene from the past with which Judith had presented him – a series of neurotic but artistic dashes across North American and Europe filled with hilarious adventures and innocent good fun – imagined instead the following: Judith sprawled naked on the bed of a young man whose poetic equipment hung primarily between his legs; Judith, her teeth stained purple by red wine, laughing in her wild way at some perfectly inconsequential joke; Judith rolling over like a cat to have her breasts stroked once more by the nameless poet before going off to her job in a health-food bakery; Judith taking out her address book so that she and the nameless wonder could exchange telephone numbers; Judith succumbing to a few last-minute caresses and being late for work; Judith finally writing down not only the name of her seducer but the name of the hotel where he claimed to have learned his amorous techniques.

Of course it had been raining; that spring it seemed that the sun came out only once a week, a brief obligatory flash at the end of a grey and inescapable chain of showers, downpours, and drizzles, so that when they had stood at the desk to register Maurice felt uncomfortably wet, uncomfortably aware of the way his thinning white hair was plastered to his scalp. And when they went to their room to deposit their bags and get ready for dinner, Judith insisted on taking a shower to get warm, so that while Maurice was sitting on the bed changing out of the socks that had gotten soaked through the holes in his desert boots, he was treated to the sight of Judith standing under the hot spray, Judith cupping and soaping herself like an irresistible young nymphet, finally Judith emerging naked and dripping, her nipples glowing like neon lights from the heat of the shower and the friction of the towel; and for the first time since their arrival in Italy he wanted her, really wanted her, but even as he stood to embrace her she turned away, an instinctive refusal that she would have denied had he accused her of it, and began dressing quickly, slapping her rosy skin to keep warm.

The comedy of the shower, Maurice was able to realize later when her leaving gave him time for reflection, was the first act of a play which he hadn't yet realized he was attending. It was only later that he deduced Judith must have made her plans several days before. This meant, for example, that while he was changing his socks and promising to buy himself a new pair of shoes, she would have been rehearsing her own part which included the big farewell scene followed by a trip to the airport and the taking of an already-reserved plane to a destination where she knew she was awaited.

At the time, Maurice was left feeling only slightly uneasy, slightly ashamed of himself for desiring Judith when she was enjoying the healthy subcutaneous bounce of her own youthful skin rather than thinking of the dirty old man to whom she had pledged herself so faithfully, so irreversibly, that for him to doubt her love and durability would have been a total betrayal of her young heart.

The second act began at dinner as Judith raised her head coyly to the waiter and asked for a bottle of something special but not too expensive. When the wine was poured, she raised her glass and toasted Maurice: 'Thank you for Italy,' she said. With that Maurice had experienced a little pinprick of anticipation, just enough to draw blood, just enough to wake him up and make him realize that something was happening. Between comments on the food, Judith reminisced about the various places they had seen. It was a thin portion of the script – like her poetry, Maurice thought later, her plays were dependent on blood and one-liners. Nonetheless the essential was established: Italy was always discussed in the past; plans for their future were referred to only vaguely, like a dream already forgotten. While she chattered, Maurice watched Judith's face. It was a face he had found immensely attractive. Her black hair was in contrast to skin so white it was almost transparent. In certain lights, though not in the light of the restaurant, he could see fine blue veins lacing her temples. Her cheekbones were strong, her nose perfectly narrow and straight, her chin the shape of a heart. The only weakness was her eyes, which were a watery green, also transparent. Looking at her eyes, Maurice wondered if they were somehow the shallow lake of his dream, with sandy infertile depths that indicated good swimming but no future.

The third act was more vigorous. A good strong climax after the dawdling over coffee and dessert. 'I've been thinking of going to England,' Judith said. They were back in the room and Judith had poured herself a glass of the brandy she had bought at the Lester B. Pearson International Airport's duty-free. 'England,' Maurice said. 'I think I'll stay here.' He couldn't believe his own calm voice. Judith was sitting on the bed. He saw a small grin break through the surface and then quickly disappear. In the two years since they had started sleeping together, Maurice had always presumed he was going to pay a terrible price for this ridiculous flirtation with youth.

'We could meet in a month or so,' Judith said.

'Are you leaving tonight?'

'In the morning.'

'Do you need money?' The surface was broken again, this time by a flush of embarrassment. Maurice remembered the final scene with his wife, a much uglier scene in which he had broken down and cried while begging her to stay. At the time he had felt a perverse pride in his ability to feel emotion, his lack of ability to control himself. Now, to his surprise, he felt no sense of bereavement at all. It was a gift of the dream, he thought to himself; the dream had prepared him.

'I have some traveller's cheques,' Judith said. 'And I can stay at a friend's. A woman,' she hastily added.

'I think I'll take a bath,' Maurice said.

'Don't you want to go for a walk? It's our last night here.'

'You go ahead.'

Then he went into the bathroom and shut the door. While he was running the water Maurice looked at himself in the mirror. He could feel his heart beating rapidly, a sense of tension. But it wasn't painful. Then he sat in the steaming tub and continued reading the mystery novel he had started the night before. There were actually a few minutes when he forgot that Judith was leaving. Then he realized that if she hadn't been leaving he wouldn't have shut the door; nor would he have read his book, because as on other nights she would have come in and sat on the toilet while he bathed and discussed the sights they were going to see the next day. This made him feel old and heavy. He tried to remember if he had heard the door close. The night his wife had announced her departure she had gone right away, taken a taxi to the house of her new boyfriend. He had been left alone in the apartment to get drunk and feel sorry for himself. But now, when he had dressed, he opened the bathroom door to find Judith lying calmly naked in the bed. She was reading, too, the sheets and blanket pulled down so that her breasts peeked out like baby seals.

'Make love to me tonight,' she said.

That was the fourth act: sex. It took a long time, Judith was more aroused than usual, and in her arousal she coaxed him along for a repeat performance. But Maurice felt his body was simply going through the routines; even while Judith sighed with pleasure, real or fake, he found himself sinking back into the calm sobriety of his dream, the warm tribal feeling of the friends he had never met. When it was over Judith told him again how much she loved him, how grateful she was for the trip to Italy. The trip, Maurice thought, had lasted only a month. What about the other two years they had shared together, or at least pretended to share? At the time they had seemed to him the highest reality he had ever experienced, an unexpected and passionate flowering after years of som-nolence, a triumph of passion over age; but that was at the time. When he opened his eyes in the morning and saw that she was gone, his first reaction was a sigh of relief. To keep young for her – he remembered she had once said of another man, one his own age, that he must wake up smelling like an overflowing ashtray – he had stopped smoking cigarettes. Now he quickly dressed and, without shaving, went down-stairs and across the street to a café where he bought a package of cigarettes. Then he ordered a beer, followed by numerous cups of strong coffee which he drank while greedily smoking as he read the sports section of an English-language newspa-per.

After he had paid his bill and was waiting for the receipt he caught sight of himself in the mirror: a red-faced man with white hair and a St. Francis fringe of beard who looked like an old-fashioned professor taking early retirement to spend his declining years touring Europe. With Judith, of course, he had been someone else – a potent older man still in the swim of sex and success – but as he counted his change – in front of Judith he had always been embarrassed – he decided to cross the street to the hotel and take a nap before lunch.

The fifth and final act of Judith's tragi-comedy began while Maurice was getting ready not for this nap but a similar one two days later. At the moment he discovered Judith had left him a note. It was in his shoe, and he had already walked on it for a dozen hours. It hit the floor with a slightly sweaty thump. He was still in Florence, still at the same hotel, still luxuriating in his new-found freedom.

Dear Maurice,
I wish I could be with you reading this note, but I guess that's like wanting to be at your own funeral. I love you very much, more than I have ever loved anyone else, and that frightens me. In one month exactly I will come back to Florence, and I will meet you at the restaurant where we had our 'Last Supper'. So if you want me, I'll be there. No questions, no answers, all I can offer you is myself.
Love

And after 'love' she had written, of course, nothing at all, because it was their habit never to sign their love notes, ever since Judith had written her poem 'Names Are Too Anonymous', which had won second prize in a national contest sponsored by the Canadian Broadcasting Corporation.

Hoping to end act five and bring the curtain down, Maurice disposed of the note. Carefully folding it up along its original creases, he held it briefly in the palm of his hand, then tossed it from the bed where he was sitting through the door of the bathroom and into the wastebasket under the sink. There was no applause. He reached for his red Michelin guide to Italy and began flipping through it. Since Judith's departure a strange and unidentifiable tune had been making its way to the surface: now, finally, he could hear it – 'The Isle of Capri'. One of the summers at the cottage, an early and unclouded summer, Eleanor had taught him to tango to 'The Isle of Capri', and so every time the song came on the radio they would leap to their feet and dance through the crowded rooms of their cottage, out onto the screened porch and then, when the black-fly season was over, down the pine-shaded path to the beach where they would strip off their clothes and plunge into the lake, humming the chorus.

Maurice lit a cigarette. It was the first time since his resumption of smoking after Judith's departure that he had smoked a cigarette in the hotel room that they had shared. He imagined Judith lying in bed with her new lover in London, idly flipping on the television set for some light entertainment between rounds. On his desk was the bottle of duty-free Scotch. Maurice stubbed out his first cigarette, lit a second one, took a tentative swallow straight from the bottle. Several times he had cut himself while shaving along the edges of his beard, to say nothing of the ragged patch on the left cheek that resulted from a slip of the scissors while giving the beard a post-shave trim. Also, last night, his glasses had fallen to the floor while he was reading himself to sleep and then he had stepped on them in the dark when he got up to urinate, so that one of the arms was bent. He felt, too, though perhaps this was only paranoia, that his skin had deteriorated very quickly. He remembered something he'd read once about essential hormones that were a by-product of orgasms; somehow their sudden cessation had made the skin of his neck extremely sensitive and he had developed an uncomfortable rash. Ordinarily, or at least formerly, he would have told Judith about it and, as with his many other physical complaints and hallucinations, she would have comforted and cured. A pill, a bottle of lotion. But now she was gone, so it was up to Maurice to go to the *farmacia*. At the crucial moment his Italian failed: while attempting to explain what he wanted he found himself absolutely silenced, waving his hands helplessly and pointing at his neck. Finally the good-natured clerk brought him a bottle which, when Maurice got back to his hotel room and translated the label with the aid of his dictionary, turned out to be very expensive baby shampoo.

He lifted the Scotch to his lips again. In Winnipeg, when he was a boy, drunks would sometimes come to the door asking for money. His mother would always refuse them cash, but if there was food in the house she would make one of her 'health' sandwiches, rye bread with cheese and jam. The prospect of a rye bread, cheese, and jam sandwich was less than appealing. Maurice went to the bathroom and turned on the hot water. When he had cleansed himself with the Italian baby shampoo he packed his suitcases and left the hotel.

Once in his car he began to drive randomly, taking the streets that were easiest to turn onto, until he found a sign for Assisi. When he got there he parked near the centre of town, hauled out his guidebook, and went dutifully to worship at the recommended sights. In front of each painting, each work of sculpture, he first read the guide to find out what he was supposed to be looking at, and then he carefully appraised what was in front of him to make sure that no detail escaped him. He stayed in the hotel that he and Judith – in better days – had preselected together, and to cover his embarrassment at eating alone he read and reread the guide at lunch and at supper. At the end of four days he had seen absolutely everything – twice – and had run out of the courage required for restaurant eating. Still consulting his book he drove to Siena. There he spent a week. But instead of looking at paintings he found himself spending his time walking aimlessly through the town. To make the evening pass more quickly he bought a bottle of wine every afternoon. This he would drink in his hotel room while writing home – at first postcards to his friends in Toronto, then two long, sentimental letters to Eleanor which ran to a dozen pages each. None of these were mailed, because when he reread them they seemed to be written in the voice of a stranger. As he ripped the letters up and put them into the wastebasket he considered returning to Toronto – a thought which crossed his mind every day, but then remembered, as he also did every day, that he had rented out his apartment for the year of his leave. The next morning he got into his car and drove on the superhighway towards Milan. His intention was to turn in the rented car at the airport and fly to Paris, where he had a cousin who worked at the British embassy. While having lunch at a roadside café he ran into an American couple who heard his halting Italian and insisted he sit with them. They were from California. He told them he was an insurance salesman from Montana. After a very alcoholic lunch the wife forced upon him her copy of her favourite book, *Even Cowgirls Get the Blues*, and Maurice, too drunk to keep driving, spent

the afternoon reading in his car. Then he got off the superhighway and found himself driving on a twisting road that led high
into the Tuscan hills. It began to rain; the rain was joined by a
thick mist. Exhausted by the hairpin turns, he stopped and
rented a room. He stayed there and read for three days. When
he started driving again he found himself in high pine-covered
mountains. There was still snow between the trees and he
became so homesick for Canada that he stopped at the next
small town and rented a room again. This hotel was owned by
a man with a brother in Vancouver, so when he saw Maurice's
passport he insisted Maurice eat with the family. After a long
drunken dinner Maurice slept as though in a coma. The next
day the owner filled him with coffee, then dragged him off to
see the hunting preserve which it was his job to guard between
seasons.

As they walked through the pine forests Maurice, breathing
the clean mountain air, felt Judith slipping away. The owner
had a rifle slung over his shoulder. When a rabbit bolted from
under a hedge the rifle was suddenly up in the air; there was a
sharp explosion and the rabbit lay bleeding its life out in the
white snow. Back at the hotel Maurice split wood for the fire
while dinner was being made. The Italian pine was fibrous and
stuck to the blade of the axe, but even when it began to rain
again Maurice kept working, feeling deep in his dream now,
more contented than he had since his summers at the cottage.

It was a week before he left. At the car the owner of the
hotel stepped forward to embrace him; for the first time in his
life Maurice put his arms around another man. It was a strange
sensation: a muscled bellied body pressing into his own. From
that point on he drove without destination, making his way
slowly to the coast and then ambling around until finally, as if
by coincidence, he arrived in Florence on the appointed day.

He could never have found the hotel on purpose, but
trapped in a maze of one-way streets he arrived. When he
checked in there was a two-week-old postcard from Judith,
saying nothing about their meeting but mentioning only that
she was in London and, again, thanking him for their time in
Italy.

Nor was Judith at the restaurant that evening. But Maurice

sat down, ordered a bottle of wine and began reading a British newspaper. By now he had a plan. After another day in Florence he would drive to Rome, spend a week walking the city, then fly back to Canada. He would arrive at the beginning of April. A perfect time to rent a cottage so that he could spend the rest of his leave living on water until he could start teaching again.

As he was thinking about this plan, a plan that had been formulating itself since the week in the mountains, he saw a family coming into the restaurant. It was unclear what drew his eye, something about the children – a girl of about ten who was very pretty and very restrained, and a brother who was somewhat younger but walked in a very strange and jerky fashion, as if he were drunk and about to fall over.

When he sat down the boy spread his arms wide, then clapped his hands to his chest while he leaned his head forward until it fell with a loud clink onto the empty soup-plate. Following the sound of bone against porcelain there was a low animal moan. The boy's mother, a plump, worried-looking woman, put her arm around him and began to murmur soothingly. The father was larger: a broad-shouldered man with a generous stomach and large ears, red with embarrassment, that protruded like rigid wings from his head. While mother soothed son, father showed daughter the menu. Her hands were folded together and her eyes closed; as her father talked she leaned over to listen, a polite little princess, her eyes finally opening to look dutifully at the difference choices.

He was sitting close to the family's table; without looking directly at them he could see the waiter approach, take their order. The father spoke quickly, as if to tell the waiter that if the food came right away there would be no further incidents. Speed, at all costs, *speed*. In fact, Maurice told himself as he started his second glass of wine, speed – so far as the boy was concerned – was exactly what was impossible because his lines of communication had been destroyed.

As if to confirm this the boy began gesticulating wildly just as the waiter turned away. Then he began to talk – or at least it might have been talking, but really what was being emitted was a new series of moans, varying wildly in tone and pitch. This time both the father and the mother leaned over him and spoke urgently. Then the mother took one of the boy's hands and held it firmly between her own.

Maurice's first course finally arrived. It was a pasta dish, the speciality of the restaurant according to the waiter, but it was covered in cheese burned black at the edges. As Maurice was taking his first bite the boy knocked his soup-plate from the table, and when his father bent to retrieve it the boy leapt to his feet and sprang towards Maurice.

His eyes were dark and burning, his face was scarlet, his mouth was twisted into a black grimace. As the boy's father tried to pull him back the boy opened his mouth wide and Maurice saw, as the boy began to scream, that he had no teeth.

Unable to stop himself, Maurice stood up to leave. The boy squirmed free and flew into Maurice's chest, wrapping his arms and legs around him and screaming into his coat.

Maurice was still shaking as he walked back to the hotel. Twice he almost stepped directly in front of cars, and both times, pulling himself back, he stumbled. He could feel the eyes of passers-by swinging to him, the way his own eyes had instinctively swung back to the boy in the restaurant. When he got to his room Judith was lying on the bed, reading. He saw his suitcase open by the dresser; the crumpled clothes had been taken out, neatly folded and replaced. Judith stood up and stepped towards him.

'I came to the restaurant but there was such a scene I thought it would be better to meet you here. Forgive me?'

She put her arms around him, gently, but as he closed his eyes his first reaction was to feel again as he had in the restaurant, a stunned inner silence as the boy clung to him, then the flurry of hands tearing at him and the boy as he had fallen to the floor, the boy still screaming until finally the father had the boy in his arms and was rushing him out the door. He remembered looking around the restaurant as he sat down again, finished his glass of wine, and asked for a cup of coffee. He hadn't seen Judith then, she must have come earlier, but he had seen the way the girl, serene, had turned to her mother and asked if they were going to wait for their meal or leave right away.

Now it was Judith who was guiding him to the bed, where she made him lie down and took off his shoes. Eventually he put an arm around her and she rolled closer to him.

'I missed you.' Her warm hand had searched its way inside his shirt, was caressing his chest as he shivered. Her eyes were closed and her face was calm and dutiful. Maurice looked up at the ceiling and then towards the door. He imagined Judith watching herself soothing him, watching herself as she extended her caresses, watching as she began to cover his neck with soft kisses, watching as her kisses moved from his neck to his chest to his belly.

'I had to learn something about myself,' Judith whispered, or at least that was what he thought he heard as she undressed him. He began to shiver again so she pulled the covers over them and lay right on top of him, hugging him to make him warm. Maurice closed his eyes. The next thing he knew it was the middle of the night and he was making love to Judith.

'I knew we would never get divorced,' Eleanor had said. That, too, in the middle of the night, after a reunion salted with its own passion. She had announced this while smoking a cigarette; Maurice sipping at a glass of water and finding himself unable to stay in bed, instead paced about the apartment thinking how odd their old furniture looked in this new place.

The apartment faced the expressway, so he was able to open the curtains and watch the streams of headlights travelling in and out of the heart of the city.

'I know it's crazy, we haven't even seen each other for two years, but I still love you. I admit I made a mistake. I didn't mean to hurt you. It's just that I had to find something out about myself. What I found was that I was an old-fashioned girl, just like the girl I always was. Let's get back together, have children, live happily ever after.'

Then she had gone to the kitchen to make coffee. While the water was boiling and Eleanor was talking about the house they would move into, the cottage they would find to rent in the summer again, the names they would give to their children, Maurice had tried to imagine himself saying no. The word wouldn't come out of his mouth so instead he simply got dressed and walked out of the apartment. On the way down in the elevator he had broken into laughter, then laughed at himself laughing.

Even driving across the city he couldn't believe he had made such an escape. He was sure the gods would strike him dead in a traffic accident, but when he got back to his apartment he was still alive. The first time the telephone rang he didn't answer it. The second time he picked it up. Eleanor told him that he was a bastard and that she never wanted to see him again. Before he could protest she hung up.

'I want us to be together forever,' Judith said. 'I want to be with you. Will you let me?'

'Yes,' Maurice said. He fell sleep thinking about the lake of his dreams, the neighbours he had never met.

RACIAL MEMORIES

THE BEARD of my grandfather was trimmed in the shape of a spade. Black at first, later laced liberally with white, it was also a flag announcing to the world that here walked an orthodox Jew. Further uses: an instrument of torture and delight when pressed against the soft ticklish skin of young children, a never empty display window for the entire range of my grandmother's uncompromising cuisine. To complement his beard my grandfather – indoors and out – kept his head covered. His indoor hats were *yarmulkahs* that floated on his bare and powerful skull; the hats he wore outside had brims which kept the sun away and left the skin of his face a soft and strangely attractive waxy white. White, too, were his square-fingered hands, the moons of his nails, his squarish, slightly gapped teeth, the carefully washed and ironed shirts my grandmother supplied for his thrice-daily trips to the synagogue. A typical sartorial moment: on the day before his seventieth birthday I found him outside on a kitchen stepladder wearing slippers but no socks, his suit-pants held up by suspenders, his white shirt complete with what we used to call bicep-pinchers, his outdoors hat – decked out in style, in other words, even though he was sweating rivers while he trimmed the branches of his backyard cherry trees.

Soon after I met him, I began remembering my grandfather. Especially when I lay in bed, the darkness of my room broken by the the thin yellow strip of light that filtered through the bottom of my door. Staring at the unwavering strip I would try to make it dance. 'Be lightning,' I would say. 'Strike me dead; prove that God exists.' And then I would cower under my sheets, waiting for the inevitable. That was when I would remember my grandfather. Standing alone with him in the big synagogue in Winnipeg, the same synagogue where he must have sought God's guidance in dealing with Joseph Lucky, looking up at the vaulted ceilings, holding his hand as he led me up the carpeted aisle to the curtained ark where the Torah was kept.

And then he showed me the words themselves. God's words. Indecipherable squiggles inked onto dried skin not so different from the tough dry calluses on my grandfather's palms.

Also full of words was the high bulging forehead of my grandfather. Everything he said to me in English, which he spoke in a gently accented cadence I had difficulty understanding, he would repeat in Hebrew, which I couldn't understand at all. Cave-man talk, I would think, listening to the guttural sounds. He showed me, too, the separate section where the women sat. I was amazed at this concept of the women being put to one side, just as later I was to be amazed to discover that when women had 'the curse' they spent their nights in their own dark beds, left alone to bleed out their shame.

My great-great-uncle Joseph, the one after whom I was named, served in the cavalry of the Russian czar. This is true, and I still have a photograph of a bearded man in full uniform sitting on a horse in the midst of a snowy woods. After two years, during which he was promoted once and demoted twice, my ancestor deserted and made his way across Europe to a boat which took him to Montreal. From there he caught a train on which, the story goes, he endeared himself to a wealthy Jewish woman who owned a large ranch in Alberta. We could pause briefly to imagine the scene: minor-key *War and Peace* played out against a background of railway red velvet, cigar smoke, and a trunk filled with souvenirs. Unfortunately the lady was married, so my uncle ended up not in the castle but out on the range, riding wild mustangs. (Also, it has been claimed, singing Yiddish folk songs to the animals as they bedded down beneath their starry blankets.)

And then my uncle Joseph struck it rich. Sitting around the campfire one night, he reinvented the still with the help of an old horse trough and a few lengths of hose. All this is according to my father; he was the historian-in-exile, but that is another story. The rest of the family claims he was only trying to make barley soup. Maybe that explains how my uncle became known as Joseph Lucky.

Having made his fortune and his name, Joseph Lucky began sending money to the relatives. We've all heard about those

Russian Jews: semi-Cro-Magnon types covered in beards, furs, dense body hair, living without flush toilets or electricity in a post-feudal swamp of bone-breaking peasants, child-snatching witches, and wicked landowners. Having helped his blood relations through the evolutionary gate of the twentieth century – to say nothing of destroying the racial purity of his adopted homeland – my uncle asked only one thing in return: that the newcomers settle in Winnipeg, well away from his field of operations. When they got established, he came to pay a visit. By this time the wealthy Jewess had died and, because of a jealous husband, my uncle Joseph had moved on from his life on the range to 'business interests'. Another photograph I possess: Joseph Lucky standing on the Winnipeg train platform, winter again, wearing matching fur coat and hat and framed by two enormous suitcases which my father told me were made from 'soft brown leather you could eat'.

This was before the First World War, before my father was born. Also before the war was my uncle's demise. What had happened was that for causes unknown he was put in jail. After a few months he wrote to his nephew, my grandfather. The letter was written in Yiddish, using Hebrew characters – the same formula which my grandmother employed to torture my mother decades later. I've seen the letter; my grandfather showed it to me when I was a child. He opened the envelope and out blew the smell which made a permanent cloud in my grandparents' house, a permanent storm-cloud to be exact, always threatening to rain down the pale greenish soup that my grandmother claimed was all her frail stomach could support.

My grandfather was a strong man. Once, when a neighbour's shed was burning down, he carried out two smoke-damaged pigs. The image of my grandfather, wearing his inevitable satin waistcoat and box *yarmulkah*, walking down the street with a sow over each shoulder has never seemed improbable to me. I can imagine him, too, poring over the letter from his benefactor. Caught between his duty to help a relative, his distaste for my uncle's way of life and his own poverty. According to my father, my grandfather never answered the letter. Instead, after waiting two weeks he gathered what cash he could and took a train for Edmonton. When he arrived he discovered that Joseph Lucky had died of food poisoning, and his body had been claimed by someone whose name had not been recorded. My grandfather always feared that his delay had killed Joseph Lucky. That is why my father felt obliged to give me his name. Also because, he always insisted, Joseph Lucky had likely died not of food poisoning at all, but had been bribed away from the jail (body claimed by an 'unrecorded stranger'! – who could believe that?) by a rich client and spent the rest of his days happily riding some faraway range.

'If you could credit a Jewish cowboy ...,' my mother would protest and shake her head. But that was where Joseph Lucky was lucky, I didn't have to be told. Somehow he had escaped being Jewish, wiggled out from under his fate and galloped off into that carefree other world where you are not under a life sentence or, to be more exact, perhaps you are under a life sentence of mortality (even an assimilated Jew finds it hard to believe in Heaven) but you have been promoted to a different part of the sentence: instead of being the object, you are the subject.

'Did you hear the one about the rabbi's wife?'

'No,' I say. We are lying in the centre of the school football field, five of us in a circle, face to face with our bodies extended like the spokes of a wagon-wheel. It is late September, a cool but spectacular twilight. At the word 'rabbi' my stomach has suddenly tensed up and my hipbones start to press against the hard ground.

'This sausage salesman comes to the door ... Are you sure you haven't heard it?' The five of us are the offensive backfield of our high-school football team: the wheel of which I am the only Jewish spoke.

'I'm sure,' I say. I look up over at the boy who is talking. The fullback. A power runner known as Willy 'Wild Bill' Higgins. He's the one we need when it's late afternoon, November, and gusts of cold rain are sweeping down the river valley and turning us into sodden little boys who want to go home. That's when Wild Bill – it's me who gave him the name – drives forward with his cleats spitting out gobs of mud, knees pumping up into the face of anyone crazy enough to tackle him.

'All right,' he says, 'forget it. Don't get your cock in a knot.'

All evening, over my homework, I'm left wondering. Something to do with circumcision no doubt. Animal sex? Two weeks ago a girl I asked to a dance told me her father wouldn't let her go out with a Jew. I'm at my sixth school in ten years but I still can't get used to breaking the ice. Can't get used to the fact that it never breaks.

At eleven o'clock the phone rings. It's another spoke of the wheel – a small spoke, like me. 'Don't let dickface get you down,' he says. The first thing I think is how glad I am that this is happening over the telephone, so my friend can't see my eyes swelling up with unwanted tears.

Idiot, I say to myself. *Thin-skinned Jew.* 'Doesn't matter,' I say aloud. 'Except that maybe I missed a good joke.'

Peter Riley laughs. He's a skinny Irish kid whose father has lung cancer. Sometimes, after school, I go home with him and we sit in the living room with his father, feeding him tea and watching him die. 'She says she only eats kosher,' Peter Riley says.

I start a fake laugh, then stop.

'Not funny?'

'Not funny to me.'

'Join the club,' Peter Riley says.

'What club?'

'You name it.'

'The Wild Bill Fan Club,' I say, a little chunk of the past – another school, another group of boys – jumping unbidden out of my mouth.

Leonard lived above the garage attached to the house my grandfather bought after he moved to Toronto to be nearer the brothers, sisters, aunts, uncles, cousins, etc. The spider's web of relatives in Toronto didn't include my own parents: they had already learned their lesson and were hiding out in Ottawa, on their way to greener fields. As a gesture to family solidarity, however, they had sent me to the University of Toronto. There I was not only to carry my parents' proud banner in the world of higher learning, but to act as unofficial delegate and/or sacrifice. Leonard, not a relative but a paying boarder, was also at the university; ten years older than I, he had the exalted status of a graduate student in religious philosophy. 'He doesn't eat kosher,' my grandmother confided to me in the kitchen, 'you can tell by his smell, but he goes to *shul* every morning and he doesn't make noise.'

In a room with my grandparents, Leonard was so well-behaved and courteous that he hardly seemed to exist. Once out of sight, however, he became the main subject of my grandmother's conversation. 'Did you see how he wiped his mouth?' she always began, as though she had spent the whole time doing nothing but watching Leonard compulsively snatch at the napkin. And then Laura, a cousin slightly older than I who had sealed her reputation by going to a drive-in at age fourteen with a married man (self-made, rich from vending-machine concessions), would point out that once again the insides of Leonard's nostrils were flaming red because – she had seen him at it through his window – every night he spent an hour yanking out his nasal hairs in order to combat his other urges.

'Wanna see my place?' Leonard invited, while we were drinking tea after a sabbath lunch.

I followed him out the back door, along a path worn through the grass, and we arrived at the metal stairway leading up the outside of the garage to Leonard's room. Immediately I found myself thinking this arrangement was ideal because it allowed Leonard to come and go as he pleased, even bringing company with him if he wanted. Or could. An unlikely possibility I thought, following the shiny seat of Leonard's grey-and-black checked trousers up the final steps.

The first thing I noticed was the mirror where Leonard was reported to carry on with his nose. It hung above a dresser from which the drawers jutted out, each one overflowing. The cartoon chaos of the room continued. Piled over every available surface were dirty clothes, newspapers and magazines, empty pop bottles, wrapping from candy-store food. Even the desk of the graduate philosopher was a tower of babble – unsteady stacks of library books interspersed with sheaves of folded paper. Ostentatiously draped over the back of the chair was a strangely mottled towel. Stepping closer I saw that the towel was, in fact, heavily stained with blood.

'War wounds,' Leonard said.

At lunch I had already noticed Leonard's soft white fingers, his unmuscled arms blotched with freckles and covered with a sparse layer of white-orange fur.

'They're crazy for it then. Ever notice?'

I shook my head.

'Read Freud. The power of taboo. Close your eyes. Imagine it. You're in the dark with the woman of your dreams. The smell of sweat and blood. Smells so strong you can taste it. Get up from the bed and your dick is dripping with it.'

My eyes weren't closed. I was looking at Leonard. His eyes were boring straight into my face. 'You some kind of a pervert?'

Leonard looked puzzled. Encouraged, I continued with a further inspiration: 'If you didn't pick your nose, it wouldn't bleed.'

Leonard shook his head. 'You're going to study philosophy, kid, you need to have an open mind. I told you the truth.'

'Don't make me laugh. No woman in her right mind would come into this rat's nest for more than five minutes.'

At which point Laura opened the door, came and stood by Leonard's chair, practically sticking her chest in his face while he patted her bum. 'Isn't this great? Look, we're going to drive you downtown and then we'll pick you up later for dinner. Isn't this place unbelievable?'

Laura and Leonard are halfway up the greys, exactly at centre ice. From where I line up on defence I can see the steam billowing from their styrofoam cups of coffee. They grin at me. 'Go get 'em,' Leonard shouts and his voice echoes in the empty arena. This is intra-mural hockey, a house-league game taking place close to midnight. The only other spectators are a few couples who have discovered that the shadowed corners of the varsity rink are good for more than watching hockey.

My legs are tired. There are lines of pain where the blades of the skates, which don't quite fit me, press into the bones of my feet. One of my shoulders has already begun to ache as a result of a collision against the boards. Peter Riley looks back at me. He is our centre. A quick skater with dozens of moves and a hard wrist-shot, he is the only one who really knows how to play. The rest of us make up a supporting cast, trying to feed him the puck and to protect our goalie, a non-skating conscript whose main virtue is that he has the courage to buckle on his armour, slide across the ice in his galoshes and risk his life.

Most games we just give the puck to Peter and he scores with tricky unstoppable shots. Now we're in the finals and they've got the strategy to beat us. Two, sometimes three, players shadow Peter, sandwiching him every time he tries to dart forward. The rest of us are often left in the open but compared to these other bigger, stronger players, we are ineffectual midgets. Somehow, however, our goalie has risen to the occasion. With a couple of minutes to go in the game we are only one goal behind.

The referee looks back at us. I bend over my stick. My rear end is sore from numerous forced landings. Riley winks at me and then nods his head for good measure. I know what this signal – our only signal – is supposed to mean: when the puck is dropped he will gain control – then I am to skate by at full speed so that he can feed it to me and send me in.

As the puck bounces on the ice I'm already driving forward, and by the time I've crossed centre ice the puck – via Riley – has arrived at my stick. I'm alone, the crowd of two is screaming. I'm going as fast as I can but I can hear the ice being chewed up behind me, long powerful strides gaining on my short choppy ones. The hollow ominous sound of steel carving ice, Laura's amazingly loud voice – I lift my stick back preparing to blast the puck before I'm overtaken – and then something has hooked my ankles and I'm sliding belly-down.

No whistle so I'm up again. Peter has somehow recovered the puck from the corner and is waiting for me to get in front of the net. This time I'm going to shoot on contact, no waiting: again my stick goes back. Then I'm swinging it forward, towards the puck, already feeling the sweet perfect impact of the hard rubber on the centre of my blade, already seeing the net billow with the tying goal. Suddenly the curtain comes down. A blast to my forehead so intense that I lose consciousness falling to the ice. Get up, dazed, glove held to my head. Start skating again, vision foggy, towards the puck, until I see that everyone else has stopped, that my glove and hockey stick are covered with red, that the clouding of my vision isn't dizziness but a veil of blood over my eye. Leonard and Laura are rushing towards me.

There are words, too. 'Jew. Eat it, Jew,' I thought I heard someone say. The words are rattling in my head like pebbles in a gourd but I'm too confused to know who put them there. Laura's got a handkerchief out of her purse, it's soaked in perfume, soft white cloth with a pink stitched border. The pebbles are still rattling in my skull and I can't stand them, have to do something about them, twist away from Laura and skate towards the big boy with blood on his hockey stick.

But Peter Riley is already there. When the boy hears me coming, turns towards me, Riley twists – twists and straightens his legs as he sends an uppercut deep into the unpadded belly. Mine enemy collapses to the ice retching. His team prepares to rush ours. By now I have felt my left eyebrow that opens and closes every time I move the muscles in my face.

Before anything can happen there is a sharp blast of the whistle. The referee, who is also the dean of men and who hands out suspensions for fighting – from the university, not just from hockey – is holding the puck and standing bent over the spot where he wants play to begin again.

'Sir,' Riley says, 'one of our players is bleeding.'

'Have his friends take him to the hospital.'

As I'm clumping along the wooden gangway, Laura's scented hanky pressed to my wound, Leonard is calling my dean a 'Jew-baiting bastard, an anti-Semitic son-of-a-bitch who would have spent his afternoons cracking open teeth to get at their gold fillings'.

By three o'clock in the morning, when I am sharing a mickey of rye with Peter Riley, my wound has been reduced to a small throbbing slice covered by a neat white patch. And Riley is telling me that the dean shook his hand as he left the dressing-room.

As I fall asleep, the words are still with me. I am lying in the dark. The first time I heard such words, such words said by other than my own, I was ten years old. I was in a new school that year, but friends had come quickly and life seemed suddenly to have grown wide and easy. Then one day, late in the fall, my friends turned on me. There were three of them. 'Jew,' one of them said. 'Jew,' said the other two. We had been standing in a vacant lot on the way home from school. Talking about nothing. One of them pushed me. A nothing push, not really a punch, something I wasn't sure whether or not to ignore.

'Jews are Christ-killers,' one of them said.

'Christ-killers,' the others repeated. The words unfamiliar to all of us.

Now I can see they didn't know what to do. Something their parents had said would have put them up to this, probably without intending anything specific.

There were more shoves. I shoved back. 'Christ-killer,' they were saying, still trying to convince themselves. 'Run,' one of them said.

'No.'

'Run,' said the biggest one. He slapped me across the face, knocking my glasses to the grass. When I bent to pick them up, he covered them with his foot. I reached anyway. As I pulled them out from his shoe he stamped on my hand.

'Run.'

I held my glasses tightly. The other two boys, the ones I had thought were my friends, had backed away. Without my glasses their faces were foggy and distorted. I put my glasses on. My friends had pebbles in their hands.

'Run.'

I ran, hating myself from the first step. As I did, a shower of rocks fell gently on my back. One boy, the biggest, chased me. I was smaller but faster. I vaulted over the fence – clearing it the way I'd had to in order to become a member of the club they had invented – the Wild Bill Fan Club – then ran to the back door as the one boy still chased after me. As I opened the door, he reached in. To grab? To punch? A reflex action? I slammed the door on his hand.

For a week I walked back and forth from school alone. Stomach broiling. At night I couldn't wait to be in bed, alone, lights out. Then finally the world of fear I'd been containing all day in my belly could expand, spread out, swallow the make-believe theatre of pretend-niceness that surrounded me during the day. In the dark, instead of daring God to show himself as I used to, I listened for the sound of convoy trucks on the road, knocks at the door, policemen's boots on the stairs. And if they weren't going to come? I eventually had to ask myself. Did that mean that in this new world there was safety after all? That my great-great-uncle Joseph Lucky truly had led us out of the wilderness and into the promised land?

One afternoon recess, during the compulsory all-school no-rules soccer game, mine enemy was delivered. Head down, dribbling the ball forward at full speed, running straight at me while being chased by fifty screaming boys. An hour later we were standing on either side of the door of the principal's office. Him with scratched cheeks from the gravel he fell into when I tripped him, plus a swollen lip from the only punch I had managed to land; me with bloody nose and ribs rearranged from the fight-ending bearhug.

I still remember the principal's suit. A blue-grey plaid too long for his short legs, worn cuffs, lapels sporting a maple leaf pin. In his hands, very small, was a thick leather strap. Without comment he reddened our palms. Then we were out in the hall again, the door closed behind us. No handshakes, no words of mutual consolation, no smiles. But by the time the school day had finished, the underground telegraph had turned us into folk heroes, victims and survivors of the principal's best, warmly united members of the Wild Bill Fan Club once more.

I am in Laura's bedroom. Laura is in her dressing gown, then takes it off to try on her dress. Laura encased in sterile white brassiere and panties surrounded by tanned skin. The body is untouched, an uninhabited countryside, a national park waiting for its first visitor; but her face is the city. A long curved jaw stubbornly set. Lips painted what Peter Riley called 'North Toronto Red'. Brown eyes, Jewish eyes, eyes which I knew my friend found sympathetic and embracing, but which to me looked hardened with all the calculations they had made.

I am in Laura's bedroom because I have been delegated the task no one wants. Why me? Instead of, for example, my father? The explanation for this lies in other stories, stories too long and intertwined to tell, stories not about Joseph Lucky and Laura and Leonard, but stories about my parents. Most of all my father who had decided by now to complete his escape and was residing (with my mother, of course – herself a subject not to be broached without lengthy explanations) in Sydney, Australia, where he was attempting to unknot the city's bus schedules.

'This is crazy. I'm supposed to talk you out of marrying my best friend.'

'So talk me out.'

'He's a shit. His father's dead and his mother drinks too much. So does he. His brother is a lawyer and makes deals with politicians. His sister goes to church on Sunday. Five years from now he'll be screwing his secretary. How's that?'

'You can do better.'

'He's a Catholic. Secretly he hates Jews but he hasn't got the guts to say it. He's marrying you in order to destroy you. When you have children he'll drag them down the basement to a priest he has hidden in the furnace and baptize them.'

'At least we'll have a house.'

'Tell me,' I suddenly say. As if I'm thinking about it for the first time, and maybe I am. 'Why *are* you marrying outside? Really why?'

Laura looks at me. For a second it seems that my question has truly surprised her, cracked the shell. Then I realize that she's only waiting for me to back down. 'I love him,' she says. Her voice is so wooden as she pronounces this formula that I can't help believing her.

'But answer my question.'

'Crazy boy.'

She crosses the room to where I am sitting on her bed. Bends over me and kisses the scar above my eyebrow. Then my lips. A slow kiss that leaves me bathed in her taste and scent. 'I couldn't marry a Jew. It would be like incest, if you know what I mean. Did I ever show you this? Grandpa gave it to me.'

Dear Nephew,
You will remember me. I am your wicked uncle, Joseph Lucky. A few years ago I came to visit you and the rest of those whom you call your family. As always, I brought gifts. As always, they were greedily snatched and then scorned. His money is dirty, they would like to say, since they have none. You alone wrote to thank me. I kept your letter, nephew, because I, a childless old man, wanted to dream about what might be possible. I imagined such things, nephew, as bringing you to live with me and making you a partner in my various enterprises. That is the letter I should have written you because you might have been the one to change my fate. Too late now. Now I am in jail, starving because despite everything you might have heard about me I refuse to eat anything but kosher food. To tell the truth, even the smell of pork chops is enough to turn this old stomach. Nephew, I beg you to come and see that I am released, or at least fed. When you arrive I will give you the name of a lawyer who can arrange things.
Love from your fond Uncle –

'What about the other letter? The one my father has?'
'There were lots of letters. Each one written as though the others had somehow failed to arrive. Not all of them were sent to Grandpa either.'
'And when he went to Edmonton?'
'He never went. No one did. They let him die because they were ashamed of him.' Laura puts on her dressing gown and lights a cigarette. 'You think Peter's cousins are on their knees right now? Begging Peter not to marry me?'
'They should be.'

An hour later I am at Leonard's. Stiffening the spine so that I can report the failure of my mission to my grandparents. 'You are the outsider,' Leonard is explaining to me, 'the perennial third man. You think it's because of your shiny metal mind. Forget it. You're outside because you're a Jew. And that's why Laura is marrying your friend. She grew up being outside and now she wants to be sure she'll be outside forever. Except that she won't because ten years from now the whole world will be people like you and Laura, people trying to get away from themselves. And you know what will happen then? Laura will decide she's unhappy. She'll start to drink or have an affair or run away to a kibbutz in Israel. The next time you see her, middle-aged, she'll say that she wasted ten years of her life. She'll ask you why you let her get married.'

'Why did I?'

'Because you want to do the same thing.'

Leonard was dressed in his *shul*-going suit. Black without stripes or flecks. Shiny seat bottom. Pockets padded with *yarmulkahs* and hankies just in case someone needed an extra. Soon we would be going to the bride's house, which was where the wedding would take place – under the supervision of a Unitarian minister who didn't seem to believe anything overly offensive.

'And you? I thought you were the one who was so hot for her.'

After my grandfather's first heart attack Leonard had evolved from paying boarder to man of the house. Now he even had a job – as a history teacher at the Orthodox Synagogue Hebrew Day School. Leonard the responsible citizen was heavier, jowled, and his hair was turning a dull grey at the temples. And then he smiled. With the memory of whatever had transpired between him and Laura, I thought at first, though what could have linked this prematurely middle-aged perpetual bachelor to the ripe and bursting Laura was hard to imagine. 'Never,' Leonard said. 'I promised myself years ago to a young woman of strong character who takes care of her mother in Vancouver.'

'And when did you meet her?'

'The summer I went to study in New York. She was on the Holocaust committee.'

'How romantic.'

Leonard gave me a look I hadn't seen since the day he explained his bloody towel. 'You're a fool. Helen is the perfect woman for me in every way.' He turned to his desk. In his student days it had been heaped with scholarly texts. But since the summer in New York, the philosophical treatises had been pushed aside first to make room for bulky volumes on the Holocaust and then, more recently, for the history primers he needed for his job. From a drawer stuffed with letters he pulled a picture of a squarish-looking woman with a young smile and a surprising splash of freckles across her nose. 'When her mother dies –'

My grandparents are waiting for me in their parlour. Like Leonard, like my grandfather, like Laura's own father waiting resignedly at home, I am dressed in a suit. An almost new suit, in fact, the one I bought a few months ago when I graduated from law school. Eventually I will wear the same suit, the same white shirt, the same gold cuff-links to my grandfather's funeral. The cuff-links were his gift to me on my Bar Mitzvah. On that occasion, a few weeks after my thirteenth birthday, I had needed new thick-heeled shoes to push me over the five-foot mark. One sideburn had started to grow, but not the other, and this unequal hormonal outburst had been accompanied by the very unmasculine swelling of one of my nipples. For some reason this swollen nipple ached when I sang, especially when my voice cracked in public, which it did dozens of times during the painful delivery of my *moftar*. Afterwards my grandfather, his breath thick with rye, had delivered me a bristly kiss and pinched my arm so lovingly that I carried the bruise for a month.

Now they are sitting stiffly and waiting, elderly patients bracing themselves for the bad news. Stubborn but helpless. I beg them to at least come to the reception, for Laura's sake. This is the compromise everyone has been hoping for – avoiding the wedding but joining the celebration.

My grandfather is looking placidly about the room. His most recent attack seems to have taken away his electricity. He is perpetually serene, almost vacant. Even his shining and muscular skull seems to have lost its power; now the skin is greyer, listless. I try to imagine what might be going on inside.

Weather?

My grandmother is twisting her hands. Everything considered, she has big diamonds. 'We'll go,' she announces. 'The mother of those bastard children was born a Jew and so the children can still be rescued, God willing, after the father has left.'

'Assimilated,' Leonard says. He pronounces the word slowly, savouring, then repeats it. First he stares at me – a Leonard who has emerged in the ten years since his own marriage, a Daddy Leonard with a rounded bulldog face, muscular cheeks, blue eyes that have spent so many long nights poring over his Holocaust documents that they have turned the skin surrounding them into dark crater-holes – then he swings his head to Laura for confirmation. She nods. Laura whom I've known forever. Laura who is prettier then ever, but whose face seems more angular because she decided to replace her contact lenses with glasses when she started taking Hebrew lessons again.

I am sitting by the window. It's still open, a souvenir from the golden warmth of the October afternoon. Now it's evening and a cold breeze sucks at the back of my neck, but no one is thinking about the heartbreak of Indian summer.

Laura is kneeling on the floor. Her floor, the floor of the living room of her and Peter Riley's North Toronto house. While she kneels she staples posters to sticks. NAZI JEW KILLER, the posters all read.

'I can't believe how *assimilated* you are,' Leonard says, pleased with himself now that he has found the word for me. 'How *typical*. I won't say you're a coward. When it comes to being punched in the face, you're ready. When they call for volunteers to get baked, you'll probably run to the train. *Bravo*. But ask you to stick your neck out and stand up for yourself – all of a sudden you turn into a lawyer for some Jew-baiting creep.'

'Listen to yourself,' I say. 'You're filled with hate. Do you think Jews are the only people in the world who have ever been killed? Even during the Second World War there were three million Poles who died. Gypsies were sent to concentration camps too. Do you think the Holocaust gave the Jews some sort of moral credit card? Do we get to trade our dead for Palestinians? Is it one for one, or do Chosen People get a special rate of exchange?'

'I have never killed anyone. But I am proud of my people when they defend themselves.'

'Violence poisons,' I say.

'God is violent,' Leonard comes back.

Bang-clack, bang-clack, goes Laura's stapler. Now she's finished her signs, a dozen of them. In a few minutes it will be time to carry them out to the family-size station wagon. While the 'family' – twin four-year-old daughters – sleeps, Peter is to babysit. And while Peter babysits, Laura and Leonard are to drive the signs out to the airport, where Leonard has been tipped off that an East German cabinet minister someone claims was once a concentration-camp guard is to arrive for intergovernmental trade discussions.

Laura and Leonard stand up.

'I'll go with you,' I say.

Leonard's face breaks open. 'I knew you would.' He moves forward, hugs me. All those years living above my grandparents and now he smells like they used to – the same food, the same soap, the same sickly sweet lemon furniture polish. I can't help smiling, thinking about Leonard's youth as I knew it: tortured nasal passages, a white towel soaked with what he claimed was menstrual blood.

We stand around for a moment while Leonard phones home. At the other end, apparently saying little, is his woman of perfect character, the devoted Helen who has borne him four children and seems to make a virtue of obeying Leonard. They live in the main house now – my grandparents left it to them – and the room above the garage is consecrated to books and pamphlets detailing the attempted destruction of the Jews. Lately they've added slides, films, one of those roll-up white screens with little sprinkles on the surface. You know what I mean.

We all drag the posters out the front door to the waiting station-wagon. A few leaves crackle and drift in the cool breeze. Lights are on in all the houses around us. It's the moment when children have gone to bed, tables have been cleared, televisions have been turned on or attaché cases opened. We're on the lawn waiting for Peter to open the back hatch when a neighbour walking his dog stops to talk. The subject of conversation is, of course, the weather, the growing possibility of snow, the desire to spend one last weekend at the cottage. Only while the neighbour is agonizing over his big decision – whether or not to dig trenches so that he can keep the cottage water turned on until Christmas – does he notice the NAZI JEW KILLER signs. He says he is going to dig trenches after all, if the weather is good, you have to think of the future, and besides he has always wanted his children to share his own dream, a white Christmas in the country.

At the airport a small band of the faithful were waiting on the fifth floor of the parking garage. We got out of the car, distributed the signs. According to Leonard's information, the former concentration-camp guard was due on an Air Canada flight from London. The plan was to meet him at the Passenger Arrivals gate.

There were ten of us. Too many, with our NAZI JEW KILLER signs, to fit into a single elevator. Laura went with the first group – Leonard too – so I was left with four strangers to descend in the second shift. One of those strangers became you, but only later. Sharing our elevator were two passengers with their suitcases. At first they paid us no attention – then, reading our signs, they shrank back.

By the time we had left the elevator and were walking towards the Arrivals gate, Leonard's group was surrounded by airport security officials and police. We raised our own signs and began to approach them. But before we could be noticed Leonard had gotten into a shouting match with one of the officials. 'Never lose your temper needlessly,' Leonard had lectured us in the Riley living room. But, as Laura told me later, Leonard had already called his friends at the television station and promised a confrontation. When photographers with television cameras on their shoulders and assistants carrying portable lights began to run towards the struggling group, Leonard turned towards them. Soon, the official forgotten, he had positioned himself in front of one of the cameras to make a speech about a country that denied its own citizens free expression while protecting foreign 'criminals against humanity'. Then there was one of those incidents that is not supposed to happen, a relic from other countries, other eras: just as Leonard was working himself to a climax, a policeman smashed his truncheon into the back of his head, sending him falling face forward onto the floor.

Later that night I could watch myself on the television news as I entered the circle of light, knelt above Leonard and turned him over so I could see on his face, running with blood, a half-smile of triumph. You weren't in the picture. 'Communist,' shouted a voice from off-camera, but no one laughed.

Driving to the liquor store Peter Riley and I are already drunk. Actually, we have been drinking all afternoon. It's the kind of day that deserves drinking, a Toronto December special that is cold but snowless, a gritty colourless day that merges pavement and sky. Peter's shirt is open. The tuft of red hair at the base of his neck has gone to flat silver; silver too is the colour of the red mop that used to peek out the holes and edges of his football helmet. To heighten the effect he's wearing a leather jacket left over from our university days; U of T 66 is blazoned across the back in white. Looking at him, at myself slumped uncomfortably beneath the seat belt, I am reminded of the men Peter Riley and I used to go and watch during the summer in Ottawa, fat and powerful men with big paunches and thick arms who played evening softball at the high school diamond. Strong but graceless, able to swat the ball a mile, but stumbling around the bases in slow motion, the evening athletes had always seemed an awesome joke to us. 'Battles of the dinosaurs', we called their games, delighting in their strength, the kaleidoscope of grunts and sweat and beer-fed curses.

At the liquor-store parking lot we climb out of the car and stand, side by side, looking up at the clouds. We aren't two baseball players, I am thinking, among other things; we are two middle-aged lawyers, partners in a small firm. We are tense, over-tired, mind-fatigued businessmen taking a day off to drink ourselves into oblivion, because it's the only cure we know for the fact that while eating lunch we reminded each other that Leonard had died exactly six weeks before. Not that either of us had ever considered ourselves admirers of Leonard. Still.

'Among other things' includes the sound of the dirt falling onto Leonard's coffin, his family's uncontrolled grief, the talk at the funeral about another martyr to anti-Semitism. You were present, silent, beautiful, though your face was pinched with cold. We started walking towards each other at the same time and before we had even told each other our names, I was asking you for your telephone number. Also at the funeral were the wide circle I see once every few years at such events. Aunts, uncles, cousins at various removes who have come not because they think of Leonard as a martyr or support his politics but because they remember Leonard as the faithful boarder who helped my grandparents through their old age, the daily *shul*-goer who, even when my grandfather was eighty years old, patiently shepherded him back and forth to the synagogue.

Some of the aunts, the uncles, the cousins at various removes are themselves getting old now. Short stocky men and women in their seventies, eighties, even the odd shrunken survivor who was born in the last century. Many of them, not all, were born in Russia and came out of the mythic peasant crucible to Canada where they gradually adorned themselves in suits, jewellery, houses, coats, stock-market investments until finally, at this group funeral portrait, they could be seen literally staggering under the weight of their success.

I find myself looking at Peter Riley's open shirt again. 'For Christ's sake, do up the buttons, you'll get arrested.'

'Undo yours,' Peter Riley says. 'In the name of the Wild Bill Fan Club, I formally dare you to undo your buttons.'

'For Christ's sake,' I say again, this time wondering why on this occasion it is Christ I invoke – Leonard must have been right. An occasion, to be precise, on which Peter Riley and I have already emptied one bottle of Scotch, to say nothing of a few beer chasers, and now find ourselves, at 4:33 p.m., in front of the Yonge Street liquor store in search of a refill. Near the

liquor store is a shop where we can buy newspapers, mix, cigarettes, ice, candies. Even twenty years ago, when we were
under age, we went there to buy Coke for our rum.

'I'll go to the liquor store,' I say, 'you get the other.'

The Scotch hits me while I am alone in the heated display
room. 'The last of the big drinkers I am not' is the sentence
that comes into my mind – spoken by my father. But my
father is dead, possibly along with whatever part of me is his
son. 'Never shit on your own doorstep,' my father also told
me. Translation: you can go to bed with non-Jewish girls, but
don't bring them home. I move down the counter and settle on
a bottle of *The Famous Grouse* Scotch whisky. When I present
my order the cashier makes a point of staring at my unbut-
toned shirt. He has straight oiled hair into which each plastic
tine of the comb has dug its permanent trench. My age or
older. Skin boiled red by repeated infusions of the product he is
selling. Looks a bit like Wild Bill near the end, I finally decide,
but not enough for me to tell him about the fan club. I look
into his eyes. Tough guy. He doesn't flinch. Meanwhile the
store is empty, we could go on staring like this forever. 'I'm
having an identity crisis,' I imagine saying to him, 'I mean I
was born Jewish but I don't feel comfortable carrying NAZI
JEW KILLER signs.'

That night I dream about the hearse, a sleek powerful limou-
sine. You aren't in the dream but the rest of us are. We're sitting behind the driver. Laura in the centre, Peter Riley and I
surrounding. Behind us is the coffin and its presence somehow
makes us even smaller than we are, reminding us that Death
is the queen bee and we humans are just worker bees keeping
Death supplied. It is nighttime, the time of night when time
does not exist.

The hearse is carrying us down University Avenue. Wide,
empty, stately, the street conducts us to the American
embassy, where there is one other car, an ambulance with its
rotating light winking 'He's nuts' into the sky. The attendants, bored, are leaning against the ambulance and talking to
the lone policeman.

Crouched on all fours, his weight on his knees and hands,

Leonard is howling like a dog at the closed door of the American embassy.

When he sees us he interrupts to wink, then turns back to his howling. After listening for a while I realize that his howl is in fact controlled, a merely moderate howl you can howl until dawn or at least until newspaper reporters arrive. I turn to relay this news to Laura and Peter Riley, but as I turn I see they have been transformed into the ambulance attendants, while I have somehow ended up on my knees, baying at the door. When Leonard tries to arrest me I leap at his throat, bringing him to the ground and tearing at him until I wake myself up with my screams.

At the funeral the men took turns throwing shovelfuls of earth on the coffin. Into the silence small stones and earth rattled against the dull wood. I couldn't help listening, I couldn't help watching, I couldn't help crying at the thought of Leonard dead. At some point I discovered you were still standing beside me. Anonymous in your black coat, bare fingers gripping each other in the frozen air, thin black shoes with the toes pressed together. When the service was over we walked towards the parking lot, climbed into my car, drove to a hotel.

Now this hotel is my train. You are my benefactress, wealthy in the dark cream skin that you inhabit, the mysterious odours of your mysterious places, your eyes that becalm everything they see. Under your protection we ride our wild animals into the twilight. Until beneath our starry blankets we find a way to sleep – out on the range, in this room which hovers in an otherwise unmarked universe, which exists for no other purpose than the mutual exploration of mutual desire. *Assimilated,* as Leonard used to say; against our non-existent will we have been assimilated into this compromised situation – two unrecorded strangers claiming each other with words sight touch smell until we raise spark enough to join our foreign bodies.

TROTSKY'S FIRST CONFESSIONS

Love is like a revolution: the monotonous routine of life
is smashed. *Ivan Turgenev*

LATELY YOU HEAR on television that depression is a chemical
condition. You are invited to imagine the victim in question,
whether yourself or some famous historical figure like
Napoleon or Virginia Woolf, as an empty silhouette filled with
clouds of skewed molecules. For such a situation, a micro-
galactic misunderstanding, Sigmund Freud is of no use. Even
his famous couch – let us not speak of those of his successors –
was apparently the scene of quackeries and depravities best
resolved by the courts. What does this say about the erotic collapse of the middle class when faced by the monstrous success
of its capitalist offspring? No one knows. Inflammatory questions are no longer permitted. If you want to ask something do
so politely and in terms of a survey. The answer will be a pill
administered in the comfort of your own home or outpatient
clinic. This pill, through processes kept secret by the drug com-
panies, will realign your nasty neurons or supply you with those
artificial hormones whose random absence need no longer ruin
your life or make you a burden to your family and friends. The
next day the sun rises on an entirely different person. A positive
thinker whose pleasure receptors are now primed to quiver and
trill with the first chirp of a bird or the feeling of toes sliding into
a pair of clean socks. Experts say, for example, that under more
auspicious chemical circumstances Virginia Woolf would have
had the sense to reject a life built on prose without punctuation,
and instead run a very successful restaurant, specializing in
Bloomsburies, the fruit tart from which the melancholic literary circle eventually took its name.

Virginia Woolf, it hardly needs saying, is dead. There is
something honest about being dead, just as being alive is nec-
essarily evasive.

This necessary evasion is what makes beginning so
difficult. Talk about not having a leg to stand on. It's that old

stork dilemma that cracked Lenin's brain and brought us Stalin, my downfall, etc. Or perhaps it is a matter of cultural disjunction. Lately I am a fanatic on the subject because I have been preparing a little paper on Walter Benjamin – an obscure literary critic who killed himself under circumstances with which I can identify, and whose greatest ambition was to present the public with a book composed entirely of quotations. One of his own: 'Quotations in my works are like robbers by the roadside who make an armed attack and relieve an idler of his convictions.'

If this is going to be Benjamin's attitude I might do better returning to Virginia Woolf, who was more a case of dysfunction than disjunction. In an earlier paper, also presented to the faculty association, I attempted to lay out a sort of schema regarding problems that rhymed. It wasn't very well received. We live in an era when – despite all the new big words – ideas are less important than biography.

In fact I have 'real-life' connections with Virginia Woolf. It all began many years ago. Even at the time I felt as though I were in the opening scenes of a movie. There I was, at the wheel of a rented car. Following a series of improbable events, events which do not require recounting, I was touring the south of England with a temporary companion.

As might be expected, it was a literary tour, long on quotations and short on convictions. At a certain point the highlight was a walk along the seawall that figures in a very famous spy novel. While reading the novel it had come to me I would have been useless as a British spy because I look ridiculous in damp tweeds and trenchcoats. Also, my father never taught me how to wear a hat. But strolling along the wall, I imagined myself not in the novel, but as the novelist himself. This was a curious sensation. Suddenly, rather than being a humble and useless intellectual of the male sex, I was promoted to being a rich and famous writer, not only a popular icon but an astute worldly man who had peered under the skirts of the Cold War and found a fortune.

Why, I asked myself, could I not do the same? As salt spray from the English Channel blew across my face, I had an image of myself pacing this wall for hours at a time, trailed by admiring secretaries taking notes while I dictated the complex Faustian story of a man who sold his soul because he didn't believe it existed. Until – perhaps at this point I would have a couple of shots of single malt – the time came, etc.

I was still half believing that I would one day return to the seawall – my Berlin Wall – to figure out the details of this masterpiece, when we came upon what seemed to be an interesting house conspicuously located on a promontory looking out to the sea. It had a sign advertising apartments to let.

We were in search of a life to believe in. Unfortunately, this is a chronic problem with me, and my temporary companions – intelligent, caring persons with both feet on the ground – always become infected by my own uncertainty. Thus begins a cycle that had already become predictable by the time of my first encounter with Virginia Woolf.

I admit, of course, that I should be able to write about my past in a more measured way. Though he had his own problems, T.S. Eliot proclaimed 'maturity of language may naturally be expected to accompany maturity of mind'. But who can wait? As with myself and my temporary companion, once you have bashed the brass lion against the door, it's too late to turn back.

The owner of the interesting house – a self-contented but anxious man – answered and surveyed our Canadian faces for signs of money. I had already learned that to the English our faces appear as barren New Worlds with a geography composed of television sports and credit cards. Therefore I said, 'The rent is no problem.' A few moments later we were in an apartment with a striking view of the sea. It had new wall-to-wall broadloom, a 'kitchenette', and a frigid little bathroom with two electric heaters. The main attraction was the view. 'This is where Virginia Woolf wrote *To The Lighthouse*,' the proprietor announced.

We looked reverently out the window. Battered gently by waves and dappled by the sun was a lighthouse. I turned back to the owner, who nodded complacently. Once again I went to inspect the kitchenette. The stove where she baked her pies had been replaced by a hotplate.

'I love Virginia Woolf,' said my companion. I knew she was

Circumstances

seeing herself sitting at a desk looking out the window at the waves and writing the book she needed to write.

According to the dictionary at hand, 'disjunction' is 'the state of being disjoined'. I once knew someone with this problem, my best friend. She was named Rebecca Thomas but it should have been Rebecca/Thomas.

Walter Benjamin's disjunction sprang from the fact, he believed, that he was a German Jew – two mutually exclusive realities, each closed to him because he was poisoned by the other. At one point he wanted to become, an ambition he knew was preposterous, Germany's 'foremost literary critic'. On the other hand he considered accepting a monthly salary to study Hebrew; although he had no interest in the subject, he was desperate for a stipend.

Apropos of my own equivalents to these problems, I once asked R/T, 'Why is my life always farcical?'

Rebecca smiled sympathetically, but Thomas answered: 'Don't worry, it's not a universal condition.'

By writing a PH.D. thesis on the Bloomsburies, followed by several learned articles published in worthy journals, R/T had become a professor of English literature. My occupation – 'Perfect for a schizophrenic,' R/T pronounced, although in my opinion she was never fully able to refute the chemical hypothesis – was the same.

Perhaps R/T should be presented in her full biographical splendour: the little squibs at the end of her articles always read: 'Rebecca Thomas was born in Regina. She received her BA from the University of Alberta in Edmonton, then was a Woodrow Wilson Scholar at the University of Michigan. Her doctoral thesis, *Linguistic Recipes of the Bloomsbury Group* was published by the University of Chicago Press.' I could add that she had thick black hair, strong squarish hands, a mouth which sometimes twitched like Marcello Mastroianni trying to decide between Sophia Loren and an ice cream cone. Bright warm eyes, an elegant neck. When I first met her she also had a husband, a science fiction fanatic who drifted off into the hyperspace of computer games, then ran away to Vancouver with their babysitter.

R/T and I became friends. At first we just knew that we were people safe to talk to at those faculty parties it was best to attend for political reasons. She made the occasional remark about my 'temporary companions', perhaps just to let me know she wasn't going to be one, and I observed initial attempts to find a successor for her departed husband.

We began to write each other memos. For example:

Professor Trotsky: It has come to my attention that during the past several weeks you have been avoiding self-improvement regarding your attire. Please report for lunch tomorrow at noon so that these and other failings can be discussed.

Or:

My dear Leon: You may be interested to know that I overheard your neo-revisionist tendencies being discussed over lunch at the Student Union. Apparently you have been making a fetish of wearing your ice pick. For your own sake I advise you to renounce personalist masochism in favour of collective silence.

Early on R/T (as I addressed her in memos) and I decided to attend each other's lectures for a few months and give each other 'honest' appraisals of each other's classroom behaviour. This could have been professionalism at its highest, the gloomy conviction that no one else is listening, or just one of the strange ways we found to amuse each other.

More recently, we resumed the habit. It was amazing for me to hear R/T again after such a gap. It seemed to me – or perhaps the years have made me a better listener – that her own linguistic recipes had changed. She was more subtle, more complex, she spoke with assurance and conviction. The edgy unsure young woman who seemed to be describing something she sensed but couldn't quite see, was now offering broadcasts from the very centre of her personal cosmology.

But although Rebecca had evolved, Thomas was unchanged. Last fall, for example, not long after the first essays had been assigned, Rebecca was just manoeuvring into position at the lectern, all wound up for a discourse on the literary-sexual politics of Virginia's relationship with her publisher-husband Leonard, when a student raised her hand. She wanted to know something about the allowable length of footnotes. Rebecca answered her question and then, as often happens when Rebecca gets distracted, Thomas stepped in.

'I was thinking,' he said and looked out the window. The students, who recognized the tone of voice even if they hadn't made the diagnosis, followed Thomas's gaze. It was a day in that monochromatic zone between fall and winter. Dark grey clouds turning black in the late afternoon. Cold rain streaming from an adjoining slate roof and making the smoky grit on the windows streak down the glass.

'Suppose I were to die in Toronto. Not now, of course. Don't be alarmed. But I was thinking that somewhere out there must be the men who will dig my grave. The trees that will be sacrificed for my coffin. The mourners who will watch the coffin slide into the earth ...'

Thomas's voice became so gloomy that the students began to shift about uneasily. Not wanting to criticize directly, I sent a memo:

R/T: Excellent lecture but heavy on the melodrama. I liked the idea of your future mourners scattered across the city, unbeknownst to each other, waiting for the event of your funeral to bring them together. Even your pompous claim that your entry in 'Who's Who' is just the dry run for your obituary. But the little darlings are still frightened of death. So am I. If you have a fatal illness and have been hesitating to inform me, leave a message on my machine.

When I returned to my apartment the little red light on my answering machine was flashing. 'Not fatal but terminal.' Rebecca's voice. Then Thomas: 'Never speak of this again.'

Those who wander in the literary alleyways of the past may recall a recent biography of T.S. Eliot, the poet and critic.

When I was a young would-be poet, Eliot was a more than minor god. I memorized many of his poems, along with various weighty epigrams like the one cited above, and would recite them to myself – or aloud – whenever I was drunk, lonely, or otherwise sensed a void that required decoration. Perhaps that is another reason that my companions have always been temporary. But my worship went much further. Eliot, a banker then editor, was noted for his meticulous appearance and personal habits. To make my hair blond, like his, I once rubbed it with hydrogen peroxide and then spent a sunny afternoon walking the streets of Toronto. In the same vein I would part it in the middle. When I received my first teaching assistantship, I went so far as to purchase a three-piece suit and wire-rimmed frames to encase my thick lenses.

I appeared in front of my class, convinced I was the young Tom incarnate; later that morning I was told I looked like Trotsky without the beard.

To go back to the recent biography: Eliot had his own cosmetic moments, but at the time of my three-piece suit I was ignorant of the best. This happened near the end of his first marriage, a bizarre relationship which made Eliot very unhappy. Although Eliot prided himself on bearing the burden of his apparently insane wife with great fortitude, Virginia Woolf once wrote to a friend that to emphasize his silent struggle, Eliot had taken to wearing green make-up, which enhanced his unhappy ghostly pallor.

Imagine T.S. Eliot and Virginia Woolf, legendary giants whose colossal shadows surely extend beyond any future a professor of literature could possibly imagine. There they are, in some Parnassian moment of the gilded past, drinking tea and exchanging a few *bons mots*. Eliot's hair is perfectly parted in the middle and he speaks with built-in punctuation. Virginia Woolf is sporting a 1920s version of a long tie-dyed skirt, and drawing sketches of her lighthouse on the tablecloth. As she looks up at Eliot the sun emerges, an unexpected shaft of light illuminates his right cheek, she sees greenish powder clinging to his pores.

I am writing this in R/T's apartment, sitting at R/T's desk.

Before the movers arrive, I will have finished: meanwhile, the relevant documents are at hand. R/T's medical reports, various of her articles and research notes. From one of the files drifts a memo never sent:

Trotsky: Enough of your political diatribes! Even the beginning practitioner will agree that cultural impersonation is the disease of our times! I accept your invitation for late afternoon 'drinks' (your use of the plural will be discussed in a separate document) on the impossible condition that you appear as your authentic self!

Why did she reject this memo? What did she send me instead? Did we ever meet, that afternoon? Certainly not our 'authentic selves', whoever they might have been. Like those who so fascinated us, R/T and I were cultural transvestites; the only state to which we could claim real citizenship was that of the disjoined. Like Eliot, obviously, the American with his British banker's suit, his perfectly cut cloak of modernist free verse. 'Henry James with anorexia' as R/T once termed him. Or Walter Benjamin, neither German nor Jew. His most attractive option, as he saw it, was to go to Paris and become an expert on the politics of Baudelaire. Unfortunately the French were only able to read his studies of Baudelaire long after his death, a suicide brought on by the fact that the French he so admired had refused him the papers he required to escape the German police by crossing into Spain. That Benjamin, whose entire work is founded on the limitations of biography, should die for the lack of a visa is another of those events for which reasoned language fails me, though Eliot promised that 'we may expect the language to approach maturity at the moment when men have a critical sense of the past, a confidence in the present, and no conscious doubt of the future'. As R/T once said about the book of a valued colleague, with this kind of load the Great Wall could have been built in a week.

This year spring is slow. *April is the cruellest month.* Overnight the temperature fell below freezing and this morning there was a new thin scattering of snow on the grass. A white dusting over the cars parked along the street. When I stepped out to buy a paper I saw a bird pecking angrily at the frozen ground. It shook its head at me, fluttered to the fence, looked up to the sky to let me know he was suing God for this fracture of the bird-God weather bargain.

I had been dreaming about my own cultural disjunction, or at least about the trip between those two cultures which are supposedly mine. In the dream I was standing on deck with my grandparents, Jewish-Russian refugees who came over by boat just after the turn of the century. Their departure was not a glittering Nabokovian tragedy of lost estates and multilingual nannies. They were happy to have escaped, and they were young, dressed in black and white like their pictures. My grandmother leaned over the rail, her kerchief snapping back in the wind and her long triangular nose poking towards the Atlantic coast. Her eyes so black, the skin around them white and smooth. By the time I met her that skin had turned soft and mottled. She would look at me affectionately but also as though I were absolutely unexpected, some strange kind of pet my parents had mistakenly invented when they were alone in their room at night.

I was snuggled beside my grandmother at the rail, her arm was around me and she smelled like baking bread. She pulled me in close against her. I was in love with her. Her smell, the clean salt wind from the sea, the lush piney shoreline drawing closer.

Then she turned me around. Behind us, a squalid city filled the sky with its smoke. Suddenly we were tramping down its muddy streets. My grandmother led us into a dirty alleyway. It was filled with garbage. Old crones peered into our faces, a dog jumped at the hamper my grandmother was carrying, then sprang back when she kicked it.

We went in the back door of a rotting wood house, up narrow twisting stairs to the apartment of her grandparents. The grandparents of my grandmother. A low-ceilinged room with a dining table and a couch on which my great-great-grandfather lay. The heavy rhythm of his breathing. Drawn over him was a thick quilt. His bearded face was turned eagerly towards me, though he did not speak.

About this and other such dreams I have no one to ask. I

myself am sliding through middle age – no one alive can remember my great-great-grandparents. No one can care. Let them die and be buried in their stale European breath. Their dead dreams that lived on the edge of crumbled empires whose name no one remembers.

Why mourn over these immigrants and their ancestors? They were always unwelcome wherever they went. They were always lying somewhere, sick, watching their children or grandchildren go out the door in search of some new haven, some new hope that would turn out to be false.

At certain times – in their ghettos, on their boats, walking the streets at night in their new land – they must have looked at the sky, seen that the stars had maintained their same configurations even though the land beneath their boots had changed. Glad to escape, happy to arrive, living in the midst of their self-made islands. Watching their children and their grandchildren step off those islands. Playing the fatal game of cultural impersonation that all of history had taught against. Looking as absurd in their adopted costumes as did Eliot in his green make-up and mascara.

We are in my mid-town, mid-rise, mid-price, mid-Toronto apartment. R/T is lying on the floor, her feet just sufficiently apart that she can, while wearing her high-heeled shoes, tap her toes together. 'You never wanted to have children with me,' she says. She is pronouncing her words carefully, which is how I know she has mixed just the right amount of Scotch into her blood.

'I would have been a terrible father.'

'No. You would have been a good father.'

It is amazing how reassuring I find her words. It is as though I've been given the seal of approval by the Canadian Standards Association. A fierce and necessary gratitude towards R/T sweeps across my desert soul. I slide to my knees and begin crawling towards her. The few times we've made love – not unsympathetic episodes scattered through the years – it has always been on the floor: in this apartment, once in a cabin we rented together, once in a car under circumstances that require much explanation but ended with showers to get rid of the bits of potato chips that we inadvertently ground between the carpeting and our consenting skins.

I kneel above her. She is crying. I bend to kiss the tears from her cheeks. This is a huge aberration. Between R/T and me, despite flare-ups of desire, there has never been the slightest pretence of temporary companionship. 'I don't want to have an affair with you,' she said when I first invited her up, lifetimes ago. 'My intentions are honourable,' I'd protested. 'I don't believe you, and you don't understand me,' she'd replied. 'With me it's all or nothing and I *know* you won't understand that.'

Immediately I'd imagined R/T casting me in the role of stepfather to the little brat she sometimes brought around the department, a spoiled fat-faced beribboned girl who gave me knowing and precocious sneering looks whenever she thought her mother wasn't looking.

She takes my face in her hands. 'You still don't understand,' she says. Although I think I do; she means we should be in a lawn-surrounded house somewhere, vibrating to the sound of running little feet. I start to withdraw but even drunk R/T is too fast for me, and soon we're rocking and rolling to our own strange beat.

Afterwards, R/T insists I come into the bathroom with her and soap her all over. This isn't the kind of intimacy I'm used to with her. I light candles for modesty's sake, make a few embarrassed jokes about hot tubs. Once R/T is actually lying in the water, and one of the candles has gone out, I regain confidence. I'm kneeling beside her, rubbing the soap up and down her body in the golden light. She's barely visible beneath the water, though her breasts float and her nipples break the surface. 'Look at them,' R/T says, flushing, suddenly embarrassed herself and trying to push them down. 'Wait,' I say, and tear some petals from the flowers she brought me and use them to make small glowing hats that bob like tiny sails on the rippling surface of the water.

When depressed, Virginia Woolf dressed in flowers. Sceptics say this strategy must have failed – she did drown herself, after all. But legends are not made of scepticism, and everyone dies in the end.

Walter Benjamin was fascinated with Kafka, whom he regarded as a fellow specialist in the problem of being someone and no one at the same time. Benjamin wrote, 'On many occasions and often for strange reasons Kafka's figures clap their hands. Once the casual remark is made that these hands are "really steam hammers". ' He also said of Kafka that 'he perceived what was to come without perceiving what exists in the present'. As always when he is writing about Kafka, one feels Benjamin is really writing about himself – for example, the above lines are from a letter Benjamin wrote in 1938, two years before his suicide. R/T in my bed. Not the night of the bath – that night we had the good fortune of perceiving the present without perceiving the future. But a few months later, when she was recovering from her second round of chemotherapy. The precocious sneering daughter had long since turned into a perfectly nice young woman, a graduate student with a big fellowship in biochemistry. R/T could not bear to bother her with the incessant cycles, remissions, collapses of her illness. 'She already went through enough with me and her father. I'll call her when I'm dying.'

Meanwhile R/T kept teaching, though it was so difficult for her to take care of herself that she eventually ended up in my apartment on a semi-permanent basis. At first it was just for a weekend – a change of beds, we joked.

That was winter. It snowed a lot, unusually, and if she was well enough I would often install R/T, covered by her favourite quilt, in my rocker-armchair by the window. With our lights out we could watch the snow beating in waves against the window. R/T would nurse a glass of sherry while I tried to drink enough Scotch to stay calm.

Often on those evenings, lights out and classical music in the background, we would pretend we were at a place we had imagined, the Modernist Cafe, where we would see Eliot, Woolf, Benjamin, and Kafka sitting at their table, drinking drinks we would invent for them, making terrible puns we also supplied.

At the end of such a visit, when R/T had gone into her premidnight doze, I would walk over to her place and get her the various files and books she had requested. Of course she was always about to be well enough to move back. Twice a week I would change the milk in her refrigerator, replace the loaf of bread, take the rotten fruit from the bowl on her table and replenish it with bright fat oranges and gleaming red apples.

In the worst weather R/T would wear her coat while she was teaching. As always she insisted on delivering her lectures standing up. Thomas hardly ever appeared; when he did it was in response to a particularly hopeless question and he would snap back something brittle and bitter. Then Rebecca would shake her head and smile, as though this eruption were a gastric accident best ignored.

After her lectures, I would drive her home. Sweaty and shaking, entirely drained, she would let me help her from the car and upstairs to bed. Sometimes it would be hours before she could speak again.

At my insistence Julia started coming to visit us. 'You're like an old couple,' she said one night when I was seeing her to the door. And she gave that old knowing smile – this time without the sneer – but how could I explain to her?

Beginning is difficult, ending has its own problems. Something about Rebecca, her mannish Thomas-like hands, the way, when she drank, she used her eyebrows for punctuation.

I would sleep on the couch and when I came in to see R/T in the morning her eyes would be bigger. This was in April, the cruellest month. Her students were used to me and it seemed the most natural thing in the world when one day, instead of taking my usual seat at the back, I moved up to the front. After I had finished the lecture R/T had prepared the week before, I told them the story of the lighthouse and said that if any one of them should ever go there, they might think about R/T. I might have liked to say something about the unconsidered perils of companionship, the temporary nature of things, the way we feel, you and I, when the evening is spread out against the sky, but I didn't. I read them my last memo and the reply R/T had left for me on my answering machine.

For a few moments there was silen_____ l__ ___ h_ _ __ ___
windows open; ther_____ ___ __ __
ing into t_
gathering

MATT COHEN was born in Kingston, Ontario. He received his BA and MA from the University of Toronto. In the late 1960s he taught political economy at McMaster University before becoming a full-time writer. Since 1969 he has published twenty books, including novels, short stories, poetry, and two books for children.

He has received critical acclaim for many of his books, notably *Emotional Arithmetic* (1990) and 'The Salem Novels' – *The Disinherited* (1974), *The Colours of War* (1977), *The Sweet Second Summer of Kitty Malone* (1979), and *Flowers of Darkness* (1981). He was short-listed for the Governor General's Award in 1979 for *The Sweet Second Summer of Kitty Malone* and was a finalist for the 1988 Ontario Trillium Award for his short story collection *Living on Water*. His short stories have twice won National Magazine Awards, and have been widely anthologized and translated. His latest novel *The Bookseller* was published by Knopf Canada in 1993.

Matt Cohen now lives in Toronto, Ontario.

LAURENCE ACLAND